**Praise for *New York Times* bestselling author**

# PENNY JORDAN

"Women everywhere will find pieces
of themselves in Jordan's characters."
—*Publishers Weekly*

"[Penny Jordan's novels] touch every emotion."
—*RT Book Reviews*

"This richly satisfying story is both sensual and
emotional."
—*RT Book Reviews* on *Master of Pleasure*

"Jordan's record is phenomenal."
—*The Bookseller*

**Penny Jordan,** one of Harlequin's most popular authors, sadly passed away on December 31st, 2011. She leaves an outstanding legacy, having sold over 100 million books around the world. Penny wrote a total of 187 novels for Harlequin, including the phenomenally successful *A Perfect Family, To Love, Honor and Betray, The Perfect Sinner* and *Power Play,* which hit the *New York Times* bestseller list. Loved for her distinctive voice, she was successful in part because she continually broke boundaries and evolved her writing to keep up with readers' changing tastes. *Publishers Weekly* said about Jordan, "Women everywhere will find pieces of themselves in Jordan's characters." It is perhaps this gift for sympathetic characterization that helps to explain her enduring appeal.

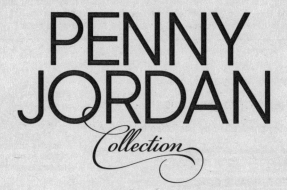

# PENNY JORDAN
*Collection*

## UNEXPECTED
## PLEASURES

HARLEQUIN®

entertain, enrich, inspire™

ISBN-13: 978-0-373-24984-8

UNEXPECTED PLEASURES

Copyright © 2012 by Harlequin Books S.A.

The publisher acknowledges the copyright holder of the individual works as follows:

YESTERDAY'S ECHOES
Copyright © 1993 by Penny Jordan

MASTER OF PLEASURE
Copyright © 2006 by Penny Jordan

Recycling programs for this product may not exist in your area.

# CONTENTS

# YESTERDAY'S ECHOES

# CHAPTER ONE

'I'M BEGINNING TO dread christenings. In fact, I only have to hear the word *baby* these days and I come over all broody...and me a mother of two hulking great teenagers. I ought to know better.

'I know what it is, of course... It's the threat of empty nest syndrome looming, with nothing to look forward to but Greg's mid-life crisis and hormone replacement therapy... Rosie...are you listening to me?'

Obediently Rosie turned towards her elder sister, and repeated obediently what she had just been told.

'Of course, plenty of women are having babies at forty these days,' Rosie heard her muse. 'Although what the kids would have to say about it...and how on earth I'd even manage to get pregnant in the first place... You've no idea how inhibiting it is having almost-adult children in the house with you. It's amazing how guilty and embarrassed they can make you feel. Mind you, talking of sex lives, how's yours going at the moment?'

Rosie felt her stomach muscles tense and prayed that her facial muscles weren't reacting equally betrayingly.

There was virtually a decade between her and her elder sister, and this had led to Chrissie's adopting an almost parental attitude to her. Although Rosie knew that Chrissie would have been outraged had *she* been as inquisitive and critical of her most intimate personal life as Chrissie was of Rosie's, she also knew that Chrissie would never be able to understand that there were times when she found her sister's questions intrusive and over-personal. After all, she knew how much Chrissie loved her and that her questions, no matter how awkward, sprang from love and concern.

And of course today she *was* feeling extra-intensely sensitive, she admitted. Christenings always had that effect on her, and it was pointless expecting Chrissie to understand that, to *know* what she was going through, to *know* about the tearing, wrenching pain within her, the sense of loss and anguish.

It was all very well for Chrissie to talk glibly about feeling broody, about having another child, to assume that she, Rosie, as a single woman of thirty-one with a business to run—a woman who, as Chrissie was always reminding her, had chosen to keep any men who approached her at a wary distance—did not know what it meant to see another woman with a child, and to feel that aching sense of deprivation within her—that tight feeling of panic and pain, of loss and fear, of so many complex emotions that she herself could barely find the words to describe them.

And then for Chrissie to make that comment about her sex life!

The Hopkinses' lawn wasn't very big; they were a very popular couple and had invited a large number of people to the christening party. Rosie winced as someone standing behind her stepped backwards, and she felt a sharp elbow accidentally striking against her, jolting her glass and causing the other woman to immediately apologise as Rosie automatically turned round.

'I'm so sorry,' she began, but Rosie wasn't listening to her.

Her whole body frozen rigid with shock and rejection, she was staring past her at the man standing several yards away watching her.

Jake Lucas! What was *he* doing here? *Watching* her! She hadn't realised that he knew the Hopkinses. If she had suspected for a moment that *he* was going to be here...

'Rosie...'

She shivered, the rigidity leaving her body as she responded to the quick anxiety in her sister's voice.

Across the space which divided them, Jake Lucas continued to watch her. She could feel the concentrated burn of that look. She knew exactly what he was thinking...how he viewed her...without having to look directly into his eyes.

'Rosie...'

This time Chrissie wasn't content with speaking to her; she was touching her as well—an elder-sisterly hand placed firmly on her arm, giving it an admonishing little shake.

'What is it? What's wrong?'

Wrong? Alarm bells clamoured violently inside her.

'Nothing... Nothing's wrong,' she denied quickly, turning her head back towards her sister so quickly that her hair spun round her, fanning out of its neat, shoulder-length cut before falling silkily back into place, its thick russet sleekness concealing her expression as she lowered her head defensively.

Jake Lucas. Even now that she was no longer looking at him, his features remained burnt into her memory so that it wasn't her sister's firm but anxious face she saw, but his, with its hard, masculine features, his mouth curling disdainfully, his hard, flinty grey eyes watching her with distaste, everything about him, even down to the way he was standing, registering his contempt for her—that and the knowledge of her which they both shared.

'Rosie, what *is* it? And don't tell me nothing. You've gone as white as a sheet,' Chrissie accused. 'Is it the sun? You should have kept your hat on; you know how vulnerable you are to sunstroke. You'd better not drive home.'

Numbly Rosie let her sister's bossy fussing wash over her, for once unable to summon the independence to remind her sister that she was an adult and not one of her children.

'It's time we left, anyway. I promised Greg I wouldn't be late. We've got the Curtises coming round this evening, and I want to make sure that Allison and Paul aren't thinking of going out tonight. I don't like them going out on Sunday evenings, not with Paul's A levels coming up and Allison's GCSEs next year.'

Rosie stayed silent, letting her sister's conversation wash over her. Jake Lucas… She tried to remember the last time she had seen him—was it four years ago or three?—but she felt too dizzy with shock to be able to concentrate.

He lived on the opposite side of town from her and their paths never crossed. He moved in different social circles, and the partnership he had in a marina on one

of the less accessible Greek islands meant that he was
out of the country a good deal.

He was closer to Chrissie's age than her own, although even her redoubtable sister had always been a
little in awe of him, despite the fact that she was a couple of years his senior.

He was that kind of man.

Awe didn't describe *her* reaction to him, Rosie acknowledged. Fear...dread...pain...panic...anguish; he
made her feel all of those, and other and even less bear-
able emotions as well.

The mere sound of his name was enough to make her
go cold with fear and shame, and to see him so unexpectedly, when she was unprepared for it and in such a
vulnerable situation, when she was already feeling so
off balance, so emotionally open to the anguish of her
past and the burden of the pain she had kept a secret
from everyone else who knew her...

Silently, she let Chrissie take hold of her arm and
firmly make her way through the tightly packed group
of people around their host and hostess.

The baby, the Hopkinses' third, was now content-
edly asleep in her father's arms. A wrenching jolt of
pain stabbed through Rosie as she watched him deftly
transfer his new daughter's sleeping weight from one
shoulder to the other while he ducked his head to kiss
first Chrissie and then her on the cheek.

'Isn't it time we saw you holding one of these?' he
teased Rosie.

His teasing wasn't malicious or unkind. Rosie and
both Neil and Gemma Hopkins had all been at school
together. Gemma was her own age. She herself was,

Rosie reminded herself bleakly, the only one of her peers now who had not experienced a committed relationship of some kind. Some of her friends were even on their second marriages.

She knew how curious people were about her, and could guess at the questions they probably asked one another about her. Always sensitive and by nature an extremely private person, she was acutely aware of how different she was, how isolated from experiences which seemed commonplace to others.

It wasn't as though she weren't attractive, as though men weren't drawn to her, Chrissie had exclaimed in exasperation four months ago on Rosie's thirty-first birthday, when she had brought up her perennial complaint about Rosie's dedication to her single state.

'I've watched you,' she had accused. 'You freeze the poor things off as soon as they try to get close to you.'

Her mother had been more understanding, but equally concerned.

'I don't understand it,' she had said sadly. 'Rosie, you were always the one who loved playing with your dolls, who always, from being a small child, talked about getting married and having children. Of the two of you, I always thought it would be Chrissie who would be the career girl. I'm not trying to tell you how to run your life, darling. If being single is what you want...'

'It is,' Rosie had told her mother fiercely, but she suspected that her mother knew as well as she did that she was not telling the whole truth.

But how could she explain, reveal to her mother, to anyone, the thing that had made her like this, the guilt, the pain, the shock of self-discovery, the realisation that her degradation and humiliation, her stupidity, had been witnessed by someone else? These had proved so painful to her that the only way she could deal with them was to try to cut herself off from them, from the person she had been before it had happened, to try to create a different person—a safer, better, more responsible, more controlled person.

How could she tell anyone about what had happened? She was too afraid of them condemning her, looking at her, reacting to her in the same way that Jake Lucas had done.

Over the years she had gone over and over it so many times in her own mind, hating herself for having allowed it to happen, for not being more aware, for not realising what was going to happen.

She knew she was not guilty of ever having done anything to encourage him; she could acquit herself of that crime. She had never come anywhere near doing or saying anything to make him think that she might actually want him. How could she have done? She had not had the least conception of what sexual desire was.

She had been a very naïve, protected sixteen, and still far too shy and immature to be sexually aware in any way.

No, she had done nothing to lead him on, but she had had that drink and she hadn't been able to stop him, and she knew enough about the world now to realise that if she were ever to tell what had happened there would always be those who would wonder...doubt... especially if they were male.

And she could never allow herself to get involved with a man without telling him, without wanting to share with him that secret, shamed, still-hurting part of herself.

And since she was afraid of allowing herself to love a man, only to discover him turning away from her with the same disgust that Jake Lucas had manifested, she had chosen instead not to take the risk of becoming emotionally committed to anyone. It was safer that way, and safety, protecting herself from hurt—these were very important to Rosie. When people commented on her manless state, she told them coolly that she was content the way she was. Normally the coolness she exhibited, the control, was enough to deter them and to protect her, but today was different.

Today she was feeling too vulnerable...too raw inside, too achingly aware of that small, sleeping bundle held protectively against Neil's shoulder and the man still standing somewhere among the crowd on the lawn, perhaps still watching her...

She shivered, feeling the perspiration break out against her skin, watching helplessly as Neil's expression changed to one of concern.

'It's the heat,' she heard Chrissie saying. 'She's always been vulnerable to it. It's that red hair and Celtic skin. I told her not to take her hat off.'

There were, Rosie decided faintly as Chrissie led her firmly away, perhaps advantages to having Chrissie for a sister after all.

She quickly changed her mind, though, when Chrissie refused to allow her to drive home.

'But I need my car,' she protested.

'Not now, you don't,' Chrissie told her. 'And if you

have got heat or sunstroke, you won't be needing it tomorrow either.'

'I've got a meeting in Chester tomorrow morning,' Rosie protested, but Chrissie wasn't listening.

'Honestly, Rosie, I should have thought at your age you'd know better,' she was complaining as she opened her own car door. 'At times you can be even worse than Paul and Allison... Now get in and I'll take you home. If we didn't have the Curtises coming round this evening, I'd take you home with me. I know you...'

Sickly, Rosie closed her eyes. She felt as weak and nauseous as if she *were* in fact physically ill, but she knew quite well whatever—or rather, whoever had caused those symptoms.

No matter how much logic she used, her senses, her reactions still continued to remind her of the trauma which lay buried in her past.

Jake Lucas. If only *he* had not been there...that night.

But he had been there...

She winced as Chrissie slammed her car door and started the engine. She was still feeling nauseatingly sick, her body clammy with shock. If only she hadn't already been caught up in the aching pain that seeing the Hopkinses' new baby had caused her, she might have been better able to control her reaction to Jake Lucas, she told herself miserably.

Her sister was still talking, still admonishing her for taking off her hat.

'You left it upstairs on Gemma's bed,' she heard Chrissie reminding her. 'You mustn't forget to collect it when you go back for your car.'

Rosie lived several miles away from her sister and

her family. She could well remember the fuss Chrissie had made when she had found out that Rosie was selling her neat, modern flat and buying a run-down, isolated farm worker's cottage.

'It will eat money,' she had warned Rosie. 'And wait until you have to spend a bad winter there. You'll be completely cut off.'

She had frowned disapprovingly at Rosie's *sotto voce* 'Please God' before going on to remonstrate again with her for her foolishness.

'I don't like leaving you here on your own like this,' she said now as she stopped her car in the lane outside the cottage.

'Chrissie, I'll be fine,' Rosie told her wearily. 'Stop fussing. I'm an adult, not a child.'

'You're still my baby sister,' Chrissie told her forthrightly, 'and if you're *that* grown-up, how come you didn't remember to keep your hat on?'

As she got out of the car, Rosie sighed. Typical Chrissie. She always had to have the last word, but beneath her rather bossy manner Rosie knew that Chrissie was genuinely concerned for her and, as she saw that concern now reflected in Chrissie's eyes, her irritation melted away.

'I'll be fine,' she assured her. 'A good night's sleep and—'

'Ring me in the morning,' Chrissie demanded imperatively. 'I'll come over after I've taken Allison and Paul to school and drive you across to collect your car.'

Rosie felt the irritation bubbling up inside her again. She had a meeting in Chester at ten o'clock in the morning. She couldn't afford to hang around waiting for

Chrissie to come and collect her, and she certainly wasn't going to cancel. It had taken her months of delicate negotiations to persuade Ian Davies to see her and she wasn't going to throw away everything she had worked so hard for.

She knew that a lot of people had been surprised when she had taken over from her father when he had retired, especially Chrissie. It had been one thing for her to work for him in his insurance agency business, but quite another for her to take over that business and run it single-handedly, despite the fact that she was professionally qualified to do so and had had several years of practical experience, working first for a much larger concern and then, for three years before he retired, for her father.

It had been very hard for her at first, getting the clients to accept her, but then she had managed to deal with a particularly complicated case and get compensation for a client who had come to her after being unable to get satisfaction from his insurance company through another broker. He had been so impressed that he had recommended her to his friends, but breaking down the barriers of male reserve and lack of faith in her abilities was a constant battle.

It didn't help of course that in her normal, everyday life she was so quiet and unassertive, and she had to acknowledge that at barely five feet two, with a very small body frame and a sometimes irritatingly delicate and feminine set of facial features, her physical appearance was perhaps not that of a woman who could withstand the occasionally slightly sneaky tricks adopted by her clients' insurers. Not that they would consider it like that.

Gamesmanship was how they preferred to think of it, a justifiable use of their power, and if someone was weak enough to be browbeaten into giving up a claim or settling for less than they had initially expected then tough luck.

But Rosie had no time for such tactics. She could be surprisingly ruthless and determined when she had to be, but there was no getting away from the fact that in the two years since her father's retirement the business had lost out to some of the much larger agencies.

She had refused to be downhearted; there was still a market…a need for someone like her who was prepared to give specialised time and attention to a client's needs. The problem was persuading the clients, not convincing herself that her skills were superior to those of a large, faceless organisation.

Which was what she was hoping to do at tomorrow's meeting with Ian Davies.

She had heard in a roundabout fashion that he was dissatisfied with his existing brokers since they had amalgamated with another firm. A fire at one of his rental premises, which had resulted in his full claim being turned down by his insurers, had increased that dissatisfaction, and Rosie had seen her chance and taken it.

He was a contemporary of her father's and, she suspected, not wholly comfortable with women taking a leading role in business. She knew that persuading him to give her his business was not going to be easy, but she was determined to at least try.

To prove to others that she was just as proficient as the equivalent male, or to prove to herself that, just because she was a failure as a woman, it did not mean that she had failed as a human being, that just because she had lost her self-respect, her sense of self-worth, her belief that she was worthy of being loved, it did not mean that every pleasure in life was denied her.

No, not every pleasure, she reflected bitterly. Just the ones she had always taken for granted that she would one day enjoy.

Like being loved and being able to love in return... Like having a child...a family.

As she opened the door and stepped into her small dark hallway, she could feel the angry, impotent tears beginning to sting her eyes.

Damn Jake Lucas... Why had *he* had to be there this afternoon...? Why wouldn't the past let her go? Why couldn't she ever seem to fight free of its destructive tentacles?

## CHAPTER TWO

Rosie waited until she felt comfortably sure that the party would be over and that all the other guests, but most especially Jake Lucas, would have left, and then rang for a taxi. There would be no need for her to disturb the Hopkinses—her car was parked outside their house and not on their drive.

It was just gone nine o'clock when the taxi driver dropped her off, the summer sky still light and the air warm.

Gemma and Neil had been lucky with the weather, Rosie acknowledged as she delved in her handbag for her car keys.

'Aha…caught you.'

She tensed automatically and then relaxed as she recognised Neil's teasing voice.

'Gemma saw you arrive,' he told her. 'Why don't you come in for a few minutes?'

Rosie started to protest, but Neil overruled her. A quick search of the road and drive had confirmed that the only other cars there beside her own belonged to Gemma and Neil, and that all the party guests had gone home.

'I didn't want to disturb you,' she started to protest,

but Neil had already taken hold of her arm and was coaxing her towards the house.

'There's something we wanted to discuss with you anyway,' he told her. 'Abby has received quite a few gifts of money as christening presents and we were wondering about starting one of these baby bond things for her... What do you think?'

Ten minutes later she was sitting in the Hopkinses' comfortable family kitchen, listening carefully as Gemma outlined their wish to provide some small lump sum for their new daughter when she was older.

The baby herself was fast asleep in Gemma's arms. Neil had gone upstairs to discover what had caused the argument they could hear taking place between their two sons. The phone in the hall rang, causing the baby to stir and cry.

'Here, hold her for me will you please, Rosie, while I go and answer the phone?' Gemma asked her, thrusting the baby towards Rosie so that she had no option other than to take her from her.

She felt warm and solid, with that undefinable but instantly recognisable baby smell.

Tensely Rosie held her, her body rigid, her stomach churning, tremors convulsing her.

Unused to being held at such a distance, and missing the warmth of her mother, the baby's cries increased.

She was still young enough to have that piercing, womb-aching cry of a new baby, and as she heard it Rosie reacted instinctively to it, cradling her against her shoulder, as she supported her small, soft head and soothed her rigid, tense body.

The baby turned her head, nuzzling into Rosie's

skin—an automatic reflex action that meant nothing, Rosie knew—and her own body's reaction to it was so immediate and devastating that she could feel herself starting to shake.

Abby had stopped crying now, apparently content with her new surroundings, snuggling sleepily against Rosie's shoulder, but for Rosie to overcome her emotions was not so easy.

She always deliberately avoided this kind of situation, making sure that she had as little physical contact with small babies as she could.

Once they were older it was different, the pain less devastating and primitive, the sense of loss, of deprivation, of agonising guilt, easier to deal with.

She heard Gemma coming back into the kitchen and immediately handed Abby back to her.

'I must go,' she told her quickly. 'I've got an early start in the morning. I'll do some work on some comparison tables for you and drop them around later in the week.'

It was only later, when she was on her way home, that she remembered that in her desperate anxiety to get away she had forgotten all about her hat.

Before going to collect her car she had meticulously gone over and over the proposals she planned to put before Ian Davies.

She was confident that they were at least as competitive as anything anyone could offer him; where she believed *she* had the advantage over much larger concerns was the personal touch.

It was almost eleven o'clock when she went upstairs

to prepare for bed. She was just about to get undressed when the phone rang.

It was Chrissie, wanting to know how she was.

Firmly she assured her sister that she was feeling fine but, ten minutes later, when she had removed her make-up and was studying her face in her bathroom mirror, she had to admit that her appearance belied her words.

She had always been pale-skinned, and for that reason had always had to protect her sensitive skin from the sun, but tonight her pallor was sharpened by tension and pain.

Shakily she turned away from the mirror, not wanting to see…to remember.

Jake Lucas. *He* had remembered. She had seen it in his eyes when he looked at her across the Hopkinses' crowded sun-dappled garden, had seen the coldness and the contempt, the distaste and dislike. It didn't matter *how* hard she worked at burying the past, at shutting herself off from it, at trying to forget it—Jake Lucas would never forget; she could not wipe *his* memory clean, could not erase his knowledge of her.

But at least there was one thing he did not know, one secret that was hers alone.

Rosie winced as she bit down too hard on her bottom lip and broke the skin.

Now she would have a swollen bruise there in the morning. She grimaced crossly in the mirror. She would have to remember to wear a concealing matt lipstick tomorrow. Her mouth was on the overfull side as it was and she had no wish to arrive at Ian Davies's office looking like some pouting little doll.

Before getting in to bed, she checked that she had everything ready for the morning. Her suit was hanging up outside the wardrobe, and so was the silk shirt she intended to wear with it.

Underwear, tights, plus a spare pair in case of accidents, were laid out ready in the bathroom.

Her shoes were downstairs, cleaned and polished, her neat leather handbag-cum-attaché case filled with all the papers she would need.

Rosie did not believe in going for a high-powered female executive image. She felt it both theatrical and off-putting for some of her smaller clients. She preferred to dress neatly and unobtrusively, so that people paid attention to what she had to say, not the way she looked.

She flinched a little, remembering how Chrissie had commented not unkindly, some time ago, that men would never be oblivious to the way she looked.

'They can't help it,' had been her half-indulgent remark. 'It's in their nature, poor dears, and let's face it, Rosie, you are very attractive.'

She had eyed her younger sister judicially before adding, 'In fact, you could be very sexy, if you wanted to be.'

'Well, I don't,' had been Rosie's fierce response.

And it was true. After all, what was the point in looking sexually attractive when she knew how impossible it was for her to follow through the promise of such looks, without at some stage having to reveal the truth.

'Don't think about it,' she warned herself. 'Just accept that that's the way things are. You aren't unhappy. You don't lack for anything.'

Apart from a lover…someone to share her life on an intimate, one-to-one basis. A lover… And a child.

IT WAS THE crying that woke her up, bringing her bolt upright in her single, almost monastic little bed, her arms crossing protectively around her body as she tried to clear her brain.

There was the familiar oblong of light cast by the moon through her bedroom window, the familiar pale colours of her simply decorated bedroom with its white bed-linen, its plain, light-coloured walls and carpet, slightly stark against the darkness of the room's oak beams.

She was not, after all, as she had been dreaming, there in that hospital ward, all around her the cries of the new-born babies, to remind her agonisingly of the child she had just lost… The child she had been so terrified she might have conceived, the child she had rejected with panic and shock, terrified of what its conception was going to mean of the way it would alter her life.

But now there was no child, and she was safe. She knew she ought to be glad…relieved. Only somehow she wasn't, and the pain inside her wasn't just caused by the physical shock of the haemorrhage which had preceded her miscarriage. And those piercing new-born cries scraped at her raw nerves like physical torture. No matter what she did, she couldn't escape from him…or from what had happened.

She was shaking, Rosie recognised, her body icy-cold. Even though it was a softly mild night, and despite her shivers her body was drenched in sweat as she fought not to remember.

It was over fifteen years ago now, almost half her own lifetime. She had been sixteen, that was all—still a child in so many ways, and yet still woman enough to grieve tormentedly for the life that was lost, for the child she would never now hold, for the ache within her that came from the emptiness of what she had lost.

Sixteen… Sixteen, and a virgin. Innocent of any knowledge of male sexuality. And yet she should have known…should have recognised.

It had been all her own fault, as Jake Lucas had so contemptuously pointed out to her.

You didn't go upstairs with someone, allow him to kiss and fondle you, without knowing where it was going to lead.

Her head had still been thick then with the cider she had had to drink. Only half a glass and she had not finished that, but she learned afterwards that it had been scrumpy, brought back from the south of England by one of the others, with heaven alone knew what added to it.

That still didn't excuse her, though. She shouldn't have drunk it, shouldn't have even been at the party in the first place. If her parents had been at home instead of away at a conference, if her sister had not been staying in the north of England helping her mother-in-law to nurse the husband who was just beginning to recover from a stroke, she would never have been allowed to go.

But they hadn't been there and, out of bravado and a fear of being laughed at by the others, she had given in to her friends' cajoling and agreed to join them.

TIREDLY SHE got out of bed. There was no point in try-ing to get back to sleep again. Not now.

And no point in reliving the whole thing all over again, she reminded herself bitterly. What good had that ever done, other than to reinforce her feelings of guilt and shame, to conjure up in front of her the sharply vivid mental image of Jake Lucas's cynical, condem-natory expression as he stared down at her half-naked body, the way she lay sprawled across his aunt and uncle's bed?

Then, still in shock, her body still aching with pain, her mind still clouded with alcohol, she had not thought of pregnancy. That had come later in a sickening wave of panic and rejection, when she'd realised that she could have conceived.

She hadn't told anyone; she had been too afraid, too aware by then of her own guilt and degradation.

A month went by and the panic became a certainty, but still she did nothing.

All around her life went on as normal, and she felt somehow that if she pretended it had simply not hap-pened…if she said and did nothing, it would all magi-cally go away. That the nausea she felt in the morning would stop, that her body's rhythms would return to normal, that the mental pictures that filled her brain at night while she slept would disappear, and that she would once again be the girl she had been before.

No one said anything to her; no one seemed to be aware of what had happened.

Jake Lucas's aunt and uncle had emigrated to Aus-tralia three weeks after the party, with their family.

Some days she almost managed to convince herself

that it had never happened, and then something would remind her: she would see a woman pushing a pram on her way home from school…or see a small baby on television. Whenever she saw a heavily pregnant woman she found herself looking the other way, as the panic bubbled up inside her.

Her mother was concerned about her and feared that she had been studying too hard for her exams.

The guilt she felt when she heard this was the worst kind of punishment. Her parents loved and trusted her. How could she tell them the truth?

And then, while they were away visiting friends and Chrissie was still with her mother-in-law, it happened.

Rosie had gone in to Chester for the day. She had some books she wanted to buy which were not available in their small market town.

She had bought the books and had just been walking out of the shop when it happened—a pain so searing and sharp that she dropped the books, her hand instinctively going to her stomach as she collapsed.

When she came round it was all over and she was in hospital.

She had lost her baby, a harassed young doctor had told her briskly, and they wanted to keep her in overnight just to check that there were no complications.

After that everyone seemed to ignore her, and it was only later that she learned that there had been an emergency that evening, with a major road accident locally.

In the confusion of that, no one realised that Rosie's family had not been advised of what had happened, and when Rosie was discharged from the hospital the next day with a clean bill of health she realised numbly that no one but her knew or needed to know what had happened.

At first she was overwhelmed with relief and gratitude for that fact, but later, when the sound of crying babies brought her out of her sleep, when the guilt over what she had done was replaced by the far greater guilt and anguish of having lost her child, she ached for someone to talk to, someone to confide in, someone with whom she could share her confused feelings.

Logically she knew that her miscarriage was probably the best thing that could have happened. She was sixteen years old, she had attended a party without her parents' knowledge, had had too much to drink and as a result... She shuddered, still not able to contemplate what had actually happened, and yet, despite knowing all that, she had still grieved for her lost child.

And still did.

She went downstairs and filled the kettle so that she could make herself a drink of herbal tea. Perhaps that might help her to get back to sleep.

She knew now that she would never have another child. How could she risk another man looking at her the way Jake Lucas had looked at her, when she told him about her past? She was too proud to want a relationship in which it remained a secret—that was not her ideal of marriage, of commitment, of sharing.

Once she realised what was happening she had, of course, tried to stop him, but he had pinned her to the bed, leaving dark bruises on her arms as he forced his way into her body, making her cry out in shock, not just at his unwanted, forced physical possession of her, but also at the emotional humiliation and degradation she was being made to suffer.

It had all been over within seconds, but those seconds had been long enough to change her life irretrievably. Even now, remembering…thinking about what had happened, Rosie was filled with self-disgust and guilt.

She had withdrawn into herself afterwards, earning for herself a reputation as a swot, as someone who would rather stay at home with her family than go out with her friends.

Her sense of shame and guilt over what had happened was so strong that she could not bear anyone else to know what she had done.

Rather then endure a repeat of the humiliation and shame, the sense of anguished guilt she had already known, she decided that her life must have another focus, that for the sake of her own sanity and self-respect she must accept that that commitment—marriage, a relationship that included a lover and the children they might have together—was not for her.

And most of the time she managed to convince herself that she was content. Except when she saw a small baby or a pregnant woman, except when she woke in the night remembering the past, except when something or someone reminded her of what had happened.

Her tea had gone cold. She looked at it with distaste.

It was fortunate that she was not superstitious, she told herself bitterly, because there could be no worse omen to precede her meeting with Ian Davies than what had happened today.

Tiredly she went back to bed, promising herself that

this time she was not going to allow Jake Lucas to disturb her much-needed rest. That this time she was not going to lie there in the darkness remembering the way he had looked at her, the way he had spoken to her, the contempt and dislike with which he had treated her.

THIS WOULD HAVE to happen to her today of all days, Rosie fumed anxiously, as she waited on the full garage forecourt for a petrol pump to become free.

After all the careful preparations she had made for this morning's meeting with Ian Davies, how on earth had she come to overlook something as vital as making sure her petrol tank was full?

The pump in front of her became free and she pulled quickly into it, ignoring the attempts of the driver behind her to cut in ahead of her.

As she unlocked the petrol cap and pushed the nozzle of the hose into the tank, for some contrary reason, instead of gushing smoothly into the tank, the strong-smelling liquid flooded backwards, spilling out on to her shoes and tights…

It was only a few small splashes, but they left a dismaying strong smell, Rosie acknowledged as she queued to pay for her petrol.

She always left herself with a good extra margin of time when she was travelling to an appointment, but this morning everything seemed to be against her. She had lost at least fifteen minutes getting petrol, and once she was actually on the motorway there was an unexpected hold-up where a lorry had shed its load and the mess was being cleaned up. She eventually arrived in Chester with only five minutes in which to find a parking spot and to get to Ian Davies's offices, and Chester was a notoriously difficult place to park.

Luckily she found a spot just when she was beginning to panic and fear that she was going to be late, and even more luckily she found in the glove compartment a long-forgotten bottle of body lotion which a friend had given her to pass on to Chrissie for one of her jumble collections.

As she used it to clean the petrol stains and smell off her legs and shoes, Rosie winced a little at its strong scent. It was a perfume designed to be worn in the evening, not during the day, and it was certainly far too strong for her taste, but at least it had removed the malodorous smell of petrol.

She reached the offices with a minute to spare, and self-consciously checked her appearance in the lift mirror, to see if she looked as flushed and untidy as her hurried rush through the centre of Chester had made her feel.

A little to her own surprise, the reflection that stared back at her from the small mirror looked cool and composed.

Idly, as she waited for the lift to carry her to the top floor, she wondered if anyone had ever thought of placing a hidden camera or watching device in a lift, and then, remembering some of the very odd things she had heard that people sometimes got up to inside them, she reflected wryly that it was probably just as well they did not.

The lift doors opened and she stepped out into the carpeted foyer, composing her features into a calm, professional smile.

THE MEETING PROVED every bit as tricky as she had expected. Ian Davies was a chauvinist who, Rosie suspected, did not entirely approve of the new role that women were playing in the business world.

Had she been a secretary, a personal assistant, someone's wife or woman friend, she had no doubt that he would have been perfectly charming to her and perhaps even have flirted with her in a courtly, old-fashioned sort of way, but it was plain to her that he was antagonistic not so much to her, but to what she represented.

But, for all his prejudices, he was still very much a business man, and Rosie saw how quickly he assimilated the advantages of using her as his broker.

'Are you saying that, had you had our business, you would have got us more compensation from our insurers?' he asked her at one point.

Firmly Rosie shook her head. She was not going to be caught out like that.

'Without knowing the full details of the arrangements your previous brokers had with your insurers, I can't say that,' she told him equably, but smiling, a little grimly, inwardly to herself as she saw that he had caught the small hint she had dropped about his brokers' private arrangements with the insurers.

She had a very shrewd idea that the brokers he was presently using adopted a policy which she herself refused to consider, and that was an agreement to let some claims go through unhindered in return for the brokers advising other clients not to proceed with theirs, or suggesting to them they should accept lower compensations.

It was her view that her primary loyalty was to her

clients and, if that meant a less easy passage with some of the insurance companies, well, so be it.

'I've brought some comparison quotes with me,' she told him as she stood up. 'If I may, I'll leave them with you.'

A little to her surprise, he accompanied her out into the foyer, but after she had thanked him crisply for his time and turned round to leave she realised why.

Jake Lucas was seated in the foyer, obviously waiting to see him, because he was now standing up, and beyond her she could hear Ian Davies saying something about taking him to lunch.

For a moment the shock of seeing him had paralysed her completely, and then Rosie turned quickly on her heel, her heart hammering furiously fast as it drove the blood through her veins, overheating her pale skin.

She felt hot and sick, filled with panic and a frantic desire to escape. It had been bad enough seeing him yesterday, but this was worse.

Frantically she tried to cling to her self-control and professionalism, but in her haste to escape she moved too quickly, and the papers she was carrying slid from her hot, tense grasp.

She bent immediately to pick them up, her face flushing with angry mortification, and then, to her horror, she realised that two pages of paper had drifted to where Jake Lucas was standing.

For a moment she was too panic-stricken to move, and could only crouch where she was, staring numbly at them, filled with sickness and terror at the thought of having to retrieve them.

When Jake himself bent down and picked them up

she could only stare at him, unable to drag her gaze from the flat metallic hardness of his grey eyes—like a rabbit trapped by a car's headlights, she thought mechanically, as he came towards her.

She struggled to stand up, and then completed her self-humiliation by half losing her balance.

The shock of Jake's hand curling round her arm was like a jolt of electricity. He was so close to her that she could see the dark line along his jaw where he shaved, smell the crisp, clean scent of his soap, see the masculine curl of the dark hairs on his arm where his wrist protruded from his shirt sleeve.

He was still holding her, still watching her... Do something, her brain screamed frantically. *Do* something...

Somehow she managed to find the willpower to get to her feet, but, as she did so, either because of her tension or the heat it had generated, she was suddenly sharply conscious of the smell of the body lotion she had used to clean her legs, and, she realised, Jake Lucas was aware of it too... She saw the slight, and very betraying, fastidious twitch of his nose, the way his eyes narrowed, the brief, downward glance he gave the lower half of her body and, while she automatically thanked him for his help and turned quickly to make her escape, she was sickly aware of the contempt that faint curl of his mouth had carried.

The look he had given her as she dragged her arm away from his grip had underlined that contempt.

He had never made any attempt to hide from her what he thought of her: that he thought she was sexually promiscuous, that she used her body as a means of getting what she wanted out of life…out of men. And he had just let her know quite plainly that by scenting her legs with that strong, voluptuous perfume she was amply confirming his judgment of her.

What business woman who wanted to be taken seriously at a professional level did anything like that? A discreet touch of something light and cool, a subtle message that said that she was a woman and proud of that fact—that was permissible and acceptable. To wear something so heavy and voluptuous gave off a very different message indeed.

On her way down in the lift, Rosie studied her reflection again. This time it was very different. Her face was flushed, especially along her cheekbones, her eyes huge and dark with emotion, the pupils enormously dilated. Even her mouth looked different somehow, softer, fuller…as though…as though she had been kissed.

Shuddering with distaste, she turned away, and when she stepped out into the street she acknowledged that she felt so emotionally raw and on edge that she was on the verge of tears.

It was just disappointment because Ian Davies had not responded more enthusiastically to her approach, she told herself as she walked back to her car. It wasn't anything to do with seeing Jake Lucas. That *had* upset her of course, but she wasn't going to let the fact that he despised her, that he was contemptuous of her, reduce her to tears.

It wasn't, after all, his judgment of her that hurt so much; it was the fact that seeing him always reminded him so unbearably of what she had done, of the way *she* had demeaned herself.

It was bad enough that *she* knew of her shame and degradation, without him having to know of it too.

But he did know, and nothing she could do could ever erase that knowledge. When he looked at her, she knew as surely as though he were saying the actual words that he was seeing her not as she was now, but as she had been then, half-naked, stupid with drink and shock, lying across his aunt and uncle's bed, while her partner, the boy who had deliberately given her that spiked drink and who had then equally deliberately semi-coaxed and semi-dragged her upstairs to his parents' bedroom, had left her, after telling her triumphantly that he had won his bet to seduce her and bring her down off her high horse.

He had not said that to his cousin, though. No, it was a very different story he had told Jake Lucas. According to him, she had been more than willing to accompany him upstairs—she had been the one to suggest it, in fact, and Rosie, too shocked and distressed to defend herself, too humiliated physically and emotionally, had done nothing to defend herself.

Thank God that Ritchie Lucas and his family had emigrated to Australia so quickly afterwards.

And thank God also that Ritchie had apparently got so drunk that evening that it had appeared that he had no recollection of what had taken place and so had been unable to boast to anyone else about it.

No, only two people had remembered what had happened—herself and Jake Lucas—and Jake Lucas did not know the real truth.

He had assumed that she was a member of the rather wild crowd that Ritchie went around with, that she was one of those girls who was foolishly experimenting with sex and drink in the mistaken belief that she was showing everyone how grown-up she was and, beneath his anger at his cousin for taking advantage of his parents' absence to throw an unauthorised party, and his obvious disgust that Ritchie had brought her upstairs to his parents' room, Rosie had been sharply conscious of the contempt he had for her.

And yet his judgement of her couldn't have been further off the mark. She had never even kissed a boy properly before that night, never mind done anything else, and, if it hadn't been that for the previous few months a small group of girls in her class at school had been making her life a misery by taunting her about her 'primness' and her 'goody-goodyness' to the extent that she was slowly becoming alienated from all the other girls and treated as someone who was 'different'…an outcast, she doubted that she would ever have allowed herself to be persuaded to even go to the party in the first place.

To discover later that she had been the subject of a cruel trick deliberately planned to hurt and humiliate her had been hard to bear, but not as hard as Jake Lucas's contempt, and certainly not as hard as discovering that she was pregnant.

At least no one but her knew about that. She bit her lip as she bent to unlock her car door, hot tears stinging her eyes.

There had been no one to grieve with her over the loss of that baby, no one to share her complex and conflicting emotions, no one to tell that, while logically she knew that perhaps it was all for the best, a part of her ached with loss and pain for that unborn child.

No, that was something that no one else knew, and sometimes she wished they did… sometimes she ached inside to be able to talk about what she had experienced: her pain, her sense of loss…her sense of guilt.

Despite the fact that it was over fifteen years ago since it had happened, sometimes she felt as close to it as though it were less than fifteen weeks, as though the wound, the agony, was still so raw that she needed to be able to talk it through with someone…that she needed to be able to publicly and openly mourn the death of her child.

But someone like Jake Lucas would never be able to understand those kind of emotions. She could just imagine his reaction. No doubt he would have told her that she was lucky things had worked out as they had, that such luck was far in excess of what she actually deserved. He would have no pity, no compassion…no understanding… He would reject her pain and her need to express it in just the same contemptuous way as he had rejected her, turning away from her to talk to his cousin, ignoring her as though she simply did not exist.

But he had come to see her afterwards.

Yes, she told herself savagely, to make sure she wasn't going to make any trouble for his precious cousin.

Angrily she put the car in gear and reversed out of her parking spot.

## CHAPTER THREE

'ANY LUCK WITH Ian Davies?'

Rosie looked wryly at her brother-in-law.

'Well, I haven't heard anything from him yet, but he didn't give me the impression that he was interested. He's one of those men who isn't really comfortable with women holding positions of authority in business. If Dad had still been running things, it might have been different.' She gave a small shrug. 'Still, it's his loss as much as ours. I suspect his existing brokers are using his business to get better terms for their other clients instead of reducing his premiums.'

'Did you tell *him* that?' Chrissie demanded.

Rosie shook her head.

'I only suspect that that's what they're doing,' she told her.

'Well, I think it's all wrong that men should still try to keep women down,' Allison announced passionately with indignation. At fourteen she was just beginning to lay claim to her independence, and was staunchly pro women's rights.

'I wonder how Gran and Grandad are getting on. They'll be in Japan now, won't they?' Paul chimed in.

'Yes, they should have arrived there by now,' Rosie agreed.

'I never thought they'd actually do it,' Chrissie marvelled. 'Spending a whole year travelling round the world.'

'It's something they've been planning for and dreaming about for years,' Rosie reminded her.

Chrissie had rung her earlier in the day to check that she was going round as usual to have supper with them, a regular Friday night ritual which Rosie always enjoyed.

'Did you collect your hat from the Hopkinses?' Chrissie asked her now.

'No, not yet,' Rosie told her.

'There's a car boot sale on tomorrow morning. Fancy coming?'

Rosie shook her head.

'I can't. I've promised to go over and see Mary Fuller to help her fill out some claim forms. Her garage was broken into on Wednesday and some things stolen.'

She stood up to leave and was surprised when Chrissie reached out to detain her.

'Not yet,' she muttered. 'There's something I want to tell you. Allison, Paul, upstairs both of you, to make a start on your homework,' she instructed her children.

Rosie frowned as her brother-in-law, too, disappeared from the kitchen, saying something about having a phone-call to make.

Chrissie had been on edge all evening, flustered and quick-tempered in a way which was out of character for her, and immediately they were on their own Rosie demanded anxiously, 'What is it? What's wrong?'

When Chrissie sat down, her eyes filling with tears, Rosie stared at her.

'Chrissie,' she exclaimed reaching out towards her. 'What is it?'

'I'm pregnant,' Chrissie told her tearfully. 'I've only found out this morning. I thought it was just my age… I mean, I *am* forty…but I've been feeling so uncomfortable, so bloated and sick, that I decided I'd go and see Dr Farrar. When she asked me if I could possibly be pregnant, I laughed at first…

'Oh, Rosie, what on earth are people going to say? Allison and Paul? I feel such a fool. A baby at my age… Would you believe it? Greg is thrilled… Isn't that just like a man?' she complained as she sniffed and blew her nose vigorously.

'I'm sorry about that,' she apologised. 'It's just been such a shock…'

'You're not that old,' Rosie assured her automatically. 'Lots of women have babies at your age, some of them for the first time, and as for Allison and Paul… You wait… I'm sure they'll understand.'

Chrissie pregnant… Chrissie having a baby… Although outwardly she knew she appeared calm, her words warm and soothing, inwardly her reaction was very, very different.

She could not be *jealous* of Chrissie, she told herself later as she drove home, having congratulated her slightly shamefaced brother-in-law who, as Chrissie had said, was quite obviously thrilled at the idea of another child.

Jealous of Chrissie… She could not be… She *must* not be. And yet, as she parked her car outside her own home, she acknowledged that she was.

Not jealous in the way that one might be of someone

else's material possessions or even someone else's apparently more fortunate lifestyle; no, this jealousy wasn't like that—it went deeper, bit more sharply, hurt her in so many different ways that she almost felt as though she wanted to scream her pain and misery to the world.

It wasn't that she didn't want Chrissie to have her baby. She shuddered at the thought. It was just… It was just that she… It was just that she what? Wanted a child of her own. A child she would have to bring up single-handedly. A child to whom she would one day have to explain and apologise for its lack of a father. Was that what she really wanted?

She didn't know what she wanted, she acknowledged later; all she did know was that the control she had always been so careful to exercise over herself and her deepest innermost feelings was dangerously close to splintering. That the pain she had thought she had buried so deep that it would never, ever surface was growing inside her, threatening to overwhelm her.

She must not let it. She must not let anyone…anyone guess what she was feeling, especially Chrissie who, for all her strength, was right now feeling very vulnerable, and who needed her love and support.

IN THE MORNING she woke up heavy-eyed and on edge. Her sleep had been disturbed by confusing, unhappy dreams from which she had woken up with tears on her face.

She must stop this, she told herself as she prepared to go and see her client. She had heard about, read about women who became obsessed with their need to fulfil their primary biological function and have a child. It filled and sometimes destroyed their whole lives, occupying them to such an extent there was no room left for other things, other relationships which might have offered them comfort and compensation.

But, deep down inside her, Rosie knew that it wasn't so much the desire to have a child that was causing her emotional anguish, but that somehow her feelings were all connected with the child she could have had but had lost. It was not just that she felt pain and on her own behalf; she felt it on that child's as well. Pain and guilt, sorrow, anger almost, because her child had never been properly grieved for, had never been allowed to be acknowledged…because she had never been able to mourn its loss and share what she was feeling with others.

But how could she have shared it? To share it would have meant admitting what had happened, revealing what she had done, how she had behaved.

Did she really want other people to know about that? Look how Jake Lucas had reacted. Did she really want to see that same contempt in other people's eyes, to know that people were talking about her behind her back, discussing what she had done…? And besides, it was all too late, over fifteen years too late.

But no matter how logically she tried to argue with herself, she still felt emotional and on edge. The thought of having to spend the next eight months or so listening to her sister talking about her pregnancy and making plans for the eventual birth of her baby made her stomach churn with tension and anxiety.

She felt as though emotionally she was stretched so tightly, so over-wound inside, that she was almost on the verge of snapping completely.

What had happened to her? This time last week she had been perfectly all right... Hadn't she? All right, so she hadn't wanted to attend the Hopkinses' christening, and thinking about it had brought everything back, resurrected the pain she was increasingly conscious of having to suppress, but she had been to other christenings and had coped. What had been so special about this one, other than the fact that Jake Lucas had been there?

Jake Lucas. It was *his* fault she was feeling like this, she decided bitterly. It was because of him that she couldn't enjoy the news of her sister's pregnancy, couldn't react with the unshadowed pleasure and enthusiasm she wanted to feel.

Jake Lucas... If only he hadn't been there that night... If only he hadn't opened the door and seen... It had all been over then anyway, her frightened struggles to escape from his cousin's too powerful grip long since subdued and the damage done.

Jake Lucas. She hated and loathed him almost as much as he despised her. She smiled bitterly to herself. Much he would care. Still, she very much doubted that he was used to being on the receiving end of such a negative emotion from her sex. He was, physically at least, a very attractive and compelling man—even she could see that—the kind of man she would have expected to have had a string of women passing through his life, but oddly he seemed not to do so. He had a wide social circle of friends, but if he had a serious personal relationship with anyone it had not reached the town's very efficient grapevine.

Good-looking, comparatively wealthy and, according to everyone else, with the kind of personality that immediately drew others towards him, he still remained single.

'Rumour has it that he fell in love with someone years ago and that he's never got over it,' Chrissie had once remarked, but Rosie had found it hard to believe her. Jake Lucas, in love? He was too hard, too detached, his opinion of himself far too high to allow him to admit into his life the turbulence of an emotion like love.

It took most of the morning for her to help her client fill in her claims forms. The burglary had upset her, and left her feeling nervous and insecure, and Rosie, who had come across the same thing with other clients who had suffered similar robberies, let her talk, knowing that this was the best thing she could do.

Would she have felt any different, would her life been any different, if there had been someone for her to talk to? But how did you tell someone, anyone, anything like that? To explain what had happened, how her baby had been conceived in the first place, would have been hard enough, but then to go on to discuss her mixed and contradictory feelings over her miscarriage... How could she tell *anyone* of the relief she had first felt...relief at the death of her child, and then go on to expect them to believe how later her feelings had changed completely, and how guilty she had felt? As though in some way she had actually willed the miscarriage on herself.

Had there been any repercussions? Jake Lucas had asked her curtly the day he had come to see her.

'No,' she had told him stoically, denying the truth, keeping it secret and hidden, just as she had gone on keeping it secret and hidden ever since; but she had lied:

there had been repercussions then and there still were now, echoing agonisingly through her life, through her.

These days there was counselling available to people who suffered trauma, but at sixteen she had been too young, and much too ashamed and frightened, to have sought out any kind of professional advice even if she had been aware that she could have done so.

All she had wanted to do when she left the hospital was to put the whole thing behind her, to lock it away in the darkest, most hidden recesses of her mind, where it could lie forgotten.

Only her guilt had not allowed her to forget it; it had driven her, relentlessly sharpened by pain. And it had been a twofold guilt.

Initially she had felt shame and anxiety because of what she had done because, even though she knew they would do all they could to help her, her parents would be hurt. She had not thought about the baby then, that had come later…a secondary and much, much worse guilt, a deep, more intense feeling of having failed another human being, of having let them down and caused them to suffer. Her baby had died and, even though logically she knew such things happened, she still felt that she was to blame, that somehow her baby had known that it was not loved…not wanted and that because of that…

And now Chrissie was having a third child. Rosie gripped the steering-wheel tightly.

She was not going to allow herself to be envious of her sister, to spoil the relationship she had with her with feelings of useless envy, to spoil the relationship she would one day have with her new niece or nephew with unhappiness for the child she had lost.

It was just gone lunchtime when she got home. On Saturday morning she normally got up early and drove into town to do her food shopping, while everywhere was relatively quiet, but today, because of her business appointment, that had not been possible, and now she realised she was virtually out of fresh food.

Not that it mattered. She didn't really feel very hungry.

But she really ought to have something to eat, an inner voice nagged her. Neglecting her health wasn't going to solve anything or make her feel any better, was it?

Grimly she pulled open the fridge door and surveyed its contents without any real enthusiasm and then closed it again.

The hot, sunny weather had continued all week, and her garden, especially the pots of flowers and herbs by the back door, all needed watering.

Originally built to house farm workers, her cottage had a very good-sized rear garden, which had been one of the main reasons Rosie had bought it in the first place.

Last summer, much to Chrissie's exasperation, she had painstakingly laid a pretty, small, stone-paved area outside the back door.

It had taken up virtually all her spare time for the whole of the summer, and Chrissie had told her forthrightly that she would have been wiser to pay someone else to do the work, leaving herself with enough free time to concentrate on her own social life.

'Honestly, Rosie,' she had told her. 'Anyone would think you *wanted* to be on your own. Every time anyone asks you for a date you tell them that you can't because you're working on that patio.'

Rosie had said nothing, not wanting to admit to her sister that inadvertently she had hit upon the truth.

Rosie assumed that it was because her job brought her into contact with so many men that she was constantly being asked out, unaware that it was her looks and personality that were really responsible for their interest.

'What's wrong with you?' Chrissie had demanded with sisterly candour.

'I just don't want to get involved,' Rosie had responded quietly.

Outwardly she had been calm, and even slightly withdrawn, but only because that was the sole way she had of controlling her inner pain.

She ached to be able to confide in her sister, to tell her what she was suffering, but she had been too embarrassed, and besides, keeping her emotions, her fears, the truth hidden had become so much a part of her that the mere thought of discussing it with anyone else caused her to feel acute terror and panic.

Instead of having some lunch she made herself a cup of coffee and then, changing into her jeans and a T-shirt, she went outside and connected up the hose-pipe.

She had a small vegetable plot which she was diligently tending at the bottom of the garden.

She was working busily in it and just starting to relax, enjoying the warmth of the sun and the peace, when suddenly she heard children's voices as some people walked past, and immediately she began to feel her tension return.

This was getting ridiculous, she told herself shakily, as she put down her fork. *She* was getting ridiculous.

Even so, she couldn't stay where she was. She hurried back to the house, angry with herself and frightened at the same time. If she couldn't bear to hear the sound of other people's children, things were getting worse, she acknowledged as she stripped off her gardening gloves outside the back door. It was the news about Chrissie's baby that had thrown her into this mood, but somehow she must come to terms with it to...

She tensed as she heard someone walking down the path that ran alongside her house.

She heard the gate squeak as it was opened, and firm, male footsteps.

She moved forward to see who her visitor was at the same moment as he came round the corner.

Jake Lucas!

Rosie froze.

'I couldn't get any answer when I rang the bell at the front,' she heard him saying. 'But your car was outside, so I thought I'd just check to see if you were in the garden.'

The shock was beginning to recede now, slowly and painfully, so that it was as though her numbed brain was only gradually coming back to life; her thought processes were slow and disjointed.

'I've brought you this. You left it at the Hopkinses' last weekend.'

Rosie stared at the hat he was holding in his hand. Her hat.

She lifted her head and looked at his face.

Why had Jake Lucas brought her hat back? What was he doing here? What did he want?

Suddenly her thoughts began to accelerate and then to skid frantically out of control as panic gripped her.

'There's something else I wanted to discuss with you as well.'

His voice was deep and calm...controlled...but Rosie still caught the note of hidden tension within it, her perceptions sharpened by her own tension and fear.

'There isn't anything you and I could possibly have to discuss,' she told him fiercely.

It was too much, his coming round here like this, invading her privacy, her peace...just as his memory constantly invaded her thoughts...her dreams...or, rather, her nightmares.

She saw that he was frowning and her heart gave a frantic bound, but she wasn't going to let him intimidate her any more with his disdain...his contempt...

Like her he was dressed casually in jeans and a cotton T-shirt but, where hers was large and loose, his clung lovingly to a torso that was surely far too athletically, firmly muscled for a man of close to forty.

His arms—tanned, no doubt by the time he spent in Greece—made his T-shirt look even whiter in contrast.

It was all very well knowing that pale skin was far healthier, safer than that which was tanned, but even so she couldn't help contrasting the cream pallor of her own arms with the warm golden-brown of his, and feeling slightly envious, Rosie admitted.

As she spoke, she stretched out her hand to take her hat from him, making no attempt to conceal her hostility and bitterness.

· Why should she, after all? *He* had never made any attempt to conceal how he felt about her. She made it plain by her body language that she expected him to hand over her hat and leave without saying whatever it was he seemed to think they had to discuss. But, instead of responding to the message of her tense muscles and shuttered face, he kept hold of her hat and took a step further into the garden, a step closer to her, so that her fingertips accidentally brushed against the flesh of his forearm.

His skin felt warm and smooth like velvet, so that for a moment she was actually tempted to stroke it and savour the pleasure it gave her to touch it. The dark hair covering his skin was much softer than she had expected. Somehow she had thought it must feel abrasive... Because that was how she saw him? Instead it felt silkily fine, distracting and confusing her.

The sensation of him jerking his arm away from her touch, just a heartbeat before she herself removed her fingers, made her face burn with shamed confusion and panic.

*She* should have been the one to withdraw first, instead of standing there, practically caressing him deliberately. As though...as though...as though she had actually wanted to touch him. And that would be what he was thinking of course... That she hadn't changed at all...that she was still the person he had believed her to be at sixteen, and so avaricious for sensual, sexual sensation that she would offer herself to any male...initiating intimacy where none was wanted.

'Ritchie is coming back.'

She was so wrapped up in her own anger that it was

several seconds before she realised what he had said, what the hard, flatly delivered short sentence actually meant.

When she did she reacted automatically, shock turning her skin even paler, as she stepped back from him instinctively, looking directly into his face, searching it frantically, half expecting to find he was simply tormenting her. But, as she met his eyes, she saw that he was speaking the truth.

Her heart started beating frantically fast, her stomach churning nauseously.

'Why... How?'

She seemed to hear her own voice from outside her body, thin and weak, taut with tension, as fear and shock poured reactively through her.

She could see the way Jake's mouth curled fastidiously with disdain, the way he stepped back from her, almost as though he believed she actually contaminated the air between them, as though he couldn't bear to be anywhere near her.

'He's married,' he told her harshly. 'He's coming over on business and decided to combine it with a holiday. He's bringing his wife and children with him. His wife wanted to see the place where he grew up.'

Children... Ritchie Lucas had children... Just for a moment she was so overwhelmed by bitterness and pain that she almost cried out, and then thankfully the agony faded, and with it the red mist of fury which had momentarily possessed her.

'Nothing's changed, has it?' she heard Jake saying in angry disgust. 'You still want him...still love him.'

He was about to say something else, but Rosie didn't let him.

She was suddenly possessed by an anger, a rage so intense that it overcame her fear of him, her awareness of his contempt and dislike, everything but her need to strike out against him, to make him suffer as she was suffering…to refute…

It boiled and raged inside her, demanding an outlet, refusing to be suppressed any longer. She was literally shaking with the force of it when she opened her mouth and told him wildly. 'Love him…? I loathe him…hate him… I've always hated him—always.'

She was shaking violently now, barely aware of the small, frantic voice inside urging her to be more cautious, but suddenly she needed to vent her emotions, her bitterness, to tell Jake Lucas how she felt, how she hurt.

It was as though the injustice of his accusation, coming on top of all that she was already suffering, had driven everything but her need to defend herself from it out of her mind.

'How *could* I love him after what he did to me? The way he forced himself on me…the way he ruined my life…?'

She was crying now, raising her hand to dash the tears away impatiently as the rage continued to burn through her, fuelling the hot outburst of everything she had kept locked inside herself for so long.

'Ritchie *forced* himself on you…?'

The sharp question sliced through her hysteria, shocking her into silence.

She was shivering, ice-cold with shock and reaction, Rosie realised shakily, as the icy disbelief in Jake

Lucas's voice cut through the heat of her emotional outburst.

'Are you trying to claim that Ritchie raped you?' he demanded acidly. 'Because if so…'

Nausea clawed at her stomach. She had to stretch out an arm towards the wall of the house to support herself and yet, despite the terror, the fear rising up inside her, despite the vivid image etched on her brain of the way this man had stood and watched her as she lay rigid on his aunt and uncle's bed, her still only youthfully developed breasts partly revealed to him, her body numb with panic and shock but her brain, her emotions rawly vulnerable to the contempt, the disgust with which he was regarding her, Rosie suddenly knew that if she backed down now, if she allowed him to use her vulnerability and pain against her so that he could reject the truth, she would suffer for that weakness for the rest of her life. She had made that mistake once; she wasn't going to make it a second time.

Curling her fingers into the window sill, she willed herself to be strong, to stand up for herself. She was a woman now, not a child.

'Because if so what?' she challenged him bitterly. 'You'd be more than happy to stand up in court and call me a liar…' Her mouth trembled, but grimly she fought for control. 'Maybe Ritchie didn't knock me unconscious and drag me upstairs…and of course, to a man like you, that is what rape constitutes, isn't it…'

'You were drunk,' Jake interrupted her flatly. He had gone pale beneath his tan, she noticed, and his eyes, the eyes she had always thought of as being so cold and unemotional, were blazing with heat.

Somehow this sign that he was, after all, capable of betraying himself with human emotion instead of making her afraid that he might lose his temper actually strengthened her determination to stand up for herself.

'Yes,' she agreed. 'Because my drink had been spiked… Deliberately, as I discovered later.' Her mouth twisted a little. 'By my so-called friends with the connivance of your cousin.' Her head lifted proudly as she tilted it back so that she could look directly at him. 'Apparently your cousin thought that it was high time I learned what life…what sex was all about…' Distaste shadowed her eyes as she looked away from him. 'So, yes, I was drunk… Mercifully… But not so much that I didn't know what was happening—'

'Just enough to ensure that you didn't do anything to stop it, is that what you're saying?'

The harshness of his voice made Rosie's skin burn.

'If Ritchie did, as you claim, force you…then why the hell didn't you say something at the time?'

'To whom?' Rosie demanded. 'You'd already shown me how people were likely to react,' she told him bitterly. 'All I wanted to do was to forget that it had ever happened. So, you see, if you've come here to warn me to keep away from your cousin because he's married you needn't have worried. Like you, he's the last person I want anywhere near me.'

She heard his indrawn breath, but didn't bother to look at him. Suddenly she felt weak and drained, her anger dissipated by her explosion of temper. She felt sick inside and very close to tears, confused and shaken by her own reaction but, most of all, desperately wishing she had not allowed him to provoke her into that verbal outburst.

What good had it done? It was obvious he didn't believe her, but then she had always known that he wouldn't. No, it had been for her own benefit that she had given in to her driven need to tell him the truth, not his.

She started to turn away from him and then stopped as she heard him saying harshly. 'If what you're saying is true—'

*If*! The anger reignited inside her. She turned her head and looked at him, her mouth curling with a passable imitation of his own disdain.

'*If*? How can it be, when *you* were there? When you saw *everything*. When you have already decided that I was just a cheap little tramp who—'

'I never thought that…'

His denial took her by surprise. She stared at him, her expression momentarily unguarded and vulnerable.

'But you…'

Grimly Rosie compressed her lips, biting back the words she had been about to say.

'It doesn't matter now,' she told him distantly. 'It was all a long time ago…'

'So long ago that you've forgotten all about it, is that it?'

Rosie tried not to shiver as she heard the sarcasm in his voice.

'Of course,' she lied bleakly. 'After all, it's hardly the kind of thing I'd want to remember, is it?'

## CHAPTER FOUR

'WHAT DO YOU mean, you're not going? Of course you are. The Simpsons are some of Mum and Dad's oldest friends,' Chrissie said firmly.

Rosie tried to hold on to her temper. Chrissie's pregnancy seemed to be making her bossier than ever, or was it simply that with her outburst to Jake Lucas she had somehow lost a little of her protective coating... her control? Rosie wondered uneasily.

She had noticed a disturbing tendency recently for her emotions to swing far more violently from one extreme to the other. She was constantly tense and on edge, looking over her shoulder, half expecting to find Jake Lucas watching her disapprovingly.

She cringed to think of that awful confrontation she had had with him. *Why* had she told him about Ritchie? What had she hoped to achieve? What had she expected him to do? Apologise... Show regret, remorse, guilt? He hadn't even believed her. He had made that plain enough.

'Rosie...' Guiltily she realised that Chrissie was still talking to her.

'The Simpsons' lunch party... You've got to go... I can't, because we're spending that weekend with Greg's mother.'

'Chrissie-'

'You're *going*,' Chrissie told her firmly. 'Or are you trying to tell me that you've got some hot date? That you're sneaking off to spend the weekend romantically tête-à-tête with someone special?'

Rosie knew when she was beaten. Though she could have pleaded work, she told herself later in the week when she surveyed her desk tiredly.

She had heard nothing from Ian Davies and she knew better than to telephone him, but she had plenty of other work to keep her busy. There had been a spate of burglaries in the area, necessitating house calls on her clients, while she helped them to fill in their claim forms.

It was a time-consuming and non-profit-making task, but she was glad to be kept busy. It kept her mind off Jake Lucas. Or at least it should have done.

Instead of relieving her tension and enabling her to put the past firmly behind her, her furious outburst against his cousin only seemed to have reactivated her pain and despair.

Would she have felt any different if he had believed her?

She frowned. No, of course she wouldn't. She didn't need absolution from him. And anyway, how could he believe her when doing so would mean having to admit that he had misjudged her? No, she didn't need his understanding, his acceptance. She didn't need *anything* from him, she told herself fiercely as she bent her head over her paperwork.

'AND SO I said to him, well, if you don't tell her, then I'm going to have to, whether she's your sister or not...

I'm not having her telling me how to bring up my children…'

'Rosie…I am glad you could make it.'

A little guiltily, Rosie returned Louise Simpson's warm hug.

'Thank goodness the good weather has held, although Jim isn't too pleased. He's worried about people trampling on his precious lawn,' Louise told Rosie ruefully.

The Simpsons' garden party was an annual event which normally Rosie enjoyed, but Jake Lucas had made her feel so hypersensitive that she felt reluctant to go anywhere, just in case she might run into either him or his cousin. Not that Ritchie was likely to be here, she reassured herself. As far as she could remember the Simpsons, like her own parents, had never been particularly friendly with his.

Taking comfort from this reassuring thought, she followed her hostess out into the sunny garden, and then froze as almost the first sound she heard was a child's voice with an unmistakable Australian accent. Panic hit her immediately.

Quickly she turned away, heading in the opposite direction, thankfully merging herself with a group of people around their host.

She stayed there as long as she could, determinedly asking Jim questions about his precious roses long after everyone else's interest had quite obviously faded.

'Better get back to my duties as barman,' Jim told her. 'You haven't got a drink, Rosie. Come with me and I'll get you something.'

She would have preferred to stay where she was,

separated from most of the other guests by the rose-hung pergola which was Jim's pride and joy, but Jim already had his hand on her arm and she couldn't refuse.

The bar had been set up on the large, paved area just outside the house. Several large groups of people were congregated around it.

One of the Simpsons' grandsons had taken over as barman, but was now quite obviously pleased to be relieved of his duties and set free to enjoy himself with his friends.

He was a shy boy of around seventeen, who blushed fiercely as Rosie said hello to him.

'The lad's got a bit of a crush on you,' Jim told her with a chuckle as his grandson disappeared. 'Can't say I blame him, mind…if I was twenty years younger…'

Dutifully Rosie smiled, refusing an alcoholic drink and asking for something cool and soft instead.

As she waited for him to pour it for her, she felt a sharp prickle of sensation at the base of her neck, a conviction that someone was watching her. Automatically she responded to it, turning her head to glance over her shoulder, and then she froze.

She was being watched, by Ritchie Lucas. She recognized him immediately, even though, unlike his cousin, *his* physical appearance had changed considerably in the fifteen years since she had last seen him.

At school, Ritchie had been considered good-looking by some of the girls, although personally she had never found his rather beefy blond-haired looks in the least attractive. To Rosie there had always been something slightly coarse and uncontrolled about the way he looked which, she had subconsciously felt, reflected his personality, so that she had always felt repelled by him. Which was no doubt why he had decided to pick on her as a victim of his callous cruelty.

Now that coarseness was very much more obvious, his skin burned a reddish brown by the Australian sun, his blond hair now more gingerish and very obviously receding. He had put on weight and, to judge from his physical appearance, was not particularly keen on exercise. He was holding a can of beer, and as she looked at him he raised it towards her, acknowledging her presence, grinning at her, ignoring the faintly anxious glance the small dark woman at his side was giving him. Was she his wife? And those two boys with her, were they his sons? Jake Lucas was standing with them, and Rosie shivered, quickly putting down her glass, her drink untouched.

She couldn't stay here now.

'Rosie, are you all right?' she heard Jim asking her in some concern.

'Yes... Yes... I'm fine... It's just that I've remembered a phone-call I should have made...'

She was gabbling, she recognised, her manner causing Jim's concern to increase as she desperately tried to find an excuse to escape.

'Business? Well, feel free to use the phone in the study. You know where it is.'

Her face burning with a mixture of guilt and anxiety, Rosie headed for the house. If she were lucky, she would be able to make her escape without anyone even noticing she had gone. She would have to phone Louise later, of course, and apologise for leaving without saying goodbye to her.

Feverishly planning what she must do, Rosie opened the French window and stepped into the cool darkness of the house.

The noise of the party receded, muted by the glass doors.

Thank goodness she had arrived a little late and had not parked on the drive, where she might have been blocked in by other cars.

She could hear voices in the kitchen, where Louise and her helpers were preparing to serve the buffet.

Feeling almost like a criminal, she held her breath and waited, hoping that no one would come into the sitting-room or see her leaving.

Her heart was beating too fast and unevenly—her body's physical reaction to her mental panic.

She started to walk across the room to the door which led into the hall. It would have been easier to go back outside and walk round the side of the house to the front, where her car was parked, but she was terrified of doing so in case she saw the Lucases again.

She was halfway across the room when she heard the French window open. Immediately she froze.

'Rosie… Not going yet, are you?'

Her heart lurched with fear. Ritchie Lucas. Had he seen her come inside and deliberately followed her, or was it simply a coincidence?

She heard him laugh. She had always disliked his laugh. He had laughed that night when she had tried to make him stop.

'Well, now, you sure have turned out fair dinkum, haven't you? A real beaut… I always did have a yen for you, you know, Rosie…'

He was, if not drunk, then certainly very close to it, Rosie recognised fastidiously as she watched him swaying slightly on his feet. He was sweating heavily, and she could smell the sour, rank scent of his body.

She wanted to turn away from him, to open the door and run, and yet at the same time she was terrified of taking her eyes off him, terrified of breaking that visual contact, clinging to it as though in doing so she was actually somehow physically keeping him at bay.

She was paralysed with fear, she recognised numbly; like an animal trapped in the beam of a car's headlights, she simply could not move, was too *afraid* to move in case in doing so she somehow brought about the very thing she most dreaded.

'Little Rosie… Who knows what might have happened between us if I'd stayed around?'

Sickly Rosie watched as he lurched towards her.

Run…run, a voice inside her screamed frantically, but she was incapable of obeying it.

He had reached her now, was stretching out his hand to touch her, the same hand which had once torn at her clothes, clawed at her skin, forced her hands behind her back while he had laughed at her efforts to escape.

She felt the panic building up inside her, and knew that everything she was feeling was clearly written on her face: the fear, the anxiety, the revulsion…

'You're not wearing a wedding ring… Good on you. Marriage is a mug's game. Gets you landed with a nagging wife and a parcel of brats. You and I could have fun together, Rosie…'

Fun… Rosie felt herself gag as her stomach heaved.

He was so close to her now that she couldn't understand how he couldn't see the revulsion on her face.

'Rosie…there you are, darling…'

Her head snapped back in shock as Jake walked into the room.

Darling… Jake had called her darling… What…?

At any other time she might almost have been cynically amused by the way Ritchie gave way to his cousin, stepping back from her as Jake stepped forward, moving aside so that Jake could stand next to her.

'I just came inside to cool down,' she heard Ritchie blustering. 'Didn't realise you and Rosie here had something going, Jake…'

'Naomi's worried about Adam. She thinks he's got a temperature. She wants to go back to the hotel.'

When had Jake taken hold of her arm in that proprietorial, possessive manner? Rosie wondered numbly, as she watched Ritchie turn back to the French window in obedience at his cousin's words.

She had started to tremble, small tremors of shock shaking her body. She tried to control them, knowing that Jake must be able to feel them, but the more she tensed her muscles, the more intense her shuddering became.

She knew what Jake must be thinking, of course, why he had laid claim to a relationship between them that never had and never could exist. No doubt *he* thought she had deliberately encouraged Ritchie to come in here after her… No doubt *he* thought she had deliberately planned the whole thing.

She turned towards him, intending to pull her arm free, but before she could do so the inner door opened and Louise came in, coming to an abrupt and obviously startled halt at the sight of them.

'Jake…Rosie…'

'We were just about to leave, Louise,' Rosie heard him saying. 'Rosie isn't feeling too well… Too much sun…'

Rosie could see the surprise and the speculation in Louise's eyes. Her heart sank. Louise had a kind heart, but she was also a terrible gossip, and Rosie could see quite plainly the interpretation she was putting on finding them together, Jake's hand resting so possessively on her arm, silently laying claim to an intimacy between them which did not in reality exist. And yet she seemed unable to drag herself free as Jake led her towards the open door and through it.

She was still trembling, still physically reacting to what had happened and to her shock, she comforted herself for her lack of will-power and for letting Jake take the initiative.

'You can let go of me now,' she told him stiffly. 'There's no need to march me off the premises like some kind of criminal. Whether you believe it or not, the last thing I want…the last person I want to be with is your precious cousin, so if you think I'm—'

'So I saw.'

Rosie stiffened at his curt tone. 'If you're trying to be sarcastic—' she began, but Jake shook his head.

'Now you're the one who's jumping to conclusions,' he told her quietly.

When she stared at him, he explained grimly, 'I saw your face, Rosie. I saw the way you were looking at him. No one, but no one, could fake that kind of re-action.'

Was he actually saying that he believed her? That he *didn't* think she had deliberately enticed Ritchie to follow her? Rosie couldn't believe it. Shock made her sway slightly on her feet, so that Jake's grip on her arm immediately tightened. She heard him curse and then say under his breath, almost pleadingly,

'Don't go and faint on me, Rosie. Not here...'

Faint...? What did he think she was? Rosie wondered belligerently. Of course she wasn't going to faint.

'I *am not* going to faint,' she told him, gritting out each word with separate emphasis.

'I'm glad to her it,' Jake told her cordially. 'But as well as not fainting, do you think you could possibly start walking?'

'You don't have to hold on to me,' Rosie told him fiercely. 'Or to see me off the premises. My car is this way,' she added as Jake ignored her.

'And mine is this way.'

Rosie stared at him and then started to protest.

'I'm not letting you drive,' Jake overruled her. 'Not in the state you're in...'

'What state?' Rosie protested. 'I'm not in any kind of state...'

Abruptly Jake stopped walking, turning her round to face him.

'No?' he said grimly. 'What is it, then? Malaria? That's the only physical cause I know of for someone shaking the way you're doing.'

'I am not shaking,' Rosie denied, but her face had

started to burn with reaction and awareness of the fact that she was lying and that he knew it.

'You might as well give up, Rosie,' he told her. 'I am not letting you drive home, even if that means physically carrying you to my car. I wonder if Louise is watching us,' he added speculatively.

Rosie couldn't help it. Immediately she looked anxiously towards the house, and then realised that he was deliberately baiting her.

'Why did you do that?' she demanded shakily.

'Do what?'

She gritted her teeth. 'Why did you tell Louise we were leaving together as if…as though…?'

'As though what?' Jake prompted her.

Rosie shook her head, suddenly overcome with reaction. She didn't have the energy to argue with Jake right now, or to demand an explanation of why he had implied to Louise that they were a couple, using that deliberately intimate 'we'…nor why he had indicated the same thing to Ritchie, either.

'Come on…let's go…'

Too drained to argue, she turned mutely to follow him, and then tensed as he slipped his arm round her, pulling her firmly, protectively almost, against his body, as though he knew how weak and vulnerable she was feeling.

Instinct urged her to pull away, but obeying that instinct was too far outside the capabilities of her shock-exhausted muscles.

It was easier simply to stay where she was, to let him guide her towards his parked car.

She was muzzily pondering on why it should feel so

comforting to be held so securely against him when she
loathed and disliked him so much, when he suddenly
stopped walking and cursed briefly under his breath.
She lifted her head automatically to look at him, forgetting how close to him she already was.

'It's Ritchie and Naomi,' he told her. 'They've seen
us and they're heading this way.'

His breath felt coolly pleasant against her hot skin.
He was smiling at her, she recognised with an odd,
frantic skipped beat of her heart, his eyes suddenly
soft and warm.

'Rosie…'

He had never said her name like that before, and
she was startled to discover how different it sounded
when he did.

She looked enquiringly at him, her brain, her emotions, her responses still not fully recovered from the
fear Ritchie had caused her to feel.

Jake bent his head towards hers; his free hand
cupped her face, his skin cool and firm against the
nervous heat of hers.

She looked at him questioningly, and then froze as
she realised what he was going to do.

It was too late to avert her face and push him away.
He was holding her too closely, the arm which had
felt so protective and comforting now imprisoning her
against him.

Anger took the place of her earlier numb shock. She
opened her mouth to demand that he release her.

'Rosie…'

She felt rather than heard him say her name, through
the movement of his mouth against her own, her body

automatically stiffening in furious reaction at his kiss, her eyes wide open and brilliantly angry; but he ignored the outraged message of her body language, sliding his hand along her jaw, stroking her hair back off her face in a slow, deliberately caressing movement, and all the time he kept on kissing her, moving his mouth lingeringly over her own, caressing her tightly closed lips with gentle deliberation, ignoring the rigid rejection of her body. He was kissing her with a mixture of tenderness and determination that was completely unfamiliar to her, his mouth stroking over her own again and again until it was impossible for her to keep her lips rigid any longer.

She felt them start to tremble, and so, obviously, did he, because the movement of his mouth stilled for a second and lifted from hers, his thumb stroking gently against her lips, applying just enough pressure to make them part slightly.

Rosie glared angrily up at him, letting him know that, while physically he might be able to dominate her, he could not control her mentally.

His eyes were open too. She saw the way they glinted between his lowered lashes as he looked first into her eyes and then down at her mouth, as though to remind her that, despite her mental and emotional dislike and rejection of him, physically she had not been able to do so, and not because of any use of brute force.

He was still looking at her mouth, and an exquisite thrill of horror ran through her as she realised he was going to kiss her again.

'No.' Her denial of him was an anguished, shaken whisper.

'Still not gone yet, Jake?'

'We were just leaving, Ritchie.'

Ritchie!

Rosie could feel the tension gripping her spine, enclosing it with ice-cold fingers of dread. Without being aware of it, she moved closer to Jake, only realising what she was doing when she felt his arm move slightly to accommodate her, and recognised with a tiny dart of disbelief that she had pressed herself so close to him that she could actually feel his heartbeat and the solid strength of the bones and muscles that underlaid his flesh. Was she really seeking protection from her fear of Ritchie with Jake?

'Ritchie, the boys are tired and hungry.'

Rosie could hear the irritation in Ritchie's Australian wife's voice.

'Oh, for God's sake, Naomi, stop nagging, will you?'

The obvious lack of love or respect in Ritchie's voice made Rosie wince. Even without knowing her, Rosie felt sorry for his wife.

She could just imagine how *she* would have felt had she been the recipient of that kind of comment, spoken in front of a stranger from a man who professed to love her, and not just in front of her, a stranger, but in front of their children as well.

She could feel Jake starting to release her, and for one blind, panicky moment she actually wanted to hold on to him, to beg him not to let her go, not while Ritchie was still here, and then she realised that he was reaching round her to open the passenger door of his car for her. Gratefully she got in, her legs unsteady, her face flushing, as she inadvertently caught a glimpse of the leering expression on Ritchie's face.

'Looks like *you* made the right decision, mate,' she heard Ritchie saying to his cousin. 'Seems to me that a fella can have a hell of a lot more fun single than married.'

Rosie saw the nervous, half pleading look his wife gave him and her pity for her increased. She obviously loved him, Rosie acknowledged compassionately. And that love quite obviously made her very vulnerable. Even the two boys seemed slightly nervous of their father and yet, as Rosie watched them walk away, she saw that, young as they were, they were already beginning to adopt their father's bullying and contemptuous attitude towards their mother.

'Poor woman…'

She spoke the words out loud without realising that Jake could hear them.

'Yes,' he agreed tersely as he slid into the driver's seat of his car and closed his door. 'Ritchie treats her abominably, and she's terrified of losing him. Part of the reason she wanted this trip to England was because she hoped that it would give them time alone together as a family. Apparently when they're at home Ritchie prefers to spend his time with his mates.'

The obvious disapproval in his voice made Rosie turn her head to look at him, a small frown pleating her forehead.

In the past she had thought there was little to choose between Ritchie and Jake; they were related by blood and, it seemed, shared a common attitude towards sex. Of the two of them she had disliked Jake more than

Ritchie because Jake had been the one to more openly show his contempt of her and to condemn her. Now Jake's reaction to Ritchie's treatment of his wife confused her.

'Naomi is very vulnerable where her relationship with her husband is concerned. Ritchie's obvious interest in you won't help her.'

Rosie stared at him.

'Ritchie's interest in *me*? But—'

'He followed you into the Simpsons' house,' Jake told her coolly. 'And Naomi saw him do so. If I hadn't intervened…'

Was *that* why he had held her, kissed her…implied that they were lovers…not to protect *her* from Ritchie's unwanted attentions, but to protect Ritchie's wife from the pain her husband was causing her?

A pain she hadn't known she was capable of feeling unfolded achingly inside her. Her fingers curled tightly into her palms, nails pressed against her skin to prevent her crying out with the intensity of it. If they hadn't been travelling at some speed she would have been tempted to wrench open the door and fling herself bodily out of the car.

She frowned as she suddenly realised that they weren't travelling in the direction of her home.

'This isn't the way to where I live,' she protested.

'No,' Jake agreed calmly, pausing for a few seconds before adding, 'I'm taking you home with me. We need to talk.'

'To talk?' Rosie stared at him, infuriated by his high-handedness. 'What about?'

The look Jake gave her made her toes curl in nervous self-protection.

'The past…' he told her shockingly. 'And the future…'

# CHAPTER FIVE

THE PAST! ROSIE TREMBLED. What was he planning to do? Grill her so relentlessly that she broke down and retracted the statements she had made about what had really happened with Ritchie?

She had already seen in his face how little he had enjoyed hearing the truth. She knew how much it must have infuriated him, hurt his pride.

And it wasn't just for the sake of his pride that he would want her to retract, either.

She had read into his comments about Ritchie's marriage a none too subtle warning off. Did he *really* think after what she had told him that she would want anything...anything to do with his precious cousin?

He must do, otherwise why the charade about pretending they were a couple? Why that kiss?

That kiss... Her heart started to thump unevenly. Against her will, an unfamiliar mixture of languor and sensuality spilled slowly through her.

She had received other kisses, and yet she could not remember a single one of them affecting her as his had done.

There had been a new dimension to it, an awareness within her of an aching sadness and pain, as though she had suddenly become aware that there could be something in a man's kiss that could stir her so deeply that she was helpless to resist it.

But she *had* to resist it. She had to remember just who Jake Lucas was, and just what the situation between them really was. That hadn't changed just because she had lost her temper and challenged his perception of past events.

He had not followed her into the Simpsons' house to protect *her*, as she had initially so naïvely imagined. He had followed her to protect his cousin's marriage.

From her?

She was the last person who wanted to threaten it. As far as she was concerned, she would have much preferred Ritchie to stay where he was in Australia.

At least he seemed to have no memory of what had happened between them. Thank God, but then, remembering how much he had had to drink, it was perhaps not as surprising that he should have forgotten, as she had once thought.

She remembered how terrified she had been all those years ago, dreading hearing that he had been boasting about what had happened, and then how stunned, how disbelieving, when it first began to dawn on her that he couldn't even remember the incident.

She had been glad, of course, but at the same time bitterly resentful that something which should have had such a devastating effect on her and her whole life had had so little effect on his.

For him there had been no guilt, no pain, no suffering, and certainly no remorse.

From what she had seen of him today, she doubted that he was capable of feeling any of those emotions, and for the first time she was thankful that the child she had conceived had been spared the discovery of what his or her father was.

No child should have to suffer that kind of burden; she could see already the effect he was having on his own children.

She shivered suddenly in reaction to what she was thinking. Out of the corner of her eye she saw Jake's head turn in her direction as though he had seen that small physical betrayal.

His terse, 'Almost there,' might almost have indicated concern coming from any other man.

But he had already shown her how little concern he had for her, how little respect for her reputation. To have kissed her like that where anyone could have seen them, to have verbally implied that they were lovers.

These might be the 1990s, couples *might* live together openly and easily without feeling it necessary to marry, believing that their emotional commitment to one another was the only bond they needed. But this was a very small market town where, while mothers and grandmothers might say bravely to their friends that of course they would never dream of pressuring their child to marry simply for the sake of convention and that children were far better off being brought up by two adults who loved them rather than by a married couple who stayed together out of duty, they still admitted privately to their closest friends that, old-fashioned though it made them, they would dearly love to have seen their son or daughter married, preferably before they presented them with their much-loved grandchildren. Rosie knew that, while her parents would never question the way she chose to live her life, they would still, deep in their hearts, be hurt by any gossip linking her name with Jake's in a way that suggested they were lovers with a physically intimate relationship that they had no plans to make permanent.

And then of course there were her clients. Many of them were her own age and some even younger, and she knew they would not be in the least concerned about what she did in her private life. But when she had taken over from her father she had taken on his clients, many of whom had expressed doubts as to her ability to fill her father's shoes, and their attitude, she suspected, would be confirmed once any gossip reached their ears. In their eyes a woman involved in a sexual relationship with a man outside marriage was not his equal, involved in a mutual partnership, but something very different. She would lose status and respect in their eyes… And their business as well?

Wearily she closed her eyes, a feeling of helpless despair and resentment washing over her.

Glancing across at her, Jake frowned. Even now, in the intimacy of his car, she still had this ability to withdraw from him, to distance herself from him.

Pain twisted unsparingly inside him. Fifteen—*sixteen* years and nothing had changed. She still had the ability to get under his skin, to touch emotions and needs that no one else had ever come even close to touching.

She hated him, of course. He had always known that. He had seen it in her eyes the night he found her in bed with Ritchie and he had seen it in them on every occasion they had met since.

Until this afternoon.

This afternoon she hadn't looked at him with hatred.

She hadn't looked at him with love, either, he reminded himself.

HE HAD BEEN twenty-three, almost twenty-four, when he'd first realised he loved her, and he had been revolted by that knowledge. She had been just sixteen, still a schoolgirl, a child, and with none of the precocious sexuality of some other girls of her age.

She had been innocent, unknowing…uncaring of the effect she was having on him.

He had fought against what he felt with all the power of his intellect and intelligence. He was a man, she was a child; his feelings were a malicious joke played on him by capricious fate, a form of sickness, madness… a danger both to him and to her.

They would pass. They had to pass. He could not really be in love with a sixteen-year-old *child* who barely knew he existed, who was closer to his irresponsible cousin in age than himself. All he had to do was to ignore them, to ignore her, and eventually they would go away without harming either of them.

And then he had found her in bed with Ritchie. It had been a neighbour of his aunt and uncle's who had alerted him by telephone to Ritchie's illicit party.

He had arrived there to find the living-room full of drunken teenagers, rock music blaring out so loud he suspected that, sober, their eardrums could not have withstood it.

Unable to find Ritchie, he had automatically gone upstairs, searching his cousin's bedroom first, only alerted to the fact that someone was in his aunt and uncle's by the light shining beneath the door.

Ritchie had been standing beside the bed, fully dressed, when he walked in, but Rosie…

He gripped hold of the steering-wheel as the echoes of the emotions he had felt then surged through him.

She had been lying motionless in the bed, sated by his cousin's lovemaking, he had thought, her clothes in disarray. He couldn't remember actually moving across to the bed, only the look on her face as she turned and saw him.

The savage jealousy which had possessed him had sickened him. If she had wanted so desperately to experiment with sex, what the hell had made her choose his cousin? he had wanted to ask her…

Why hadn't she come to him?

But he had already known the answer, of course. She barely even knew that *he* existed. She probably believed herself to be in love with his cousin and, knowing that Ritchie was shortly leaving the country, that she was unlikely ever to see him again, she had wanted to consummate that love.

Later he was glad that the width of the bed had separated him from Ritchie, otherwise, he suspected, he might not have been able to control the savage murderous impulse which had possessed him.

That he had been jealous—blindingly, achingly, tormentedly jealous—of his cousin had been one thing and bad enough; that he should have physically wanted to punish him, to destroy him almost, because of that jealousy had been another.

He remembered the terrified white-faced look Rosie

had given him once she had pulled her clothes on; then he had thought it was that she had recognised what he had been feeling... Now...

He glanced at her. Her eyes were open now, but she was looking away from him, out of the window.

To discover that she had not gone willingly with Ritchie as he had believed, to hear her say that her drink had been deliberately spiked, that his cousin had deliberately planned to hurt and humiliate her...to hear her accuse him of being a part of the reason why she had said nothing...nothing...of what had happened... had made no complaint...no protest...

And this afternoon he had seen in her face confirmation, if he had needed it, of just exactly what she did feel about his cousin.

*Why* had he been so blind? Why hadn't he realised then...?

Why hadn't he questioned events more deeply? Why, out of his love for her, had he not somehow known what she had chosen to keep hidden from him...from everyone...?

When she had needed him most, when she might have *turned* to him as a confidant and a friend, through his own behaviour he had caused her instead to turn away from him, to believe that he despised, condemned her.

Even if he had not loved her he could *never* have done that. She had been a child...a baby still.

But she had not been a child the day he had gone to see if there had been any repercussions from her relationship with his feckless cousin. Then she had been all woman, cold, distant, remote, while her eyes blazed her defiance and bitterness.

He had thought then that she had somehow blamed him because Ritchie had gone, never coming close to realising what she was really feeling.

But he knew now!

His face hardened as he turned into the private road that led to the small, exclusive development of houses of which his own was one.

Rosie, turning her head to protest again that she had no wish to go home with him nor to listen to anything he might want to say, saw his expression and, shocked by the harshness of it, instead said nothing.

She was still suffering the effects of her run-in with Ritchie, she told herself shakily, as Jake brought his car to a halt on the brick-set drive to his house.

The house, although modern, was built on traditional lines, and like its neighbors was set in a mature wooded landscape, so that the warmth of its brick façade blended comfortably with its green backdrop.

His manners, at least, were very different from his cousin's, Rosie acknowledged, as Jake opened the car door for her and waited courteously for her to get out. Where Ritchie had terrified her with his physical strength and brutality, Jake intimidated her with his watchful distancing of himself from her, with the contempt she had believed he had always felt for her.

She had been conscious of that watchful distance even before he had found her with Ritchie, nervously wondering what it was she had done wrong that made him focus on her like that. She had been in awe of him even before that night, she admitted as she waited for him to unlock his front door.

But she wasn't in awe of him any more. Why *should* she be? And she wasn't going to allow him to intimidate and browbeat her into retracting what she had said about Ritchie.

The house had a good-sized rectangular hallway, immaculately decorated and furnished, but bare of any signs of being lived in.

There was no evidence of any family clutter, no pictures, no flowers, none of the things which, in Rosie's view, went to make a home.

As though he had read her mind, Jake turned his head and said wryly, 'Sterile, isn't it? That's partly because I'm away so much in Greece, and partly because Mrs Lindow, who comes in to clean for me once a week, says she "can't be doing with clutter and flowers making a mess all over the place".'

'I can see her point,' Rosie responded tactfully.

'But you'd have them anyway...mess notwithstanding.'

His comment startled her. She looked up at him, confused by the expression in his eyes, but still unwilling to admit how often she did buy flowers, simply for the pleasure that seeing and smelling them gave her, and then kept them even when their petals had actually started to fall, reluctant to condemn them to the dustbin until the very last one had died.

'I thought we'd be more comfortable in the sitting-room,' she heard Jake saying as he opened one of the doors off the hallway and waited for her to precede him into the room.

Like the hall, it was immaculately decorated and furnished, and like the hall it too was somehow too perfect and sterile, apart from the huge Knole settee in front of the fire.

'It belonged to my grandmother,' Jake told her, watching her study it. 'The designer who organised the décor here for me wanted to throw it out, but I wouldn't let her. Instead we compromised and had it recovered, although in some ways I still prefer the original scuffed velvet...'

'It looks very comfortable,' Rosie responded inanely.

Why was he treating her like this, almost...almost gently, as though he was concerned...afraid for her...?

'It is,' he assured her. 'Try it...'

Without ever having intended to do so, Rosie discovered that she was sitting down on the settee and being dwarfed by the depth and comfort of it.

She heard Jake laugh. 'You look like a little girl on her best behaviour at her grandmother's Sunday tea party,' he told her.

Rosie flushed because that was exactly how she *had* been feeling, uncomfortably aware of the elegance of the settee's silk covering and the fact that her lack of height meant that when she sat back in it her feet could not comfortably reach the ground.

'You can't sit on it like that,' Jake told her. 'Take off your shoes and make yourself comfortable.'

'Oh, no...I couldn't...the fabric...'

'The fabric is only fabric,' Jake told her wryly. 'Possessions are never more important than people. We've got a lot to talk about, Rosie. Would you like something to eat? You missed the buffet at the Simpsons'.'

Rosie shook her head, knowing that, despite the fact that she had eaten nothing since her breakfast, she was far too on edge to do so now.

'A drink then...tea...coffee...?'

*Why* didn't he just get on with it? Rosie wondered grimly. Was he deliberately playing on her tension, trying to gain the upper hand so that when the crunch came...?

She shook her head.

'Well, I'm going to have something,' she heard him say. 'I shan't be a minute.'

He was barely that, returning just as she had finally decided she couldn't stand the excruciating agony of either sitting with her back ramrod-straight or being unable to bend her knees and had admitted that he was right and that the only way she was going to be able to sit comfortably on the settee was if she removed her shoes and curled up on it.

She was just doing this when he walked in, carrying a bottle of wine and two glasses.

When he filled them both and offered one to her, she shook her head.

'It's only wine,' he told her mildly. Instantly her face was suffused with colour, as she wondered if he was deliberately taunting her with what she had told him about her drink being spiked the night of the party. She couldn't tell him that alcohol was something she never touched. It would make her look too weak and vulnerable.

Instead, reluctantly, she accepted the glass from him. The dark red liquid glowed richly in its plain glass, the only touch of colour in the otherwise neutral room.

When she held the glass in her hand, the liquid almost seemed to warm her flesh through it.

She took a sip, surprised to discover how much she liked the warm, fruity taste.

It *was* only wine, she reminded herself, and only one glass, and then, as Jake seated himself at the other end of the settee and turned to face her, she took another nervous sip.

This was it. This was the moment when he challenged her, demanding that she retract what she had said about Ritchie.

'Rosie…the night of the party—'

'I don't care what you say to me…how much pressure you put on me, I'm not going to change what I said,' she told him fiercely. 'What I told you was the truth.'

'Yes, I know…'

His quiet words silenced her. She stared at him and then took a hasty, tense gulp of her wine, grateful for the warmth that spilled through her from it, driving out the icy fingers clutching apprehensively at her muscles.

'You… You *believe* me…'

He nodded his head and she felt a huge surge of emotion rush through her. She took another gulp of wine.

'You believe me now, but you wouldn't have believed me then…'

She saw the look on his face and deep within her something splintered sharply, painfully.

'You wouldn't,' she repeated, denying what she had seen in his eyes.

He bowed his head.

'I *saw* the way you looked…the disgust…the contempt…'

She watched as he twisted his glass in his hands. There was something different about him now, as though…as though the distance he had always placed between them had somehow gone.

'Those were for me,' he told her in a low voice. 'Not for you. I *did* think you'd gone with Ritchie willingly, though. I thought you believed you were in love with him.'

Rosie shuddered. 'I hated him even then. He was always making fun of me…taunting me because I didn't…' She ducked her head uncomfortably.

'Because you were a virgin,' Jake supplied for her.

She couldn't speak, her emotions too raw and painfully close to the surface to allow her to. She nodded instead, taking another sip of wine, hoping it would steady her.

When Jake had brought her here to talk, the last thing she had expected was that they would be having such an extraordinarily intimate conversation…that he would accept so readily, so easily what she had to say… that he would say, and mean it, that he believed her.

She felt dizzy with the unexpectedness of it, lightheaded…*light-hearted* almost, as though some huge weight had been lifted from her.

'I felt so ashamed…so…so guilty and afraid…'

'The guilt was Ritchie's.' He paused as he looked at her, and then added in a low voice, 'And the shame mine.'

'It's all a long time ago…and none of it matters now,' Rosie told him jerkily.

What on earth was she saying? Of *course* it mattered. *She* had never forgotten what had happened…his disgust…his contempt… Only he had just said that they had never been directed at her, but at himself.

'This afternoon…were you leaving the party because you'd seen Ritchie?'

His abrupt switch from the past to the present caught her off guard.

'Yes,' she admitted. 'I saw you both…' She bit her lip when she realised what she had admitted, and realised from the bleak look he gave her that he had recognised all that she had not said.

'I suppose I deserved that,' he told her. 'I'm sorry if Ritchie upset or frightened you.'

'Well, at least he didn't remember…about the party. He was very drunk that night.'

'But not too drunk to rape you.'

The harshness of his voice startled her, making her body go tense.

'I can understand why you want to protect Naomi,' she told him. 'But I'm no threat to Ritchie's marriage.' She gave him a small, bitter smile. 'Far from it. Your Draconian measures this afternoon to keep me away from him really weren't necessary. He's the last man I'd want in my life, even if he wasn't married…'

She drank her wine quickly.

'I wish you hadn't said what you did in front of him, implying that you and I… If it gets round and people start to gossip… I know it isn't supposed to matter these days, that a woman is as entitled as a man to enjoy her sexuality—' She knew her face was burning, but she was determined to say what she felt must be said.

'But you don't want anyone thinking that you're enjoying *yours* with me, is that what you're trying to say?' he interrupted.

He sounded angry now, more like the Jake she knew, his voice harsh and tense.

'This is a small town,' she told him uncomfortably, 'where people sometimes still make old-fashioned judgements. If it weren't for the business... I—'

'You'd what?' he demanded. 'Be quite happy for people to think that you and I are lovers?'

He moved towards her and automatically she jerked back from him, her skin burning red beneath the cynicism in his eyes.

'It isn't that,' she protested automatically. 'It isn't you...'

Helplessly she saw the way he tensed, pouncing on her words.

'Not me,' he repeated softly. She saw him breathe in, awareness glinting in his eyes as he asked her quietly, 'Tell me something, Rosie. How many men...how many lovers have there been since my cousin raped you?'

To her horror, Rosie felt her whole body start to tremble. She could feel the emotion welling up inside her, the tears clogging her throat, the pain, the panic, the grief, all burning through her in a relentless, unstoppable tide.

'None... None... I didn't... I couldn't... There wasn't—'

'Rosie... Rosie...'

Almost before she could even blink Jake had covered the distance between them, taking her gently in his arms, removing the now empty glass from her hand, holding her as tenderly and carefully as though she were merely a child…a baby…

A baby…

The sound of anguish she made was smothered against his shirt, the tears she hadn't realised she was crying soaking through the cloth.

She tried to stop, to pull away, to regain control of herself and her emotions, but Jake wouldn't let her. Instead he was talking to her, crooning almost, soft, reassuring words, telling her that it was all right for her to cry, that it was all right for her to show him her pain, to share her anguish and bitterness.

Distantly she heard the small warning voice that urged her to think, to stop, to cease this act of idiotic self-betrayal with a man whom she had always thought of as her enemy.

And yet who better to share what she was feeling with? Who could understand more…know more?

'Let it all go, Rosie,' she heard him telling her gently. 'There's no need to hide it any more. You have every right to feel pain and anger.'

She realised that he was stroking her hair, the slow movement of his hand not just reassuring her but giving her as well a physical contact with him that some part of her needed.

It was as though by touching her, holding her, talking to her he had almost become a part of her as well as a part of her past.

Words, phrases, emotions, all of them jumbled and turbulent, tumbled from her lips as her control broke. Somehow she was sixteen again and saying all the things she had not been able to say then, expressing all the agony, the guilt, the anger he had caused her to feel.

Once she actually bunched up her fist and pummelled it fiercely against his chest as she relived physically the emotions he had caused her to suffer then, which she had never been able to express.

It didn't occur to her to question *why* the focus of all those emotions should be Jake and not Ritchie. She was not capable of such logical thought, but Jake was.

As he held her and let her emotions pour from her like poison from a lanced wound, he ached with sorrow and guilt for all that she had suffered.

*Why* had it never occurred to him that she might not have gone willingly with Ritchie? Had it been any other girl but Rosie, he must surely have done, but, in the seething torment of love and jealousy which had seized him, in the blinding belief that she felt for his cousin the desire she would never feel for him, he had not stopped to question her willingness to be there.

Now he realised that the dazed, transfixed stillness of her body had not been caused, as he had so jealously believed, by sensual satisfaction, and was not the aftermath of sexual completion, but on the contrary had been caused by terror and shock and had been her mind's way of escaping from the horror of what had happened to her.

Ritchie hadn't been violent with her, just rough, she had told him when he gently probed her memories. He had used force to overpower her, but the sexual act itself had been over quickly.

Her memory of it was not one of pain but one of

shock and shame that she had not somehow guessed what he had intended and been able to stop him.

As he held her and listened to her, he knew that there were no words to express what he was feeling, no relief from the burden of his own guilt.

He couldn't bear to think of what it must have done to her to have kept such a traumatic event to herself, to have felt that there was no one she could confide in, no one who could support and help her, and he could bear it even less knowing that *he* should have been that someone and knowing that, far from being that someone, as he ought to have been, he had actually caused her trauma to increase.

All these years she had kept all that locked away inside her. No one knew better than he how hard it was to lock away any kind of emotional pain, and he considered himself to be an expert on the subject, but somehow *she* had done so, stoically bearing the burden of self-contempt and guilt he had unknowingly given her.

He knew without her having to tell him why there had been no other men in her life, no other man who might have shown her that she had every right to enjoy her sexuality, to take pleasure and joy in it.

*He* was to blame for that as well.

She was still leaning against him, her body a sweet, warm weight against his own. She was trembling slightly, physically exhausted by the intensity of her emotional turmoil and by reliving the past.

He held her closer, resting his jaw against the top of her head, closing his eyes against the acid burn of his own tears. Not tears for himself—he didn't deserve them—but for her.

He tried not to think about how it could have been…
how she might have turned to him, how they could have
been united by a close bond of friendship and understanding, even if she could never have loved him.

Or maybe even that might have happened as well…
Maybe she *might* even have trusted him enough to let
him show her what the physical expression of love and
desire between two people really should be.

He felt his muscles tense his desire for her—no longer an old hunger, but a sharp, immediate need.

He was old enough now to know that his love for
her would never disappear…never change, and he knew
enough of his own nature to accept that he was not the
kind of man who could ever inflict on someone else,
even if they never actually realised it, the role of being
second best. Better to remain on his own than do that.

He looked down at the silky russet wing of hair that
concealed Rosie's face.

He had hurt her, almost destroyed her. *He,* not
Ritchie. It had been *his* reaction, *his* imagined judgement of her…*his* imagined contempt for her that she
remembered far more clearly than Ritchie's offence.

She was still trembling, but she had stopped crying…stopped talking.

EXHAUSTED, ROSIE LAY against Jake's chest. She could
feel the heavy, slightly uneven thud of his heartbeat,
smell the special personal scent of his body warmth.
Instinctively she nestled closer to him, comforted by it.

She had got it wrong, Jake had told her. He had never
blamed her, never felt contemptuous of her, and instinctively she had known that he was telling her the truth.

With that knowledge, with that barrier between them removed, had come an overwhelming need to talk about the past, to let the emotions she had kept dammed up inside her spill out.

Now she felt drained and shaky, light-bodied and empty, cleansed of all her corrosive, bitter memories. She lay in his arms, too weak to move, her physical actions still governed by her emotional needs, and the strongest of all those was her need to be close to him, to just lie here and be held by him, safe, protected, comforted, her pain shared and understood.

She closed her eyes sleepily and then opened them reluctantly as Jake said her name, lifting her head to look at him.

He watched her sombrely, and then lifted his hand to gently move her hair off her face, tucking it behind her ear.

Abruptly she remembered the way he had kissed her outside the Simpsons' house, and automatically her glance slid to his mouth, her own lips parting, her lungs expanding as she had to gulp in air.

No one else had ever kissed her like that, made her feel like that, made her forget everything but the sweet intensity of the pleasure curling slowly through her.

Jake bent his head and her heart started to hammer frantically fast.

Was he going to kiss her again? Would it feel the same this time? Would she…?

She touched her lips nervously with her tongue, wetting their dryness, her body tensing as she heard the way he said her name.

Somewhere within her a stern voice warned her that

she was being deliberately, dangerously provocative, but she didn't want to listen to it. She wanted him to kiss her, she recognised with a fierce lurch of her heart. She wanted him to hold her, to touch her, to...

Impulsively she reached out and touched him, placing her palm against his jaw. Her breathing quickened with the sudden sensual awareness that flooded her.

'Rosie.'

His voice sounded different as he said her name, thickened, slurred. He turned his head so that his lips touched her palm, caressing it.

A deep shudder went through her, her eyes unwittingly imploring as she reached up towards him.

'Rosie...'

He had intended to protest, to stop her, to explain to her that what was happening to her was just an automatic physical reaction to the emotional turmoil she had just experienced, but instead, as she reached up to him and he felt her breath against his mouth, he ignored what conscience told him he should do and instead stroked her parted lips with his tongue, tasting the richness of the wine she had drunk, feeling the way her mouth and then her whole body quivered openly in response to him, feeling the way his *own* body responded as though galvanized by a surge of sensation he was totally powerless to control.

He heard the soft murmur she made in her throat as he kissed her, felt the soft, vulnerable warmth of her body as she pressed closer to him, and knew that she was not really aware of what she was doing.

His hands touched her face, exploring its delicacy, tracing the shape of her ear, the line of her neck, feeling her shudder violently beneath his touch, and was helpless to prevent himself from deepening his kiss in response to that shudder, tasting her with his tongue, feeling her brief, hesitant shock before she melted against him, opening her mouth fully to him, her hands moving urgently over his back, so obviously impatient with his shirt and the barrier it made between her touch and his flesh that he tugged it out of the way himself, whispering against her mouth how much he wanted her to touch him, and how much he wanted to touch her.

Jake wanted to touch her... Rosie tensed and opened her eyes.

Her hands were pressed flat against the hard, warm flesh of his back, her mouth was soft and swollen from his kiss—the kiss she had silently implored him to give her.

She was trembling violently, aware of so many conflicting emotions that she could scarcely make sense of what she was feeling.

'Touch me,' Jake had told her, and then he had told her as well how much he wanted to touch her.

Now he was holding her, his mouth gently caressing her throat, his hands...

She shuddered as she realised how close his hands were to her breasts. All she had to do was to move very slightly and then he would be touching them.

Would the fingertips which had traced the bones of her face so delicately and sensuously arouse the same pleasure within her if they touched her breasts?

Her body's response to her thoughts made her catch her breath in shock as she felt the fierce pulse of desire that arced through her.

'Rosie…what is it? What's wrong?'

Unable to answer him, she wrapped herself around him, clinging shakily to him, half exalted by what she was feeling and half afraid, but not challenging the extraordinariness of what was happening, or the fact that it should be *this* man who was causing her to feel like this, to experience desire and need, to suddenly know that behind the fear and self-loathing of herself as a woman lay a sensuality that was strong and powerful enough to sweep aside and overcome all the trauma of the past if she let it.

'Rosie…'

She felt Jake hold her, move her, as though he were going to push her gently away from him, but, as his hands slid against the silk of her dress and came into contact with the soft fullness of her breasts, he went very still.

Rosie tensed as well, scarcely daring to move, to breathe…unable to initiate the touch her senses suddenly craved, but longing, aching for him to touch her, to gently remove the barrier of her dress and the silk bra she was wearing beneath it and to caress her breasts with the same care and tenderness with which he had touched her face…to make her feel whole again…clean again, to let her experience a man's desire and to express her own.

And yet, when he did as she had wished, she was suddenly overcome with tension and panic, freezing with a cold fear which could not be dispelled by the warm touch of his hands against her body.

'Rosie…it's all right…it's all right…'

As she heard his voice, heard its reassurance and

steadiness, felt him gently release her, the band of fear imprisoning her snapped.

'No…please…don't stop…I want…'

The husky, stammered words pierced him like darts of acid fire as Jake watched her…loving her…wanting her…knowing that, in her emotionally wrought state, she *believed* she wanted him…knowing that he had no right to take advantage of her confusion, and knowing, as she raised her mouth to his and started to kiss him, that there was no way he was going to be able to resist her…to stop…

This time when he caressed her breasts the icy coldness of fear had gone, and in its place was a sensation so achingly sensuous and pleasurable that it was Rosie herself who arched her body up towards him, her hands holding his head, her fingers sliding fiercely into his hair, her head dropping back against the damask fabric of the settee as gently, watchfully at first, and then, as he realised that the sensation of his mouth caressing her nipples had not frightened or distressed her, finally giving in to his own passionate need to express his desire for her, he suckled on the hard points of flesh until the needle-sharp darts of sensation that pierced her made her cry out frantically in shocked pleasure.

Drugged with arousal and need, Rosie moved closer to him, and then abruptly she realised what she was doing, and what could happen if she didn't stop.

Jake felt her tension, her withdrawal, and lifted his head to look at her. Her eyes had gone blank with shock and panic.

Had his touch, his caress…his love reminded her of Ritchie? Disgust and pain welled up inside him.

'Rosie, please…'

He had been about to beg her to forgive him, but Rosie misinterpreted the anguish in his voice and shook her head before he could finish, her eyes still registering the intensity of her emotions.

'No… No… I can't,' she told him. 'I couldn't go through that again…I couldn't endure killing another baby…'

Rosie was barely aware of what she was saying, driven by the weight of her pain and guilt, by the knowledge of how easily she had forgotten the past…forgotten what had happened… She was sickened by how easy it would have been for her to give in to that ache still pulsing through her and to encourage Jake to make love fully to her.

How *could* she have forgotten what happened with Ritchie…the baby she had conceived, the panic and anger she had felt, the guilt and pain when she had lost it, the way that loss had haunted her, shadowing her life?

She was so wrapped up in her own thoughts, so shocked by her own lack of control, by the speed with which her physical desire had overwhelmed everything else, obliterating all that she ought to have felt, that she was completely unaware of what she had said and what she had revealed until she heard Jake demanding harshly, 'What baby? What are you saying? You told me…'

Realising what she had done, what she had betrayed, Rosie focused on Jake's face.

The panic that hit her was so intense, so strong, that it was like an icy tide physically engulfing her, swallowing her up and dragging her down into a dark, roaring void.

She came out of it slowly and reluctantly, not wanting to remember what happened, accepting the glass of wine Jake was giving her, distantly aware of his tension, but withdrawing from it.

She felt thirsty, her throat and mouth dry, but when she asked Jake for another glass of wine he frowned slightly, pausing before pouring it for her.

She drank it greedily, needing its warmth, its numbing benevolence, frowning uncertainly as she glanced down at her body and realised that, although her dress was fastened, she wasn't wearing a bra beneath it.

Her nipples pulsed and ached, openly erect beneath the silk.

She suddenly felt overwhelmed by a desire to close her eyes and go to sleep. She yawned and then yawned again, ignoring the sharp urgency in Jake's voice.

'I'm tired,' she told him petulantly. 'I want to go to bed.'

She stood up, her eyes widening in shock as she felt the room sway around her. The two extra glasses of wine she had insisted on having were making her head swim, confusing her thoughts. She yawned again, and closed her eyes.

Jake caught her as she staggered. By the time he had placed her carefully on the settee she was already deeply asleep.

And drunk? On three glasses of wine? A heavy, rich red wine, and she had not had anything to eat, he reminded himself. Add to that the emotional turmoil she had been through, and perhaps it was not surprising that her body and her mind wanted to find escape in sleep.

He ought to take her home, but he couldn't let her go until she had explained that frantic, pleading statement she had made to him.

*Had* she conceived Ritchie's child? When he had gone to ask her she had told him coldly that she had not conceived. But then, given what he knew now, was it likely that she would have told him anything else?

He bent grimly over her, picking her up.

Luckily Mrs Lindow always kept the spare beds made up. She could spend the night in one of them and then tomorrow they could talk.

Whether she had conceived Ritchie's child or not made no difference to the way he felt about her, to his love for her.

But if she had… He flinched as he recognised what such an event must have done to her…on top of all that she was already suffering.

There was no point in trying to wake her now. As he carried her towards the door he paused and looked down into her sleeping face, brushing his mouth gently against hers.

'I love you, Rosie,' he whispered against her lips and, even though he knew she could not have heard him, her mouth seemed to soften into a slight smile.

An omen for the future?

## CHAPTER SIX

BECAUSE HE WAS determined there *was* going to be a future for them, Jake acknowledged as he carried her upstairs and carefully laid her down on the bed in the guest bedroom before removing her dress and then going to get one of his shirts to put on her before he pulled the duvet up over her.

She was so deeply asleep that she had barely stirred while he undressed her, and now he stood beside the bed, looking down at her.

It was just as well that she had called a halt to their lovemaking. He knew well enough that the passion and intensity of her response to him had been caused not so much by any personal desire for him, but by the release of all her pent-up emotions.

He would take things slowly with her, give her all the time and space she needed to feel comfortable with him. And if at the end of that she still rejected him... Love could not be forced, he reminded himself, and nor would he want to do so. But if he could keep her close to him, showed her that she could trust him...

He bent and touched her face gently, unable to resist the temptation to do so, and then, straightening his back, he went downstairs.

In the sitting-room Rosie's empty glass was on the

floor beside the sofa and with it, almost tucked beneath the sofa, was her bra.

He picked it up and took it upstairs, placing it with her other clothes, remembering the way she had responded to him when he had kissed her breasts, the eager feminine response her body had given him. It wasn't just her physical response he wanted, though. It was her love as well.

Rosie woke up reluctantly, conscious of the dryness of her mouth, of the unfamiliar deepness of her sleep, of the way her head ached.

She moved it slightly on the pillow, frowning as she realised she was not in her own bed.

Immediately she remembered what had happened, her face flushing with mortification as she remembered the way she had cast aside all her normal restraint, all her self-control…the things she had said… the things she had done… Most especially the things she had *done*… Her face burned hotly as she shuddered in mute self-disgust.

It must have been the wine. That and the shock of seeing Ritchie…of discovering that Jake Lucas had not disliked and despised her.

Shock did odd things to people.

Including inciting them to physical desire… She pushed the thought aside, throwing back the duvet and then tensing as she realised what she was wearing…or rather what she wasn't wearing.

Jake must have undressed her before putting her to bed…undressed her and then wrapped her in one of his own shirts.

Beneath its fine cotton covering she could see the flushed areolae of her breasts. They had looked like that last night after Jake had kissed them. A tight ball of angry guilt exploded inside her.

How *could* she have behaved like that, let such a thing happen—*wanted* such a thing to happen, and to the extent that, if she had not suddenly remembered the danger that lay in having sex with someone without taking precautions against conception, this morning she could well have been waking up in Jake's bed, not this one... In Jake's bed...perhaps even in Jake's arms...?

The feeling that swept over her appalled her. What was happening to her? Twenty-four hours ago, the last man she could ever have imagined as her lover had been Jake Lucas, and now... She didn't want him as a lover now either, she told herself fiercely. All she wanted to do was to get up, get dressed and get away from here as quickly as she possibly could, so that she could forget that the whole thing had happened.

What had possessed her to break down in front of him like that...to tell him things she had never imagined she would ever share with anyone, to reveal to him emotions, fears, needs so private that she had thought she would never be able to express them to anyone?

And yet strangely it had been easy sharing them with Jake... *He* had made it easy.

Until that moment when she had remembered, realised what she was doing, and she had cried out to him her fear of conceiving another child that she might lose.

She closed her eyes, trying to blot out her memory of the look on his face.

Where was he now? Downstairs waiting for her to put in an appearance...so that he could question her?

Anxiously she looked towards the door and realised that her clothes were on a chair several feet away from the bed, neatly folded with a note propped up against them. The note read,

Had to go out for an hour. Made fresh coffee at 10.00 am. Aspirins in cupboard if needed.

Fresh coffee... She closed her eyes; she could almost smell it...taste its hot, reviving flavour. As for the aspirins... She grimaced to herself before swinging her feet on to the floor and then wincing as her head pounded painfully.

Her bedroom had its own bathroom, well equipped with everything that she might need, including a new toothbrush. Jake's Mrs Lindow did her job very well, even if she didn't like fresh flowers, Rosie admitted. A hot shower, followed by a final cold rinse that made her skin tingle and the breath lock in her throat, helped to bring her properly round from her deep sleep, a much deeper sleep than she ever seemed to enjoy in her own home.

The silk dress was remarkably uncreased, although Rosie grimaced a little at having to put on clothes she had already worn.

She also felt acutely aware of the fact that the dress was quite obviously not the kind of thing she would have worn for her normal daytime activities. It looked what it was, she decided fretfully as she hurriedly brushed her hair. A 'going somewhere' dress, totally unsuitable for something like yesterday's party, and totally unsuitable for a Monday morning.

If only her car were outside and she could simply drive home. As it was she would have to ring for a taxi and hope that it arrived before Jake did.

The thought of seeing him, of knowing what he was thinking…remembering…made her shudder with self-loathing.

How could she have been so undisciplined, so uncontrolled?

She had been under a lot of stress recently, both from her work and from far more personal emotions. Look at the way she had reacted to Chrissie's announcement about the baby.

The baby… She tensed abruptly, forgetting her desire to escape before Jake returned.

She had told *Jake* about her baby. Or as good as. How *could* she have done that? *Why* had she done it?

The rest of the evening, the fact that she had both wanted and encouraged Jake to make love to her, and the uneasy fear-cum-anger those memories had been causing her, suddenly faded to nothing. They were nothing in comparison to her final, her *unbelievable* act of self-betrayal in telling Jake about her baby.

She closed her eyes, remembering the sharp incredulity in his voice as he questioned her, the deep anger in his eyes. She could recall them so clearly that she was forced to marvel at the brain's apparent ability to function independently of its owner's befuddled state.

She *had* to get away from here and fast, she told herself in panic.

She had to get away from Jake and to keep away.

She hurried downstairs and into the kitchen, glancing tensely at the clock on the wall as she looked around for a telephone and a directory.

Half-past ten. She couldn't have woken up much after Jake had gone. She had half an hour before he came back.

If she was lucky she might just be able to get away.

She saw a telephone mounted on the wall, but couldn't see any directory with it. The rich smell of the coffee distracted her, and she was looking longingly towards it, tempted to pour herself some, when without warning the back door opened.

She tensed immediately, her body feeling as though the blood was draining quickly from it as she went cold with shock, only it wasn't Jake who came in, it was his cousin's wife, and with her was an older woman whom Rosie knew vaguely. She was approximately the same age as her own mother, and Rosie seemed to remember that she had been very friendly with Ritchie's parents when they lived locally.

Both women came to an abrupt halt as they saw Rosie. Naomi Lucas spoke first, her thin, tanned face relaxing a little, the smile she gave Rosie genuinely warm and friendly as she apologised quickly for startling her.

'Jake gave me a key and told me to come and go as I pleased. Helen is taking me shopping, and I asked her if we could stop off on the way to warn Jake that Ritchie and the boys are likely to descend on him.' She pulled a slight face and Rosie recognised the tension behind her smile.

'Ritchie isn't very good with children. Jake is much

better. Australian men, or at least the more traditional of them, don't always take easily to the responsibilities of parenthood.'

It was on the tip of Rosie's tongue to point out that Ritchie was not an Australian but British, but she caught back the words, reminding herself that Naomi was Ritchie's wife and obviously loved him, while she disliked him and felt antagonistic towards him.

The friendliness of Naomi's manner surprised her a little, as the previous day she had felt that the other woman was regarding her with some hostility.

Feeling both uncomfortable and vulnerable, and all too aware of the speculative glances Naomi's companion was giving her, Rosie was just wondering how on earth she could make some rational explanation for her presence here in Jake's kitchen when Naomi smiled at her again and said warmly, 'I hadn't realised yesterday that you and Jake were together... I'm sorry if I seemed a bit offhand. I guess Jake would have got round to introducing us officially sooner or later. We've only just arrived here, after all. Is Jake going to be long?'

Rosie could neither move nor speak. The shock of what Naomi had just said had robbed her of the ability to do either.

She had known yesterday, of course, that Jake's behaviour was bound to give rise to some speculation and gossip, but this morning she had told herself firmly that if she ignored it and just pretended nothing had happened then everyone else was bound to follow suit. But now, with those casual, friendly words, Naomi had unsuspectingly, but very, very definitely, made that completely impossible.

She could see Helen Steadings—she had just managed to recall the woman's name—looking speculatively at her and taking in the significance of the silk
dress she had been wearing yesterday afternoon and
was still wearing this morning, and Rosie felt her face
start to burn painfully and betrayingly.

She might just as well have stood in the town square
and told everyone that she had spent the night with Jake,
she recognised bleakly as she saw Helen Steadings's
speculation turn to certainty.

To Naomi it might not be important that she and
Jake had spent the night together, and Rosie knew ra-
tionally that these days there was nothing unusual in a
couple of her and Jake's age having a sexual relationship if they chose to do so, but Helen Steadings knew,
as well as Rosie did herself, that Rosie was simply not
in the habit of having that kind of relationship. Her heart
sank as she recognised the interested curiosity in Helen
Steadings's scrutiny of her. It was not even as though
she could come up with any logical or reasonable excuse to explain away her presence in Jake's house in
Jake's absence, something strong enough to refute
Naomi's innocent assumption that they were established
lovers, and anyway, Rosie acknowledged sickly, it was
too late for that now.

The time for that had been immediately after Naomi
had started to speak, not now, far too many telling seconds later.

'Well, I guess there's no need for us to wait for Jake
now,' Naomi was saying cheerfully. 'You must both come
over to the hotel and have dinner with us. Jake can—'

'Jake can what?'

Rosie's stomach muscles cramped involuntarily as she heard Jake's voice and realised that she had been so caught up in her dismay that she hadn't heard him returning.

Neither, it seemed, had Naomi, because she turned round quickly, smiling at him, exclaiming, 'Jake…I didn't hear you come in…I was just saying to Rosie that the two of you must come and have dinner with us… I called to warn you that Ritchie is in charge of the boys and that they might all descend on you.'

It was instinct rather than habit that made Rosie step back into the shadow of the kitchen's large dresser. If she could have disappeared altogether she would have been only too happy to do so, she acknowledged miserably.

'Why didn't you tell us about Rosie?' she heard Naomi demanding teasingly. 'I had no idea until yesterday that the two of you…'

Rosie thought she had successfully stifled the small moan of protest she could feel rising in her throat, but Jake had obviously heard it because he lifted his head and stared straight at her.

His eyes looked different this morning, silver rather than grey, alive with a warmth she had never seen in them before… It must be for Naomi, she decided wretchedly. It certainly couldn't have been caused by her. Her stomach trembled nauseously as she remembered the previous evening.

How on earth, *why* on earth, had she got herself involved in such an appalling situation? Thank God her parents were away. Hopefully the gossip might have died down before they returned. Chrissie would hear it, though-Chrissie! What on earth was she going to say to her sister?

Chrissie was bound to demand to know what was going on, why *she* had not been told anything about Rosie's supposed relationship with Jake Lucas. Outwardly she might not show it, but inwardly she would be hurt by what she would perceive as Rosie's secretiveness.

And yet Rosie knew that she could *not* tell her the truth, that not even to her own sister could she betray her own lack of self-control, of self-respect.

It had been Chrissie who, when she was a teenager, had sternly pointed out to her what boys thought about girls who had no respect for themselves. An old-fashioned view now, perhaps, but one which Rosie suspected her sister still held.

What on earth was she going to say, to do…? She could feel the panic starting to build up inside her. Perhaps she could appeal to Helen Steadings…ask her to forget what she had seen…heard; perhaps…

'We haven't told *anyone* yet, have we, darling? Not officially.'

Jake's voice broke into her frantic thoughts. He was coming towards her, his smile as tender as his voice.

'Selfishly we wanted to keep the way we feel about one another to ourselves for a little while longer. We haven't even told Rosie's family yet…'

Immediately Naomi pounced, clapping her hands together in excitement.

'Jake, you mean that you and Rosie…? When do you intend to get married? Will it be while we're here?

What a pity the boys aren't younger, they could have been pages…'

Rosie made a strangled sound in her throat. Jake was standing in front of her, shielding her from sight, but he could see her and she could see him. She knew he must be able to see the panic in her eyes, and the shamed guilt.

Why on earth had Jake had to bring her back here with him last night? If he had simply taken her straight home, none of this would have happened.

'Is there going to be an official engagement party?' she heard Naomi asking. 'Or—'

Jake turned round. 'That's for Rosie to decide,' she heard him saying easily. 'As for a wedding—' he turned back to Rosie, his eyes sombre as he reached out and touched her face gently, tenderly, causing her to stare at him in dumb bemusement '—naturally, Rosie wants to wait until her parents get back for that, don't you, my love?'

His love… Rosie swallowed. What on earth was he doing…saying…? Didn't he realise that with every word he uttered he was making things a hundred, a thousand times worse, not just for her, but for both of them?

Where initially she had been pleased, grateful almost, to him for giving her presence in his home, in his bed, a covering cloak for semi-respectability, now she was appalled that he could have let things go so far.

To protect her…to protect both of them by concealing the fact that her intimacy with him had been caused by her own lack of self-control, that it had in fact been a potentially tawdry and merely sexual encounter, was one thing; to go over the top in the way he had just done and to imply that they were making plans and as good as engaged…

And that was what he *had* done. She could hear Naomi asking excitedly if she had as yet chosen her ring, and exclaiming to Helen Steadings that she was thrilled to bits with Jake's wonderful news.

It isn't true, Rosie wanted to tell them, none of it's true. But just as though Jake sensed the impulse exploding inside her his thumb brushed lightly against her mouth as though to silence her.

It did more than that…much, much more. Her senses and emotions, presumably still heightened by tension and stress, reacted immediately to his touch, flooding her with sensuality and awareness, reminding her of how she had felt the previous evening when he had touched her…kissed her. She could actually feel her body starting to tremble, her self-control starting to slide. A feeling of helpless anguish filled her, anger against herself and against Jake too, humiliation because of the way she felt and because she was sure he must know what was happening to her as well.

Ever since she had woken up she had been telling herself that what had happened last night could never have done so if she hadn't been upset in the first place, if she hadn't drunk all that wine, more than enough to have a disastrous effect on someone who normally never touched alcohol at all. That had been her protection, her escape, her defence against what had happened, and now with one light touch Jake had destroyed those protective barriers, showing her that physically she was as vulnerable to him, as responsive to his touch sober as she had been drunk.

She heard Helen Steadings saying something about them having to go. Jake moved away from her, escorting the two other women to the door, but not before Naomi had hugged her briefly and told her how pleased she was about their news.

It wasn't Naomi's fault, Rosie reminded herself while Jake was walking them to their car. Naomi wasn't the one who had drunk three glasses of wine and then proceeded to pour her heart out to Jake…to cling to him and make those small moaning sounds of pleasure which still echoed hauntingly in Rosie's own ears.

No, but she *had* come round here this morning and she *had* brought Helen Steadings with her and, but for that, Rosie might just have been able to escape without anyone knowing that she had spent the night here under Jake's roof.

All right, so there *had* been that small incident at the party but, alarmed as that had made her at the time, it had been nothing compared to this.

When Jake walked back into the kitchen she was still standing where he had left her. The look on her face made him ache to take hold of her and comfort her, to tell her that everything was going to be all right. Instead he simply asked calmly, 'Would you like some coffee?'

Coffee. Rosie stared at him. How could he stand there so calmly offering her coffee after what had happened? Anger boiled up inside her, her self-control snapping.

'How *could* you do that?' she demanded shakily. 'How *could* you let them think that you and I…that… we are about to get engaged…? Have you any idea what you've done?'

Rosie could hear her own voice rising, sharpening with hysteria.

Abruptly she stopped speaking. She must not allow herself to get out of control; her own panic increased her tension, and with it her awareness of her vulnerability.

'What would you have preferred me to do?' Jake asked her quietly. 'Allowed Helen Steadings to continue to think, as she so obviously was doing, that you and I were indulging in a hole-and-corner sexual fling? Is that really how you want to be gossiped about?'

'Why should *you* care how people gossip about *me*?' Rosie demanded tautly. 'You're a man; no one will think the worse of you for having a relationship that's merely sexual—'

'*I* would,' Jake contradicted her flatly, the vehemence in his voice startling her into looking straight at him. His eyes had lost that silver warmth they had had earlier, she recognised, and were once again the cold metallic grey she remembered. 'I'm not some sexual stud intent on chalking up a tally of conquests,' he told her in fierce disgust. 'My reputation is every bit as important to me as yours is to you, Rosie. *I* don't want to be judged as sexually promiscuous any more than you do. Having people talking behind my back speculating about what kind of relationship we have is every bit as repugnant to me as it is to you.'

Rosie shivered as she listened to him. *How* did he know so much about her, about the way she felt, the way she reacted? How could he know those things when everything she had done last night must surely have given him completely the opposite impression?

'But to let them think we were virtually engaged…
discussing marriage…'

Jake turned away from her, removing the filter from
the coffee machine. His voice was slightly muffled as
he told her, 'Engagements can always be broken, you
know…relationships allowed to quietly fade…'

Relationships?

'We don't *have* a relationship,' she protested frantically, and then as Jake turned round and looked at her
she felt herself flushing to the roots of her hair.

There was no need for him to point out that last night
she had virtually offered herself to him, inviting an intimacy she had never come anywhere near wanting to
share with anyone else.

'We can't do this,' she told him in panic. '*I* can't
do it…'

She turned away from him, feeling her body start
to shake with tension.

Logic told her that what she really ought to do now
was to talk the whole thing out with him so that they
could find some sensible and workable solution to the
situation, but emotionally she knew that she just wasn't
strong enough to do so.

She wanted to go home, to be on her own, to shut
herself away from everyone and everything to give herself time to build up her defences, and to feel whole
and safe again.

Just being here with Jake made it impossible for her
to do any of those things. He undermined and unnerved
her even without trying. She couldn't even look at him
without remembering last night, without remember-

ing the scent and taste of his skin, the feel of his hands on her body.

'I want to go home.'

She sounded more like a petulant, frightened child than a mature adult, she recognised bitterly as her taut demand filled the tense silence.

'If I could use your phone, I'll ring for a taxi.'

There, that sounded better, more positive, more adult. More the persona she was used to projecting on the outside world. The inner person, the vulnerable, frightened person she had betrayed so stupidly to Jake last night, was one she always kept hidden, known only to herself, but now Jake knew about that person as well. She wanted to take back that knowledge, to wipe his memory free of it.

'There's no need for that. I'll drive you—'

'No.'

Her denial was sharp and instant, and laced with panic, she recognised.

'I...I have to call and pick up my car.'

'There's no need. I did that this morning.'

Rosie stared at him. 'You... But... Did anyone see you?' she asked him quickly.

'It's too late to worry about that now, Rosie,' he reminded her wryly. 'The horse has already bolted.'

# CHAPTER SEVEN

EXPERIENCE...LIFE HAD taught Rosie that the best way,
the *only* way for her to deal with emotions and situa-
tions she couldn't control was simply to blot them out
altogether, not so much to pretend that they hadn't happened, but rather to refuse to allow herself to admit that
they had; and this was precisely what she was doing
now, or at least what she was trying to do, she admitted
as her concentration wavered from the pile of work on
her desk and her thoughts slid helplessly towards Jake.

It was almost twenty-four hours since she had last
seen him now. Twenty-four hours since he had driven
her home and seen her courteously and safely inside
her front door. Twenty-four hours...more now, since he
had publicly linked them together as a couple.

Every time her telephone rang she tensed, half afraid
to answer it, but on each occasion the caller had been
ringing with a legitimate business enquiry.

She had barely slept the previous night, too afraid to
close her eyes in case she started thinking about Jake...
remembering... But what was there to think about, after
all? Just a few sorry minutes of indiscretion and stupidity, that was all, but, no matter how often she tried
to tell herself that her behaviour had merely been the
result of too much tension and too much to drink, that

didn't stop her from being filled with shame and anguish over what she had done and from being afraid that, in some way, having once behaved so…so wantonly, she was somehow vulnerable to doing so again.

Again… No…she wouldn't do that… couldn't, surely? She was in such a state of panic that the telephone had rung several times before she heard it. She reached automatically for the receiver, speaking into it and then only just managing to mask her surprise when she realised that it was Ian Davies on the other end of the line.

He had been reading through her proposals and projections, he told her, and had been very impressed by them. He wanted to arrange another meeting so that they could discuss them at greater length.

Quickly Rosie opened her diary, agreeing the date he was suggesting.

'Oh, and by the way, we must have dinner together one evening; the four of us—you and Jake and Anne and myself.'

As she replaced the receiver, Rosie couldn't help wondering angrily if Ian Davies's apparent change of heart towards her had anything to do with the gossip he had obviously heard about Jake and herself.

And if it had, what would his reaction have been had the gossip labelled her as Jake's casual sexual partner as opposed to his 'fiancée'?

It was all wrong that, as a woman, her professional and business capabilities and expertise should be judged on her personal life, but she had known from the moment she realised that her name was going to be linked with Jake's that there *were* people locally who would take that kind of attitude, she reminded herself bitterly.

She stared at the telephone, half wishing that she had told Ian Davies that she didn't want his business, her female pride outraged by his old-fashioned attitude; but if she was to maintain her father's success she could not afford to indulge in that kind of sentimental self-indulgence, she reminded herself hardily. No.

After all, no man would do so. But then no man was ever likely to suffer the patronising attitude she had just come up against, she told herself fiercely. She wanted to be judged professionally on her own merits, not on some reflected glow from the business acumen of someone else—a *male* someone else.

She was still seething inwardly at the injustice of the attitude of Ian Davies and of all men like him when Chrissie burst into her office.

'Rosie, how could you?' she began bitterly, launching her angry attack before Rosie could even greet her, never mind ask her how her weekend had gone. 'Have you any idea of what an idiot you've made me look? When Sara Lewis told me the news this morning, I didn't have the faintest idea what she was talking about, and of course *she* realised straight away. She would... And now it will be all over town that you and Jake—'

Rosie froze.

'That Jake and I what?' she interrupted Chrissie huskily.

Had Chrissie heard that she and Jake had spent the night together? Were people gossiping about her, speculating on just how long she and Jake had been having a secret sexual relationship before they were found out...

before she was found out? After all, no one was going to condemn Jake for having sex with her, were they? No, their condemnation, their criticism, they would all be reserved for her, Rosie acknowledged miserably.

Chrissie was glaring at her, her face still flushed with anger. It was so unusual for Rosie to take the initiative and interrupt her that she had actually silenced her, but not for long, Rosie recognised, her heart sinking.

'That you and Jake are planning to get married, of course,' Chrissie told her tartly. 'What else?'

The relief that filled her was so intense that it was several seconds before Rosie recognised its shaming significance. If people were going to gossip about her, she was obviously so much a product of her small-town upbringing that she actually *preferred* to hide behind the deceit Jake had concocted to conceal the truth rather than to let them know what had really happened. Was she really so hypocritical?

If there had just been herself to consider it would be different but there was Chrissie and her family. Chrissie's children were just at an age where they would be vulnerable to any kind of adverse gossip about members of their family, and then there were her parents, and the business...

'Why on *earth* didn't you *say* something...tell me...' Chrissie was demanding furiously. 'Honestly, Rosie, I don't understand you...I mean, it isn't as though the two of you were indulging in some kind of sordid, clandestine sexual fling. *That* I could understand your wanting to keep secret.'

Rosie flinched, wishing she could shut out her sister's bluntly corrosive comments. Chrissie had no idea of the effect of what she was saying, of course. Why should she have?

'Have you any idea of how much of a fool you've made me look? My own sister is on the verge of getting engaged, and I don't know a thing about it...

'As it is, I'm sure that Sara knew quite well that I was lying when I told her we'd decided to keep the whole thing quiet because you and Jake hadn't decided on a final date for the wedding as yet.

'Rosie...*why* didn't you tell me? I had no idea you were even seeing Jake, never mind... To come home and find out that everyone else but me does know... and to have that cousin-in-law of his going on and on about what a pity it is that her two boys are too old to be pages, and how she'll have to buy her outfit over here because of the difference in seasons... Honestly, Rosie, I just don't understand you. To tell someone who's a virtual stranger before you'd said anything to me...especially when the parents are away.'

To her dismay Rosie realised that, behind her anger, Chrissie was very genuinely upset and close to tears. Wretchedly guilty at having upset her, especially so early in her pregnancy, she said the first thing which came into her head to try and soothe her.

'It isn't definite that Jake and I *will* get engaged. The whole thing's been exaggerated. If there had been anything to tell you, Chrissie, I would have done so—'

'What do you mean it isn't definite?' Chrissie interrupted her grimly.

As she looked into her sister's face, Rosie recognised that her attempt to soothe her had had almost the op-

posite effect and that, if anything, Chrissie looked an-
grier than ever.

'You spent the night with him, Rosie. Oh, yes, I
heard all about *that*,' she added scathingly. 'Of course,
I know you're an adult and old enough to make your
own decisions, but with Allison coming up to such a
vulnerable age, I hope she isn't going to start thinking
she can follow your example… It was bad enough finding out from someone else about your engagement, but
if you're trying to tell me that—'

Suddenly Rosie had had enough.

'That what? That Jake and I made love…had sex?
Why shouldn't we? As you've just pointed out, we *are*
adults. I'm your *sister*, Chrissie, not your daughter, and
if people in this town haven't got anything better to do
than to gossip about something which is none of their
business…none of anyone's business apart from Jake's
and mine…'

She heard the outraged hiss that Chrissie gave, but
ignored it, all the tension, fear and misery she had kept
dammed up boiling up inside her and refusing to be
contained.

'Why *should* I have to tell you or anyone else what
I'm planning to do? Did *you* tell me that you weren't
using any form of birth control and might conceive another child…'

This time she did respond to Chrissie's outraged
gasp, her temper leaving her as quickly as it had come,
leaving behind it a cold feeling in the pit of her stomach
and a shakiness to her muscles, plus the miserable sense
of having been both unfair and unkind to her sister.

She saw that Chrissie obviously thought so as well, because she was as pale as she had been flushed before.

'I can see there's no point in trying to talk to you while you're in this kind of mood,' Chrissie told her as she turned towards the door. She paused and looked at Rosie. 'I'm sorry if you think I'm prying,' she added stiffly.

She had gone before Rosie could open her mouth to stop her and to apologise for her own behaviour.

Chrissie had been wrong to burst into her office demanding explanations, but she had had every right to feel hurt at what she saw as being deliberately excluded from something which was apparently common knowledge to others.

There was no chance of her being able to tell her sister the truth, though, Rosie recognised. Not after Chrissie's outburst about the effect of her behaviour on Allison's moral outlook.

That too had been an unfair comment, but this unexpected pregnancy had put Chrissie on edge, making her far more dramatically emotional than usual.

Pregnancy *had* that effect on some women, especially in the early months. Rosie remembered how she had felt... How...

She closed her eyes, balling her hands into tight, tense fists. Hadn't she got enough misery to think about without adding that?

She would *have* to find some way of placating Chrissie, of course. But how? The last thing she wanted was Chrissie taking an authoritative and stage-managing role in her supposed engagement and marriage plans. She wouldn't put it past her sister to actually almost steamroller her and Jake into marriage. It was just as well that their parents were away and not due to return for several months. Not even Chrissie would expect her to get married in their absence; by the time they did return, they could have brought their relationship to a discreet end as Jake had suggested.

None of this would have happened if Jake hadn't laid such public and unnecessary claim to her, she told herself wrathfully ten minutes later as she paced her office, trying to think up some way to appease Chrissie without inflaming the situation any further. Now if she had not drunk those three fateful glasses of wine… Angrily she turned on her heel and stared blankly out of the window.

It was as much Jake's fault as it was hers, she told herself stubbornly. More, because he had been the one who had first pretended…

A few words…a kiss; *that* could have been explained away. Her presence in his house so early on a Monday morning, wearing the same dress she had been seen out in the previous day…that had only one logical explanation. Only one explanation people would want to believe.

She would *have* to find some way of making amends to Chrissie; a small, worried frown creased her forehead. She hated being at odds with her sister, who, she knew, beneath her outer bossiness did genuinely love her and had been hurt.

She picked up the telephone receiver and dialled her sister's number, sighing under her breath when there was no response.

She would just have to go round there this evening,

and in the meantime she would just try to find some excuse that Chrissie would find acceptable.

An hour later, when she was still having trouble concentrating fully on her work, she acknowledged that if she was to get through her day's workload she would now have to forgo lunch. The pad on which she had scribbled down Ian Davies's name caught her eye. Was it really less than a week ago that she would have been overjoyed to learn that he was offering her his business?

She still would have been overjoyed if she had been offered it for the right reasons, she reminded herself.

The phone rang, breaking her concentration. She reached for the receiver, freezing as she heard Jake's voice.

'I'm at home,' he told her. 'We need to talk. Could you call round here?'

'Now?' Rosie questioned angrily. Her heart was beating far too fast and she suddenly felt slightly dizzy and sick. The last person she wanted to see was Jake, but as she tried to concentrate on thinking up an excuse that would not betray her vulnerability she heard him saying quietly,

'Yes… If you could… It *is* rather important…'

What was rather important? Rosie wanted to demand, but he had already replaced the receiver, quite obviously taking her agreement for granted.

As she stepped into the reception area, she wondered if she was being oversensitive in thinking that Jane, who worked for her, was looking at her rather speculatively.

'I…I have to go out for a while,' she told her, conscious of the fact that her face was burning hotly and that she felt as guilty as a small child telling a fib.

The first thing she saw when she pulled up outside Jake's house was Chrissie's car. She stared at it, her heart sinking, and then reluctantly opened her own car door.

Jake must have been watching for her, because he had opened the front door and was coming towards her almost as soon as she had locked her car.

He was wearing a suit, dark grey, with an immaculate white cotton shirt and a discreet silk tie. He didn't look like the man who had held her and touched her, who had stroked her and kissed her...who had made her body ache and burn. This was the old Jake—the formidable, austere, disapproving Jake who had haunted her.

She stood still, panic and dread flaring inside her, her expression unknowingly betraying what she was feeling so that Jake cursed under his breath.

He had promised himself that he would take things slowly, that he would use this opportunity fate had so unexpectedly given him to put their relationship on a fresh footing. He had told himself that now that he knew the reasons why she had always held him at a distance and rebuffed him he could surely find a way of slowly overcoming them.

Logically he knew that just because he now knew what had caused her aversion to him that did not mean that anything would change, but emotionally his heart had cried out that surely it was impossible to love someone so much and for so long and for that love not to be returned. Sexually she was responsive to him. To him... Not to his cousin, not to anyone else... To him.

Now, as he saw the panic in her eyes and sensed how tempted she was to turn round and run, he reached out to her, shocked by the icy-cold tension of her skin.

'Your sister's here,' he told her.

'Chrissie…'

She had flinched when he touched her, but she hadn't pulled away.

'She arrived in a bit of a state,' he added, watching her. 'I gather the two of you had a bit of an upset…'

The dazed, frantic look was leaving her eyes now, the pupil no longer dilating quite so painfully.

*Why* was it that, when she *knew* it was the most dangerous thing she could allow, she was letting him touch her…hold her? Rosie wondered bleakly. It wasn't just because the touch of his hand on her arm was warming, soothing. Soothing… That wasn't what the rapid acceleration of her heartbeat was telling her.

'You're cold. Let's go inside.'

Numbly she let him take charge, calmly ushering her inside.

She tensed on the threshold to the sitting-room, her eyes going instinctively and betrayingly to the Knole settee.

If Jake was aware of what she was doing, he gave no sign of it. Instead he was smiling at Chrissie, who was sitting on the edge of one of the fireside chairs, her expression strained and nervous.

'Rosie…I'm sorry about…about what happened earlier,' Chrissie began, before Rosie could speak.

'Jake…Jake has explained to me that he had asked you not to say anything until he'd completed the negotiations for selling his share of the marina business.

He told me that you'd wanted to tell me, and that you had intended to do so this last weekend.' She made a wry face. 'I suppose I didn't help, bursting out with our news about the baby the other Friday, not giving you a chance to get a word in edgeways. I suppose I did rather over-react this morning. I should have re-alised you wouldn't deliberately keep something like this from me. It was just…just that I felt so hurt hear-ing it from someone else…'

'I know,' Rosie told her contritely. The pain gripping her stomach muscles was beginning to ease. She had Jake to thank for Chrissie's calmer mood, she recog-nised, and for shouldering the blame for keeping their 'news' from her.

'I *am* pleased for you…of course,' Chrissie contin-ued, 'and I *do* understand why you both felt that you had to make your relationship public in view of what happened on Sunday. As Jake said, the last thing any of us would want is for people to start speculating that the two of you might be having some sordid secret affair.'

She got up and walked across to Rosie, hugging her.

'I'm sorry, Rosie,' she told her in a muffled voice. 'I was rotten to you earlier. I came round here intend-ing to tell Jake what I thought of the pair of you, and instead he made me see how difficult I was making things for you…'

Rosie didn't say anything. She couldn't. Every word Chrissie said to her was increasing her guilt tenfold.

It was left to Jake to take hold of her hand and draw her closer to him, close enough for him to place his arm around her waist, holding her against the warmth of his body, causing nervous, fluttery sensations of quicksilver apprehension to race through her.

'We do understand, don't we, darling?'

As he spoke he turned to look at her, his free hand gently brushing her hair back off her face and lingering against her skin just long enough to make her nerve-endings prickle sensitively and her mouth feel as though it had started to swell slightly, as she remembered how she had felt when he kissed her.

He was looking at her mouth now, she recognised. Looking at it…and lowering his head as though… He couldn't possibly be going to kiss her, surely? Not in front of Chrissie? Not when they both knew…?

'Rosie…'

Her mouth quivered as she felt the warmth of his breath against her sensitive skin. Her eyes were already closing, her body turning in towards his, her hands pressed flat against his chest.

He kissed her gently, lingeringly, and the ache of need that pulsed inside her was so keen and sharp that for an instant she almost forgot that Chrissie *was* there, so great was her need to cling to him and return his kiss, to feel his mouth harden with passion, to feel his body…

Abruptly she surfaced from her dangerous fantasy, her face flushed with guilty heat.

Mercifully Jake wasn't watching her, and had turned away from her as he released her, but Chrissie was. And, as they looked at one another, Rosie recognised the message in her sister's eyes.

Chrissie knew that she loved him. She *loved* him! The shock seemed to go on forever, seeping into her

slowly, briefly numbing her, and then receding, allowing the space it had left behind to be filled with the raw
acid burn of her terrified panic.

'Look, I'd better be going,' she heard Chrissie saying but, as she turned automatically to go with her,
Jake stopped her.

'I'll see you out,' he told Chrissie.

'I'm sorry I made such a fuss,' Chrissie apologised to
her, giving her another hug. 'This baby is playing havoc
with my hormones, I'm afraid… Still,' she grinned at
Jake, 'if you and Rosie don't waste too much time, he
or she could have a cousin to grow up with.'

She wanted to leave, to get away right now, to go
somewhere where she could be alone to examine her
pain in private…somewhere where she could lock herself away so no one else could see or suspect what was
happening to her.

How *could* she be in love with Jake? Rosie asked
herself helplessly as she watched him escort Chrissie
to her car and knew that it was impossible for her to
follow her.

She and Jake were supposed to be in love; *she* was
in love…what woman in love would rush away from
her lover, refusing the opportunity to share a few minutes' privacy with him? Especially after the way Jake
had kissed her…a kiss which Chrissie had very obviously interpreted as a restrained expression of his desire for her.

But *she* didn't want Jake to desire her. She didn't
want him to touch her, kiss her, arouse her, expose her
to the newly discovered dangers of her love for him.

No wonder he made her feel so on edge, so nervous… Had some part of her known all along…felt all along? Was *that* why she had reacted so intensely to him all those years ago? Had something in her recognised it even then?

She heard Chrissie drive away.

Panic exploded inside her.

She didn't want to be on her own here with Jake.

But it was too late now to try to escape. She heard the front door open and then close again, and her fear increased.

## CHAPTER EIGHT

'I DIDN'T REALISE YOUR sister was expecting another child.'

Rosie didn't look round as she heard Jake come into the room—she didn't dare; but as she heard the quiet calmness of his voice her panic was stoked by a sudden flare of anger.

He was taking things so calmly, so easily. Didn't he have *any* idea of what it was doing to her...of what *he* was doing to her?

As he studied her rigid back, Jake's heart sank. She didn't want to be here with him, he knew that. It hurt him, knowing how much she wanted to get away from him, but he clamped down on his desire to make things easier for her, to open the door and let her walk through it.

Deep inside him there was a growing awareness that there was another and far more important door that was locked and barred, holding her imprisoned behind it.

Was he deluding himself in believing that he might be able to help her find its key and set herself free?

There was such a lot of pain locked up inside her, such a burden of anguish and unhappiness. He had heard it in her voice the night she had told him she had conceived Ritchie's child, had seen it in her eyes just now when Chrissie had mentioned her own pregnancy.

He was a man and could only guess at how it felt to be a woman; he was afraid of being clumsy and careless, adding to what she was suffering rather than taking away from it, but he also knew that he could not stand by and watch her suffer the way she was doing right now.

It angered him on her behalf that no one else had seen that suffering. Were they all blind, those who purported to care about her, or was it that his love for her made him extra specially perceptive of her feelings? Or was it that she had let down her guard more with him than she ever had with anyone else?

He took a deep breath, knowing that however gently he led up to it nothing was going to make it any easier for either of them.

'Rosie,' he said quietly. 'There's something we need to discuss.'

Rosie heard him, but made no response. Jake paused and, when she made no movement other than to stiffen her already eloquently taut, rejecting back, he cursed under his breath and continued as gently as he could, aching to reach out and touch her, to hold her, to protect her, but knowing that he must not do so.

'The other night you told me that you had conceived Ritchie's child… What happened to that baby?'

Rosie felt the shock like the sudden impact of something so cold that it almost burned. She wasn't prepared for this…hadn't guessed…hadn't imagined. She had thought he wanted to discuss their supposed relationship, not…

Who did he think he was? What was he trying to do to her? Hadn't he hurt her enough…more than enough over the years? What right did he have to pry into this, the most painful and private part of her life…her heart?

She felt the pain burn up inside her, the anger…the guilt…the bitterness.

She turned round, her eyes glittering with a mixture of tears and emotion, her voice raw as she choked out, 'What do you think happened? I killed it…I killed it…'

As he heard the agony in her voice Jake felt his scalp tauten and muscles tense. He could see what she was going through, hear it, feel it, taste it almost, on the emotion-laden air that enveloped her.

Instinctively he wanted to comfort her, to help her, to take away from her the appalling burden of her pain and guilt. She had been a child, that was all, a child whose only guilt had been her own innocence, and yet she was punishing herself as though she had been an adult.

'Rosie. Rosie…you mustn't blame yourself. It wasn't your fault, you were only a child. I know it must have hurt, having to take the decision to have your pregnancy terminated, but—'

He saw the colour leave her face, her mouth twisting in a bitter, corrosive smile.

'But what? I did the right thing? Of course, you *would* think that, wouldn't you? How like a man…' She started to laugh, her voice sharp-edged with a hysteria that sent anxiety arcing through him. 'Well, it wasn't like that. *I* wasn't the one who made the decision. Life…fate…my baby—the baby I'd told constantly since I knew I was carrying it that I hated—was the one who did that…'

Rosie saw from his face that he didn't understand what she was saying.

'I miscarried,' she told him harshly. 'I lost the baby by accident. It knew, you see. It knew it wasn't loved.'

Silently Jake watched the tears pouring down her face, cursing himself for his crassness, his stupidity, his lack of insight. Why on earth hadn't he guessed... realised...? He *loved* her. He should have sensed... known...

For all these years she had contained the pain that was now spilling out from her, years when he could have reached out to her, could have—*should* have been there to help her...to hold her...even if it could only have been as a friend.

Why *hadn't* he realised, that day he had gone to see her, to check if there had been any *repercussions* as he had so clinically put it, that she was lying to him, that she was afraid...that she was alone and facing a trauma which would blight her whole life?

If he had not been so wrapped up in his own feelings, his own jealousy, his blind, prejudiced belief that she thought herself to be in love with Ritchie, might he not with his supposed maturity have seen that she was concealing something, that she was afraid?

Couldn't he have found a way to encourage her to confide in him, to lean on him...to draw support from him?

She could have had her baby. He would have gladly provided her with all the support she might have needed...all the love. Given the chance, he would have married her and loved them both, but he had turned his back on her, left her to suffer...

'My baby died because I didn't want it. I killed it by denying it my love...but I did love it...'

He couldn't stand any more.

He crossed the space that divided them, taking her in his arms, ignoring her attempts to push him away, wrapping his arms around her so tightly that she couldn't move, holding her, rocking her, telling her that she wasn't to blame, that these things happened... that of course she had loved her baby and that of course he or she had known that.

'If anyone is to blame it must be me,' he told her.

Rosie stiffened. 'You...'

She had stopped crying now, but she was still trembling. Her body felt weak and cold, hollow and empty, drained. She felt much as she had done after her miscarriage, she recognised light-headedly, as though there was an empty space inside her which had previously been filled but, whereas with her miscarriage she had ached with pain over that emptiness, with this one there was a sense of release, of relief.

She tried to concentrate on what Jake was saying. How could it be *his* fault?

'That day when I came to see you...I should have guessed...should have seen—'

'But there wasn't anything to see,' Rosie told him. 'I—'

Jake shook his head.

'I didn't mean that kind of "seeing", Rosie...I meant...' He stopped abruptly, causing her to frown up at him.

'What?'

'It doesn't matter,' he told her. 'What *does* matter is

you, and the way you've blamed yourself…suffered…
You were very young, Rosie. Perhaps your body simply wasn't fully ready for motherhood.'

Rosie ducked her head. He was only reiterating what
they had told her at the hospital. Then she had felt too
much guilt, too much anguish to listen to them, but
now logically she knew that both they and he were
probably right.

That didn't lessen her sorrow, though. Her sorrow…
Not her guilt…not that agonising, clawing mixture of
anger and misery which she had been suffering so fre-
quently and intensely recently; that, she recognised,
had gone, leaving behind it a kinder, gentler emotion.

Had that change been brought about simply by the
act of talking about what had happened, by giving vent
to her emotions, by being able for the first time to actually acknowledge what had happened…what she had
felt…by acknowledging the right of her child to have a
proper place in her past and her memories, instead of
being hidden away, his or her existence denied?

Jake was still holding her. She tried to move away
discreetly but, far from relaxing, his arms actually
seemed to tighten a little more securely around her.

It felt good being held like this by him, her body supported by his, surrounded by its warmth, its protection,
his heartbeat soothing the frantic pace of her own. In
her dreams she had imagined being held like this, she
recognised, had craved this kind of male comfort and
warmth, had longed for someone who would hold her,
listen to her, understand her…love her…

Immediately she tensed. Jake did *not* love her. He

felt compassion for her, and a certain amount of guilt, but he did not love her.

And she was not a child, not a teenager any longer, even if the emotions she had been reliving…venting in his arms had belonged to that era of her life. She was a woman, an adult, and it was time that she put the past behind her, accepted that there was no going back and altering it, accepted that her perceptions of it were coloured by the emotions she had felt then, by the immaturity which had been a part of her then.

She had believed that Jake despised her, condemned her for what she had done, but she had learned now that he had done no such thing. Couldn't she just as easily have allowed her guilt over her miscarriage to be equally biased and destructive? She would never forget her child, never cease regretting that she had lost it, but somehow now that loss was easier to accept, that pain easier to endure now that she shared it with someone else.

For years she had focused all her antipathy and bitterness on Jake; she must not make the mistake now of forcing him to become some kind of emotional support system for her, especially not when she knew that she loved him.

Right now he felt responsible for her…and responsive to her? It would be dangerously easy to use those feelings and to try to convince them both that they could become something else.

Some deep-seated feminine instinct told her that it would be the easiest thing in the world right now to increase Jake's awareness of her, to trade on his obvious compassion for her. All it would take was for her to lift her head, to look at him…to look at his mouth…

She felt the tremor of her own body and acknowledged, with a small pang of shock for her previous lack of awareness, how very strong her physical and emotional responses would be once they were aroused, how very, very much she wanted right now to make love with Jake.

To set the final seal upon the past and free herself completely from it? Or because she loved him…because a part of her was ready to use the smallest excuse it could find to encourage him to want her?

It wouldn't be all that difficult; physically he was responsive to her, aware of her…physically he desired her.

She wasn't sure how she knew that, but she did know it, sensed it, felt it, and in a female way was proud because of it.

But to encourage that desire, to take it and make use of it, would ultimately damage them both, but most especially her. She wasn't strong enough for a relationship which would be based on such a dangerously destructive mixture of compassion and desire on his part, and love and need on hers.

No, if there were ever to be that kind of intimate relationship in her life, then it must be based on emotions that were equally balanced. And besides, to allow…to encourage Jake to make love to her when she knew how widely different their reasons for making love would be would be to cheat and deceive him.

Jake heard her sigh, and felt her lift herself away from him. This time when she pressed firmly against his chest, silently demanding that he release her, he complied.

'I'm sorry,' she told him shakily.

'Don't be,' he responded. 'There's no need.'

He had released her fully now. She was just about to step back from him and turn away when he said softly, 'Rosie...'

'Yes?'

She looked up at him and then tensed as she saw the way he was looking back at her, at her mouth...just as she had so recently imagined he might do.

Quickly she turned on her heel, terrified of giving in to her need to fling herself back into his arms and whisper to him how much she wanted him...loved him.

'I...I must go...'

Jake saw her to her car, and then stood watching her until she had driven out of sight.

The phone was ringing as Rosie let herself into her house. She dropped her bag and ran to answer it, a small thrill of disappointment stabbing through her when she realised it wasn't Jake but Chrissie.

'Rosie...I've had a wonderful idea,' Chrissie announced. 'Why don't you have your engagement party here in the garden? There's masses of room. We could hire a marquee.'

An engagement party. Rosie's heart sank, but she couldn't summon the energy to dampen Chrissie's enthusiasm, nor to destroy the olive branch she knew her sister was extending to her.

'It sounds a marvellous idea,' she fibbed weakly. 'But I'm not sure what Jake's plans are...'

Promising Chrissie that she would discuss the party with him, she replaced the receiver.

Chrissie was *her* sister, she reminded herself, and it was unfair of her to shift the responsibility for persuading her to drop her plans for an engagement party on to Jake's shoulders, but he seemed to have the knack of dealing with her sister. Chrissie listened to him and obviously respected his judgement, while she had always considered Rosie to be her 'little sister' and still tended to treat her accordingly.

An engagement party… Wistfully Rosie tried not to dwell on how different things would be if she and Jake really were planning to marry…if he really did love her.

Enough of that, she told herself firmly. She had plenty of other things to think about, such as work. It was too late to return to the office now, but she had plenty of paperwork she could do here at home.

She went into her sitting-room and switched on the fire, opening the flap of her pretty walnut bureau, which she had inherited from her grandmother, and sitting down to work.

AT NINE O'CLOCK Rosie stopped working to make herself a light supper. After she had finished eating and cleared away, she went back to her work, switching on the sitting-room lamps as she did so. The summer light had started to fade, and as she passed in front of her sitting-room window she saw a car coming down the road.

When she realised it was Jake's, her heart missed a beat.

He had probably only come round because Chrissie

had been on to him about her wretched party, she told herself as she went to let him in.

She opened the door before he rang the bell, standing back to let him in.

'Has Chrissie—?'

'Rosie, there's something—'

Both of them stopped.

'You first,' Jake offered.

The way he was smiling at her made her feel as though she had suddenly been wrapped in something warm and cherishing, Rosie reflected shakily. It was an unfamiliar experience for her, and a dangerously beguiling one, betraying her into responding to Jake's warmth with a smile that made him catch his breath in love and hope.

Quickly she told him about Chrissie's phone-call, pulling a wry face as she admitted, 'I'm afraid I used you as an excuse for not going ahead.'

'I've had Naomi plaguing me, wanting to know if we've set a wedding date yet,' Jake told her. 'I've referred *her* to you...'

Rosie laughed.

'That wasn't why I came to see you, though...'

Rosie paused in the act of ushering him into her sitting-room.

'I was worried about you...being on your own after what happened this afternoon...' He had turned his head away from her as though half ashamed of his own concern for her, his voice slightly muffled.

As she watched him, Rosie was overwhelmed with emotion. He was so caring, this man, so completely the opposite of all the things she had once thought him. *Why* hadn't she realised sooner…known sooner that…?

That what? That she loved him.

Tears pricked her eyes. This was so unfair…so…so unendurable, after all she had already endured.

She turned her head away from him, afraid that he might somehow read the truth in her eyes.

'That…that was thoughtful of you…'

How formal she sounded, how distant, but she couldn't, dared not, let him see what she was really feeling.

'Rosie… About…about the baby…'

She tensed immediately.

'You have every right to mourn him or her, you know, every right to grieve… Forgive me if I'm saying or doing the wrong thing, but I just wanted you to know that if you can't bring yourself to talk about it to anyone else, someone closer to you…well, I'm always here, you know…'

She hadn't meant it to happen…hadn't planned for it, hadn't encouraged it in any way at all, but as she turned towards him he must have taken a couple of steps towards her.

'Rosie…'

The way he said her name made her whole body quiver. She looked up at him and knew immediately that it was the wrong thing to do.

He wanted her—she could see it in his face, read it in the way his glance dropped slowly to her mouth.

She could have stopped it even then, could have turned away from him, stepped back from him, filled the tense silence with some comment which would have banished the tension between them, but she did none of those things; instead she looked back at him, deliberately letting her own glance linger on his mouth, knowing, as surely as she knew that he could see the warm flush staining her skin, that he knew what she was offering him.

There was no rush, no awkwardness, simply the sensation of being enfolded in his arms, followed by the warmth of his mouth slowly caressing her own, exploring and caressing it, as delicately as though he thought she was something precious and fragile with which he had to take great care.

Hesitantly she opened her mouth and kissed him back, unsure at first, her heart thudding frantically fast; and then, after he had responded to her, shown her, whispered to her how much he wanted her, how much he needed her, her confidence grew, her aching need for him driving out the warning voices urging her to stop now before it was too late.

Only it was already too late. It had been too late from the first moment he touched her. Now she had no defences against the combined emotional and physical longing for him. When he touched her, her body trembled violently in response.

He kissed her mouth and then her throat, his hands warm against her body, tender and patient, not rushing or forcing her. As she clung to him, she could feel the heat coming off his body, sense the desire he was straining to control, but strangely the knowledge of his desire neither alarmed her nor filled her with distaste, as had always been the case in the past with other men.

Neither, when he kissed her, did she see behind her

shuttered eyelids an image of his cousin tainting her pleasure in his touch, destroying her ability to respond to him.

'Open your eyes, Rosie,' he told her huskily, as he kissed the corner of each eye. 'I want you to look at me when I touch you. I want you to see *me* when I kiss you…I want you to know who it is who's making love to you.'

Obediently she did as he said, unaware of the effect that her languorously enlarged pupils were having on him.

He touched her face with his hands, cupping it, not daring to let himself touch her body. If he did!

He could feel his own physical response to the thought of touching her, of smoothing his hands over the silky warmth of her skin, of caressing every single inch of her with his mouth, of showing her…giving her all the pleasure she had never known, of helping her to be proud of the sensuality that nature had given her.

He could feel his heart hammering against his ribs, his throat aching with tension and need… He buried his mouth against her throat, feeling her tremble violently against him, seeing in the golden shadow of the lamplight the sudden thrust of her nipples against her clothes.

Heat swamped him. Before he had registered what he was doing, never mind stopped himself, his hands slid to her waist, holding her, his head dipping down, his mouth covering her nipple, caressing it, his mind haunted by his memories of how often he had dreamed of touching her like this.

After one violent shudder of shock, Rosie simply

clung quiescently to him, too stunned, too devoured by the physical and emotional sensations his passionate caress had aroused to do anything else.

How could it happen that simply the heat of his mouth, its dampness against her skin, the rough brush of his tongue even through the layers of fabric that separated her flesh from it could cause such a frenzy of sensation inside her, could unleash such an aching, a need, a pulsing, that it was all she could do to stop herself from pressing his head against her breast, from wrenching aside the intrusive fabric that prevented her from experiencing his heated, passionate suckle against her naked flesh?

She wanted to feel him touching her like that, kissing her like that, all over her body, but she had no idea she had voiced that need until he lifted his mouth from her breast and whispered to her, 'Do you, Rosie? Do you? Come here, then, and let me show you how much *I* want to love you like that…'

He had just started to unfasten her blouse when she suddenly shook her head. Immediately his fingers stilled, his eyes watching her, waiting.

'Not here…' she told him huskily, her skin flushing as she looked beyond him towards the half-open door.

It was so hard for her to say the words, to explain to him how she felt…what she wanted, to tell him that, although she knew already that what she would experience with him would be nothing like that other time, she still wanted it to be upstairs in her own bed where, no matter what might happen afterwards, or what the future might hold, she would have the memory of being physically wanted and desired, of being shown tenderness and joy, of knowing what this physical thing between a man and a woman really should be, to destroy for ever the tainted memories of the past.

As she struggled to find the words to express what she was feeling and what she wanted, it seemed that somehow Jake had read her mind for her, because he watched her sombrely for a few seconds and then said quietly, 'No. Not here.'

As she walked nervously towards the door, the light fell on the damp patch of fabric pulling tautly against her breast. Heat flooded through her, weakening her, making her sway slightly on her feet.

Instantly Jake was holding her, supporting her, his arm wrapped round her.

They went upstairs in silence.

Outside her bedroom door she paused, hesitating, suddenly filled with doubt and panic. What if he didn't really want her after all? What if he was simply doing this because he felt sorry for her...what if?

As she looked towards him, she saw that he was very obviously physically aroused; her skin flushed, her body responding to what she had seen, filling her with a longing that made her tremble openly.

She didn't realise Jake had misinterpreted the reason for that tremor until she heard him saying softly, 'It's all right, Rosie. You don't have to do this. If you'd prefer me to leave...'

Her eyes gave her away before she could speak, filling with such anguish that Jake felt as though someone was physically tearing at his guts.

He was close to forty years old. He had promised himself he wouldn't rush her, wouldn't panic her, wouldn't let his own needs, his own love, get in the way of his desire to help her, to put her first…but when he saw the look of helpless aching, longing dilating her eyes…

'I want to see you,' she told him shakily. 'I want you to see me…'

She stopped speaking, unable to explain that she wanted their intimacy to be open and free, clean and wholesome…shared. That she didn't want it to be something covert and hidden, dark and furtive.

'I want to see you,' she had said, and Jake had heard beneath the defiance in her voice the tiny thread of all her past fear.

He ached in helpless anger and pain for her, but knew that if he voiced what he was feeling she would immediately reject his emotions, driven by pride and the need to protect herself.

Instead he told her wryly, 'There isn't an awful lot to see. A man's body doesn't possess the same beauty as a woman's…' As he spoke he looked down at her, and Rosie felt her heart thud frantically against her ribs as she recognised his desire for her.

Was he saying that he found *her* body beautiful— the swollen curves of her breasts, the swell of her hips, the roundness of her body with its female mysteries?

And he was wrong when he said a man's body did not possess beauty.

His did for her, she recognised as her glance skimmed hesitantly over him. His skin was tanned from the time he had spent in Greece, his arms and legs tautly muscled where hers were more gently structured, his nipples smaller, flatter but, like hers, taut and hard. If she touched them, kissed them, suckled on them, would he experience the same thrill of sensation that his mouth had given her?

Her skin burned at the thought, her hand clenching against her side as she resisted the urge to reach out and touch him, to stroke her fingertips through the soft silk of his body hair, to breathe in the scent of him, to release all her inhibitions and to show him with her hands and her mouth just how much she wanted and needed him.

'Rosie…'

She looked at him, her expression open and unguarded. What he saw in her eyes made Jake reach out for her, groaning helplessly under his breath as his senses reacted to that unspoken message of longing and need.

'Hold me, Rosie,' he whispered against her mouth. 'Hold me…touch me…love me…'

Perhaps after all this was what she needed most: not to be shown the power of her own sexuality, but to be allowed to discover the weakness of his, its vulnerabilities and needs, to be allowed to discover that a man's body was just as vulnerable as a woman's, that she had just as much power to wound and hurt him as he did her, to discover what her touch could do to him.

Against her mouth he whispered thickly, 'Whatever it is you want, Rosie…whatever it is you need, you can have…'

I want *you*, Rosie wanted to tell him. I need you…I love you…but she didn't say the words. Instead she reached out tentatively and touched him, tracing the shape of his shoulder, exploring the warmth of his skin, feeling the way his flesh responded to her touch, see-ing in his face that he had told her the truth when he said he wanted her.

What she was learning now…experiencing now were things she should have known years ago, Rosie acknowledged as her heart filled with wonder at the way he reacted to her, at the way he let her see just what she was doing to him, but more unexpected than all of that was the way her own body responded to what she was doing, the way touching him, watching him, kiss-ing him, just simply watching him, aroused her.

When she pressed her lips to the flat plane of his stomach and hesitantly caressed it with the tip of her tongue, the shudder that went through him made her own body ache so sharply that she immediately froze.

'Rosie…it's all right,' Jake started to reassure her, but she shook her head, her face burning with the force of what she was feeling as she took his hand and placed it against her body, and then watched him, uncertainly wondering if she had done the right thing. If she should have waited for him to touch her.

As soon as he touched the moist, intimate heat of her body, Jake knew what was happening to her.

'Rosie…' He kissed her mouth, her breasts, and then her stomach, all the time gently caressing her, trying to fight down his own need so that he could let her body tell him what it wanted…take its own pace.

When he kissed the inside of her thigh she trembled and tensed, but she didn't try to push him away.

His need to touch her, taste her, love her…and to show her what that love could be ached through him.

Rosie… He said her name, helplessly aware of his

self-control slipping, unable to resist his need to know her in this most intimate of all physical pleasures, feeling her tense as he opened his mouth over her, telling himself that he would stop the moment she wanted to do, and then becoming so lost in the pleasure of knowing her, tasting her, feeling her body's first quivering response to his intimate caress, that no power on earth could have made him release her.

He felt her body move against him, lifting, twisting…heard her sharp, frantic cries, felt the tug of her fingers in his hair as she tried to push him away, but wouldn't, *couldn't* let her go, not until he had felt the small, sharp quivers of sensation twisting through her body become a series of intense, pulsing contractions that he could physically feel as he caressed her.

Even after it was over, he still caressed her, gently kissing the inside of her thigh, stroking her skin, moving slowly up over her body, touching her, loving her, until he reached her mouth and saw the imprint of her own teeth on her bottom lip and the tears still seeping slowly from her closed eyes.

She was trembling, he recognised, shivering almost like someone in shock. He wrapped his arms round her, holding her, rocking her.

'It's all right, Rosie…it's all right…'

Rosie didn't speak. She couldn't. She was still in shock, still appalled by the intensity of her sexual response to him. Now that she knew…now that he had shown her… How on earth was she ever going to be able to forget?

Panic burned inside her. It would have been bad enough just to know that she loved him emotionally, but now there was this as well. This unwanted knowledge of all the nights ahead of her when she would lie awake, remembering…wanting…aching…knowing that the intensity of the physical peak she had just reached was something that could never be found through mere physical intimacy, that it was something that could only be experienced through love.

Never again would she know the pleasure Jake had just shown her.

She bit down hard on her bottom lip and then cried out as her teeth touched her already bruised skin.

Immediately Jake's hold on her tightened.

'It's all right, Rosie… Go to sleep now… It's all right…'

Go to sleep. How on earth could she sleep? She didn't want to sleep…she wanted… She yawned hugely and then yawned again. Wryly Jake watched her, pillowing her head against his shoulder as her eyes closed, and then reaching out to switch off the light before retrieving the duvet and pulling it over them both.

ROSIE WOKE UP abruptly, conscious of something missing, but not sure what it was until her brain cleared and she realised she was on her own.

'Jake…' She said his name sharply, not really expecting any response, tensing when he suddenly appeared in the open doorway.

She stared at him in the semi-darkness, her heart beating fast.

'I…I thought you'd gone.'

Thought or hoped? Jake wondered grimly as he walked towards her and sat down on the edge of the bed.

He had broken all the rules, done all the things he had promised himself he would not do, and now he was going to lose her—he could see it in her eyes. She could hardly bear to even look at him.

'Rosie—' he began, but she wouldn't let him speak, interrupting him, saying fiercely, 'You don't have to say anything, Jake. It should never have happened. We both know that. It was all my fault...I should never—'

'*Your* fault...? If any blame lies with anyone, it lies with me, not you, Rosie.'

She turned to look at him. He could see the way her eyes shone in the dark, feel her tension and vulnerability. She didn't seem to realise that as she sat up the duvet had slid away from her body, or was it that she simply didn't realise what effect the sight of her naked breasts was having on him?

'*I* was the one who started it,' he reminded her gently.

'But I didn't stop you...I wanted...' Rosie bit her lip, shaking her head, knowing how close she had just come to blurting out how she felt about him.

'I'm not a total fool,' she told him stiffly. 'I do know that sex is different for men than it is for women...that a man doesn't necessarily have to feel any emotional involvement with a woman...to...to want to have sex with her...'

It was like trying to pick his way across a minefield, Jake recognised as he tried to unravel what she was really saying to him.

'Not to have sex,' he agreed, watching her, wondering if that really had been pain he had seen in her eyes before she turned her head away from him or whether he was deluding himself.

What more did he have to lose? he asked himself grimly. Only his pride, and what the hell did that matter?

'Not to have sex, Rosie,' he repeated, reaching out and gently cupping her face, sliding his hand along her jaw and firmly turning her face towards his own. 'But to make love…that's different…and I did make love with you, Rosie, even if *you* only had sex with me.'

She had gone very still and silent, her face showing no trace of emotion or reaction at all.

'And I do love you, Rosie…have loved you for a very long time…' his mouth twisted wryly '…a very long time. Have you any idea what it does to a man to have to admit that he's fallen in love with someone who's still virtually a child, even if physically she might look like a woman? Have you any idea what it did to me to find you in bed with Ritchie?'

Now she did show some reaction, her body tensing, pain flickering in her eyes.

'You don't have to say this to me, you know,' she told him fiercely. 'I'm not going to fall apart just because I've suddenly discovered that I love you, Jake. You don't have to feel sorry for me…to pretend…'

For a moment he was too stunned to speak, to take in her muffled, fiercely spoken words.

'I know why you made love to me, you know,' she continued without looking at him, her words low and rushed. 'I know you did it because of…of Ritchie. I know you just wanted…don't want your pity, Jake,' she told him harshly. 'I don't want—'

'What?' he demanded savagely, his control suddenly deserting him as he grabbed hold of her shoulders and almost shook her. 'You don't want what, Rosie? Me... my body, my need, my desire, my love...? Well, you've got them whether you want them or not, and I'll tell you something else, shall I? All those things you don't want from me, I *do* want from you...all of them and more. I want you, Rosie. I want your emotions, your needs, your desires...your love...your life...I want all of it. All of it...all of you, and if you say one word more to me about pity or compassion—' He stopped abruptly, shaking his head. 'Rosie, I'm sorry...I shouldn't—'

He felt her hand tremble as she reached out and touched his mouth.

'No... No more words,' she told him thickly. 'Don't tell me, Jake... Show me...show me...'

He could feel the way her body shook as she kissed him and wound herself around him, the small frantic kisses that betrayed her emotions and aroused his own.

This time, when he made love to her, it was the powerful pulse of his body within her own that brought her to the peak of her own pleasure.

Later, snuggled up against him, she heard him murmur in her ear, 'That marquee Chrissie was talking about... How about using it to celebrate our wedding?'

'So soon?' Rosie protested. 'My parents—'

'They'll be there. Chrissie will see to that, and besides...' In the darkness he kissed her gently and then touched her stomach. Immediately Rosie knew what he meant.

'I wouldn't want our child to think it wasn't conceived in love any more than I would want you to think it,' he told her softly.

CHRISSIE WAS OVERJOYED when they told her the news.
'Leave everything to me,' she told them firmly.

'WHAT'S THIS?' Rosie asked Jake uncertainly as he handed her a small, gift-wrapped box.

They had been married just over three months, and she had never been happier. The shadows thrown by the past had completely disappeared and no longer held any fear or threat for her. They had just come back from a fortnight's holiday in Greece, Jake having decided to retain his interest in the marina project but to take a smaller active part in its management.

'I don't want to be away from you,' he had told Rosie when they had discussed it. 'Your own business means that you won't always be free to come with me...'

And so, rather than ask her to put their relationship before her work, he had been the one to make that decision and that choice.

'You're more important to me than anything else in my life, Rosie,' he had told her. 'I've loved you for too long, wanted you for too long, to let anything come between us now that we are together.'

She hadn't told him yet that she suspected she was soon going to have to look for a partner to take over her role in her business because she had conceived their child.

Now, as she unwrapped the gift he had given her and saw the small gold teddy bear dangling from its delicate chain, she wondered if somehow he had guessed after all, but then he said quietly, 'I'm not sure if I've got the dates right... I thought it must have been about this time...' and she realised that this gift wasn't for the child *they* had conceived together, but for the one she had secretly lost.

Tears burned her eyes as she went into his arms.

'I don't ever want you to think you can't grieve for him...talk about him,' he told her huskily as he held her. 'Or that I've forgotten what you went through... what you suffered...or how I wasn't there for you when you most needed me.'

Rosie shook her head. 'Oh, Jake...'

'Don't think I don't realise what it must have cost you to have Ritchie here when we got married. To treat him normally...to—'

'Ritchie doesn't bother me,' Rosie told him truthfully. 'If you want the truth...what happened with him...it doesn't worry me any more, Jake. Losing my baby—that was different, although I accept now that it wasn't necessarily because I'd willed it to happen. You've driven out all my bad memories and replaced them with good ones.'

She kissed him and then smiled mischievously at him. 'It's a pity you bought this, though...' she told him.

'A pity?' Instantly he frowned. 'Rosie—'

'Because now you're going to have to buy another one,' she told him, watching his face as he realised what she was actually saying.

'Are you pleased?' she asked him after he had finished kissing her.

'Pleased?' He held her tightly, his voice raw with

emotion as he told her, 'You're having my child. Pleased doesn't come anywhere near describing how I feel.

'I loved you for so long without thinking you could ever love me, Rosie. Sometimes I still can't quite believe that any of this is real, and then I look at you, hold you…touch you…love you, and I see in your eyes that it is real, that you do love me.

'Of course I'm pleased,' he whispered against her mouth. 'Come here and let me show you how much…'

'Mmm… That sounds like a good idea to me… A very good idea,' she whispered dreamily against his mouth as he began to kiss her.

\* \* \* \* \*

# MASTER OF PLEASURE

# CHAPTER ONE

SASHA TURNED HER head to look at her nine-year-old twin sons. They were playing on the beach like a pair of seal pups, wriggling and wrestling together, and jumping in and out of the waves that were washing gently onto the secluded Sardinian shoreline.

'Be careful, you two,' she warned, adding to the older twin, 'Sam, not so rough.'

'We're playing bandits.' He defended his boisterous tackling of his twin. Bandits had become their favourite game this summer, since Guiseppe, the brother of Maria who worked in the kitchen of the small boutique hotel that was part of the hotel chain owned by Sasha's late husband, had told them stories about the history of the island and its legendary bandits.

The boys had their father's night-dark hair, thick and silky, and olive-tinted skin. Only their eye colour was hers, she reflected ruefully, giving away their dual nationality—sea-coloured eyes that could change from blue to green depending on the light.

'Told you I'd get free.' Nico laughed as he wriggled dexterously out of Sam's grip.

'Careful. Mind those rocks and that pool,' Sasha protested, as Sam brought Nico down onto the sand in a flying tackle that had them both laughing and rolling over together.

'Sam, look—a starfish,' Nico called out, and within a heartbeat they were both crouching side by side, staring into a small rock pool.

'Mum, come and look,' Nico called out. Obligingly she picked her way across to them, crouching down in between them, one arm around Sam, the other round Nico.

'Come on. And I'm the Bandit King, remember.' Sam urged Nico to get up, already bored with the rock pool and its inhabitant.

Boys, Sasha thought ruefully. But her heart was filled with love and pride as she watched them dart away to play on a safer area of smooth sand. She turned to look back towards the hotel on its rocky outcrop, while still keeping her maternal antennae firmly on alert. This hotel was, in her opinion, the most beautiful of all the hotels her late husband had owned. As a wedding gift to her he had allowed her a free hand with its renovation and refurbishment. The money she had expended had been repaid over and over again by the praise of their returning guests for her innovative ideas and her determination to keep the hotel small and exclusive.

But with Carlo's death had come the shock of discovering that the other hotels in the group had not matched the financial success of this one. Unknown to her, Carlo had borrowed heavily to keep the business going, and he had used his hotels as collateral to secure his loans. Bad business decisions had been made, perhaps because of Carlo's failing health. He had been a kind man, a generous and caring man, but not the kind of man who had taken her into his confidence when it came to his business and financial affairs. To him she had always been someone to be protected and cherished, rather than an equal.

They had met in the Caribbean, with its laid-back lifestyle and sunny blue skies, where Carlo had been investigating the possibility of buying a new hotel to add to those he already owned. Now, in addition to having to cope with the pain of losing him, she had had to come to terms with the fact that she had gone overnight from being the pampered wife of a rich man to a virtually destitute widow. Less than a week after Carlo's death his accountant had had to tell her that Carlo owed frighteningly large sums of money, running into millions, to an unnamed private investor he had turned to for help. As security for this debt he had put up the deeds to the hotels. And, although she had begged her business advisers to find a way for her to be able to keep this one hotel, they had told her that the private investor had informed them that under no circumstances was he prepared to agree to her request.

She looked back at her sons. They would miss Sardinia, and the wonderful summers they had all enjoyed here, but they would miss Carlo even more. Although he had been an elderly father, unable to join in the games of two energetic young boys, he had adored them and they him. Now Carlo was gone, his last words to her a demand that she promise him she would always recognise the importance of the twins' Sardinian heritage.

'Remember,' he had told her wearily, 'whatever I have done I have done with love—for you and for them.'

She owed Carlo so much; he had given her so much. He had taken the damaged needy girl she had been and through his love and support had healed that damage. The gifts he had given her were beyond price: self-respect, emotional self-sufficiency; the ability to give and receive love in a way that was healthy and free of the taint of destructive neediness. He had been so much more to her than merely her husband.

Determination burned steadfastly in her eyes, turning them as dark as the heart of an emerald. She had been poor before—and survived. But then she had not had two dependent sons to worry about. Only this morning she had received a discreet e-mail from the boys' school, reminding her that fees for the new term were now due. The last thing she wanted to do was cause more upheaval in their young lives by taking them away from the school they loved.

She looked down at her diamond rings. Expensive jewellery had never been something she'd craved. It had been Carlo who had insisted on buying it for her. She had already made up her mind that her jewellery must be sold. At least they had a roof over their heads for the space of the boys' summer holidays. It had hurt her pride to ask Carlo's lawyers to plead for them to be allowed to stay on here until their new school term began in September, and she had been grateful when they had told her that she'd been granted that wish. Her own childhood had been so lacking in love and security that from the very heartbeat of time when she had known she was pregnant she had made a mental vow that her child would never have to suffer as she had suffered. Which was why…

She turned her head to watch her sons. Yes, Carlo had healed so much within her, yet there had been one thing he couldn't heal. One stubborn, emotional wound for which she still had not found closure.

The worry of the last few months had stolen what little spare flesh she had had from her body, leaving her, in her own eyes, too thin. Her watch was loose on her wrist as she pushed the heavy weight of her sun-streaked tawny hair back off her face and kept it there with one slender hand.

She had been eighteen when she'd married Carlo, and nineteen when the boys had been born, an uneducated but street-smart girl who had been only too glad to accept Carlo's proposal of marriage despite the fact that he was so much older than her. Marriage to him had provided her with so much that she had never had, and not just in terms of financial security. Carlo had brought stability into her life, and she had flourished in the safe environment he had provided for her.

She had been determined to do everything she could to repay Carlo's kindness to her, and the look on his face the first time he had seen the twins, lying beside her in their cots in the exclusive private hospital in which she had given birth, had told her that she had given him a gift that was beyond price.

'Watch, Mum.' Obediently she obeyed Sam's demand that she watch as he and Nico turned cartwheels. One day soon they would be telling her not to watch them so closely. As yet they hadn't realised just how carefully she did watch over them. Sometimes, with two such energetic and intelligent boys, it was hard not to be over-protective—the kind of mother who saw danger where they saw only adventure. Her own thoughts silenced the ever ready 'be careful', hovering on her lips. 'Very good,' she praised them instead.

'Look, we can do handstands too,' Sam boasted.

They were agile, as well as tall for their age, and strongly built.

'You have made good strong sons for me, Sasha,' Carlo had often praised her. She smiled, remembering those words. Their marriage had bought her time and space in which to grow from the girl she had once been into the woman she was now. The sun glinted on the thin gold band of her wedding ring as she turned again to look at the hotel on the rocks above them.

She had travelled all over the world with her late husband, visiting his chain of small exclusive hotels, but this one here in Sardinia had always drawn her back. Originally a private home, owned by Carlo's cousin, Carlo had inherited the property on the cousin's death, and had vowed never to part with it.

GABRIEL STOOD IN the shadow cast by the rocks and looked down onto the beach. His mouth twisted with angry contempt and something else.

How did she feel now? he wondered, knowing that fate had reneged on the bargain she had struck with it, and that the security she had bought with her body was not, after all, going to be for life. How had she felt when she had learned that her widowhood was not going to be one of wealth and comfort?

Had she cursed the man she married, or herself? And what of her sons? Something dark and dangerous ripped his guts with razor-sharp claws. Just watching them had brought to the surface memories of his own childhood here on Sardinia. How could he ever forget the cruel, harsh upbringing he had endured? When he had been the age of these two boys he had been made to work for every crust he was thrown. Kicks and curses had taught him how to move swiftly and sure-footedly out of their range. But then he had been an unwanted child, a child disposed of by his rich maternal relatives, abandoned by his father, to be brought up by foster carers. As a boy he had, Gabriel acknowledged bitterly, spent more nights sleeping outside with the farm animals than he had inside with the foster family, who had learned their contempt of him from his mother's relatives.

Gabriel believed that such an upbringing either made or broke the human spirit, and when it made it, as it had his, it hardened it to pure steel. He had never and would never let anyone deflect him from his chosen path, or come between him and his single-minded determination to stand above those who had chosen to look down on him.

His maternal grandfather had been the head of one of the richest and most powerful of Sardinia's leading families. The Calbrini past was tightly interwoven with that of Sardinia. It was a family riven in blood feuds, treachery and revenge, and steeped in pride.

His mother had been his grandfather's only child. She had been eighteen when she'd run away from the marriage he had arranged for her, to marry instead a poor but handsome young farmer she had believed herself in love with.

Strong-willed and spoiled, it had taken her less than a year to realise that she had made a mistake, and that she loathed her husband almost as much as she did the poverty that had come with her marriage. But by then she had given birth to Gabriel. She had appealed to her father, begging him to forgive her and let her come home. He had agreed, but on condition that she divorced her husband and left the child with his father.

According to the stories Gabriel had been told as a child, his mother hadn't thought twice. Her father had paid over a goodly sum of money to Gabriel's father on the understanding that this was a once and for all payment and that it absolved the Calbrini family from any responsibility towards the child of the now defunct marriage.

With more money than he had ever had in the whole of his life in his pocket, Gabriel's father had left his three-month-old son and set off for Rome, promising the cousin he had left Gabriel with that he would send money for his son's upkeep. But once in Rome he'd met the woman who was to become his second wife. She had seen no reason why she should be burdened with a child who was not hers, nor why her husband's money should be wasted on it.

Gabriel's foster parents had appealed to his grandfather. They were poor and could not afford to feed a hungry child. Giorgio Calbrini had refused to help. The child was nothing to him. His daughter had also remarried—this time to the man of his choice—and he was hoping that within a very short space of time she would give him a grandson with the lineage his pride demanded.

Only she hadn't, and when Gabriel was ten years old his mother and her second husband had both been killed when the helicopter they were in crashed. Giorgio Calbrini had then had no alternative but to make the best of the only heir he had—Gabriel.

It had been an austere, loveless life for a young boy, Gabriel remembered, with a grandfather who'd had no love for him and had despised the blood he had inherited from his father. But at least under his grandfather's roof he had been properly fed. His grandfather had sent him to the best schools—and had made sure that he was taught everything he would need to know when the time came to take over from him and become the head of the house of Calbrini. Not that his grandfather had had high hopes of him being able to do so, as he had made plain to Gabriel more than once. 'I have to do this because I have no choice, because you are the only grandson I have,' he had told Gabriel, ceaselessly and bitterly.

Gabriel, though, had been determined to prove him wrong. Not to win his grandfather's love. Gabriel did not believe in love. No, he had wanted to prove that he was the better man, the stronger man. And that was exactly what he had done. At first his grandfather had refused to believe Gabriel's tutors when they praised his grasp of financial politics and all the complexities that went with them. But by the time he was twenty Gabriel had quadrupled the small amount of capital his grandfather had given him on his eighteenth birthday.

Then, three weeks after Gabriel had celebrated his twenty-first birthday, his grandfather had died unexpectedly and Gabriel had inherited his vast wealth and position. Those who had predicted that he would never be able to step into his grandfather's shoes had been forced to eat their words. Gabriel was a true Calbrini, and he possessed an even sharper instinct for making money than his grandfather. But there was more to his life than making money. There was also the need to make himself emotionally invulnerable.

And that was exactly what he was, Gabriel reflected now. No woman would ever be allowed to repeat his mother's rejection of him and go unpunished.

Especially not this woman.

He could hear Sasha speaking to her sons, the sound of her voice, but not her words, carried to him by the breeze.

Sasha! By the time Gabriel was twenty-five he had become a billionaire. A billionaire who trusted no one and who kept the women he chose to warm his bed as exactly that—bedmates and nothing else. The rules he laid down for his relationships with them were simple and non-negotiable. No talk of love, or a future, or commitment; absolute fidelity to him while they were partners; absolute and total adherence to his safe sex and no babies policy. And, just to make sure that this latter rule wasn't broken 'accidentally on purpose', Gabriel always took care of that side of things himself.

Over the years he had endured his share of angry, bitter scenes, with weeping women who had thought they could change those rules and then learned their mistake. Magically those tears had quickly dried once they were offered a generous goodbye gift. His mouth twisted cynically. Was it any wonder that he had become a man who trusted no one, and most of all a man who despised women? So far as Gabriel was concerned there wasn't a woman in existence who could not be bought. His mother had shown him what women were, and all the other women he had come into contact with since had confirmed what she had taught him when she had abandoned him for money.

Not that he didn't enjoy the company of women, or rather the pleasure of their bodies. He did. He had inherited his father's good looks, and finding a willing female partner to satisfy his sexual needs had never been a problem.

'Sam, don't go too far. Stay here, where I can see you.' Sasha's words reached him this time, as she raised her voice so that her son could hear it. A caring mother? *Sasha?*

Like his bitterness, the past wouldn't let go of him. It was here around him now, gripping him so tightly that he could feel its pain.

After his grandfather's death he had had closed up his grandfather's remote and uncomfortable house in Sardinia and bought himself a yacht. With financial interests in property, it had made sense for him to travel, looking for fresh acquisitions both material and sexual. And if a woman invited him to use her for his sexual pleasure then why should he not do so? Just so long as she understood that once his appetite was sated there would not be a place in his life for her.

By the time he was twenty-five he had also already made the decision that when the time came he would pay a woman to provide him with an heir—a child to which he would make sure *he* had exclusive rights.

Gabriel watched Sasha with cold-eyed contempt. Six weeks ago, just after his thirty-fifth birthday, he had stood beside the hospital bed of his dying second cousin—the Calbrini family was extensive, and had many different branches—listening to Carlo pleading for *his* help for the two sons Carlo loved more than anything else in the world.

The same warm breeze that was playing sensually with Sasha's long hair was flattening the thick darkness of his own to reveal the harsh purity of a bone structure that bore the open stamp of Sardinia's human history—the straight line of his Roman nose a classic delineation of masculine features that echoed the works of Leonardo and Michelangelo, coupled with the musculature of a man in his prime. Centuries ago the Saracens had invaded Sardinia, leaving their mark on its history and its inhabitants through the women they had taken and impregnated. It had been Carlo who had told him that legend had it that boy children born to such women were said to possess the physical stamina and legendary merciless cruelty of the men who had fathered them. Gabriel knew that there was Saracen blood in his own family's past, and he knew too that it showed in his attitude to life. He had no mercy for those who double-crossed him.

Eyes as golden and as deathly watchful as those of an eagle studied the two boys. Privileged, and loved by a doting elderly father. Their childhood was so very different from his own. The sunlight gilded his skin, warmly gold rather than deeply olive. He looked on the promise Carlo had begged from him as an almost sacred trust, an admission from his cousin without words being spoken that he was entrusting his sons to Gabriel's care because he did not trust their mother—because

on his deathbed he had finally been prepared to admit
that she could not be trusted.

But still Carlo's last words to him had been of her.

'Sasha,' he had told Gabriel. 'You must understand…'

He had been too weak to say any more, but there had
been no need. Gabriel knew all there was to know about
Sasha. Just like his mother, she had walked out on him.
The memory of that was like a constant piece of grit
rubbing against his pride, exacerbating the darkness
within him. She was unfinished business, the cause of
a blow to his pride against which it had banked a debt
of compounded interest—which he was now here to
claim in full.

A ROAR OF protest from one of the twins caused Sasha
to turn to look in maternal anxiety, and then to call out,
'Stop fighting, you two.'

Something—no, *someone*—had moved between her
and the sun. Immediately she shielded her gaze to see
who it was.

There were moments in life that happened both so
quickly and yet so slowly that they could never be ignored or forgotten. Sasha felt the abrupt cessation of her
heartbeat, then a suffocating sense of shocked disbelief,
streaked with fear and panic—and something else so
painful that she refused to give it either life or a name.
She listened to the slow heavy thud of her heart as
though it belonged to another woman, distantly aware
of it propelling the blood into her veins, keeping her
physically functioning while, emotionally, every nerve

felt as though it had been tortured and then severed. Just one word was torn from her throat.

'Gabriel!'

## CHAPTER TWO

JUST ONE WORD, but it was so filled with anger, shock and fear that it seemed to reverberate between them.

Sasha had to tilt her head back to look up at Gabriel, and she could feel the panicky beat of the pulse at the base of her throat. She resisted an urge to place a covering hand over it.

'What are you doing here? What do you want?' It was a mistake to ask him that. He would be able to hear the panic in her voice and see how she was having to fight to control her fear. The way his mouth was twisting into that cruelly unkind and satisfied smile she remembered so well told her that.

'What do you think I want?'

His voice was so soft and gentle that it could almost have been the tender stroke of a lover's touch against her skin, or the brush of an angel's wings. Just for a second her body reacted to the memories it evoked. She was seventeen again, a desperate bundle of aching, emotional need she had kept hidden beneath a shield of bravado. Her body was bereft of its sexually challenging armour of short skirt and minuscule vest top, and her long hair, with its amateur blonde streaks, was still damp from the shower Gabriel had insisted she have. She was watching him watching her, overwhelmed by the feeling, the longing suddenly shooting through her; knowing for the first time in her life what it felt like to experience physical sexual desire. And she wanted him, *desired* him so very badly.

A door had swung open on her past. She didn't want to see what lay behind it, but it was already too late. She remembered how she had been too impatient to wait for him to come to her, running to him instead. He had caught hold of her, holding her at arm's length whilst he studied her naked body. Even her flesh had signalled its eager readiness to him, her breasts firming and lifting as she imagined him touching her there. But when he did she had realised that her imagination had not had the power to tell her just how his touch would feel, or what it would do to her. The flesh of his fingertips had been hard and slightly rough, the flesh of a man who worked and lived physically, not just cerebrally. She had shivered, and then shuddered with uncontained delight when he had slowly explored the shape of her breasts. The erotic roughness of his touch had increased her arousal so much that she had suddenly become aware of not just how much she wanted him, and how excited she was, but how ready her body was for him, how hot and wet and achingly sensitive that most intimate part of her had felt. As though he had sensed that, too, Gabriel had trailed his hand down over her body, smoothly and determinedly. When he had allowed it to rest on her hip, cupping the gently protruding bone, she had been seized with impatient urgency and the need to feel him caressing her more intimately.

Had she then moved closer to him, openly parting her legs, or had he been the one to propel her closer to him, moving his hand to her thigh? She couldn't remember. But she could remember how it had felt, how she had felt, when he had bent his head to kiss the smooth column of her throat at the same time as he had stroked apart the swollen lips of her sex to dip his fingers in the slick moist heat that was waiting for him. She had almost reached orgasm there and then.

A shudder punched through her. What was she doing, thinking about that now? She could feel the strain of her own emotions. Fear? Guilt? *Longing?* No, never again. The girl she had been was gone, and with her everything that that girl had felt.

Sasha looked down towards the beach, where her sons were still playing, oblivious to what was happening, and then looked quickly away, instinctively not wanting to contaminate them with what was happening to her. Her sharpest and most urgent need was not to protect herself but to protect them. As she looked away she stepped to one side, as though to draw Gabriel's attention to her rather than her vulnerable young. There was nothing she would not do to protect her sons. Nothing.

Gabriel tracked the involuntary movement she made away from the two boys. Carlo had claimed that she was a very protective mother, but of course she would have been while she believed that Carlo was a wealthy man and her role as their mother gave her unlimited access to that wealth. Carlo, like many men who come to fatherhood so late in life, had worshipped the flesh of his flesh, evidence of his potency. His heirs... Now the heirs to precisely nothing. Gabriel's tiger-eyed gaze pounced on the visual evidence of their privileged cosmopolitan lifestyle—expensive Italian clothes, healthy American teeth, upper-class English accents, their flesh and bones that of children who had from birth been well fed and nurtured. At their age he had been wearing rags, his body thin and bony.

He switched his gaze from the beach to the woman in front of him. She too had good teeth, expensive teeth—paid for, of course, by her doting husband. Her doting and now dead husband. Her hair was cut in the kind of style that looked artless but, as Gabriel knew, cost a fortune to maintain. The 'simple' linen dress she was wearing, with its elegant lines, no doubt possessed a designer label, just as her hands and feet with their uncoloured but carefully manicured nails spoke of a woman who had the kind of confidence that came from enjoying position and wealth. But not any longer. What had she felt when she had learned of Carlo's death? Relief at the thought that she would no longer have to give herself to an old man? Avaricious pleasure at the belief that she would now be wealthy?

Well, she would have one of those two feelings to keep, he acknowledged brutally, although probably not for very long. She must be close to thirty now, and if she wanted to find another rich old man to support her she would discover she was competing with much younger, unencumbered women. The kind of women who fawned around *him* wherever he went.

One of Gabriel's mistresses had once told him that it was his Saracen ancestry that gave him the dark and dangerous side to his nature that his enemies feared and his women loved. For himself, he believed that any child growing up as he had done—unwanted, harshly treated, both physically and emotionally—quickly learned to give back as good as it got. A child who had to literally fight off the farm dogs for a scrap of bread was bound to develop a hard carapace to protect both his flesh and his spirit.

An unexpected smile dimpled his chin as he watched Sasha swallow and saw the telltale darkening of her eyes, but there was no warmth to that smile. 'Yes, it must have been hard for you, lying there in bed, letting an old man take his pleasure with your body and being unable to give you any pleasure back. But then, of course, you had all that money to pleasure you, didn't you?'

'I didn't marry Carlo for his money.'

'No? Then why did you marry him?'

Ah, now he had her. He could hear the uneven ratcheting of her breath escaping from her lungs. How well he knew that fierce need to protect oneself from a death blow. Unfortunately for her it was too late. There was no protection for her here.

'It certainly wasn't for love,' he taunted her unkindly. 'I saw him just before he died. He was in the hospital in Milan. You, I believe, were in New York—shopping. Very conveniently you had also boarded your sons at their school, in order to give yourself the freedom to do so.'

All the colour bled out of her face. Infuriatingly Gabriel recognised that even now, almost bleached of blood and life, she still managed to look impossibly beautiful.

Sasha was terrified she might actually faint, so great was the pressure of her anger. She had gone to New

York in secret, to meet with yet another specialist to see if there was some way that Carlo might be saved. She might not have loved her husband as a woman, but she had been grateful to him for all that he had done for her and for the twins. The decision to ask the school if the boys could board was not one she had made without a great deal of soul searching. For her, the boys' emotional security was always paramount, but she and they had owed Carlo a huge debt. What kind of person would she be if she had not done absolutely everything she could to find a way to give her husband more time with them? It wouldn't have been possible to travel to New York to seek a second opinion with the boys. And then there had been the added worry of how it would affect them to watch Carlo slowly dying. She had needed to be on hand to visit the hospital and then the hospice sometimes twice or three times a day. Carlo had wanted to die in Italy, not London, where the boys were at school. She had made what she had believed was the best decision she could at the time, but now Gabriel was pinpointing the guilt that still nagged at her for having had to leave the boys at school for a term.

'You know, of course, that the business is ruined and that all he has left you is debt?'

'Yes, I know,' she agreed bleakly. There was no point in even attempting to conceal the reality of her financial situation from him, or trying to explain to him how she felt about Carlo. He would not understand because he was incapable of understanding. Their shared experience of damaged childhood years, instead of forging shared bonds of mutual compassion, had turned them into the bitterest of enemies. He would never understand why she had left him for Carlo, and she would never tell him—because there was simply no point.

'I suppose I should be honoured that you've actually come to gloat in person. After all, you weren't at the funeral.'

'To watch you cry crocodile tears? Even *my* stomach isn't strong enough for that.'

'But it is, of course, strong enough for you to come here and verbally stone me. It's been over ten years, Gabriel. Isn't it time—'

'Isn't it time *what*? That I claimed the debt you owe me, along with its accrued interest? I'm a man who likes payment in full, Sasha. Carlo knew that.'

Something—either old knowledge or female instinct—iced down her spine in a cold trickle of awareness she didn't want but couldn't ignore.

'What do you mean? What did Carlo know?'

'He knew that when he asked me to lend him money that money would have to be repaid.'

'*You* loaned Carlo money?'

Gabriel inclined his head. 'Against the security of the deeds to his hotels. He had overtraded, and badly. I told him that, but he believed he could borrow his way out of trouble, and since we were family I could not refuse him the help he wanted. Unfortunately for him he did not manage to turn the business around. Fortunately for me his debt was covered by his assets. My assets now. Including this place, of course.'

Sasha stared at him.

'Yours?' She couldn't comprehend what he was saying. 'You mean that *you* own this hotel?'

'This hotel,' he agreed, 'and the others. And your

home, the money in your bank, the clothes on your back. It all belongs to me now, Sasha. Everything. Carlo's debt is repaid,' he told her softly, 'but yours to me is still outstanding. Did you think it had been forgotten? That I wouldn't bother to seek retribution?'

She wanted desperately to look at her sons, to reassure herself that they were there, whole and safe, and that none of this could touch or harm them. But she was afraid that somehow just looking at them would draw Gabriel's attention to their vulnerability.

Instead she drew in a deep, unsteady breath and said, 'You seek retribution from me? I was the one who was the victim in our relationship, Gabriel. You were the one who—'

'You were the one who sold herself to the highest bidder.'

Somehow she made herself look at him. 'You left me with no other option,' she told him quietly.

It was, after all, the truth. She had gone to him looking for all those things she'd never had, still able to believe that miracles could happen, even for girls like her, and that all the wrongs in her life could be made right. She had still trusted in her dreams then. She felt pity for the girl she had been, was glad that she was gone, and even more glad to be the woman who had taken her place.

Before Gabriel could say anything else she demanded, 'What is it exactly that you want, Gabriel? I assume you haven't wasted your precious time coming here just to gloat? Or did you think it would be amusing to throw us out personally? Well, I'll save you the bother. It won't take us long to pack.' Of all the luxuries she would have to give up this was the one she would miss the most. The luxury of pride. Because she knew so well just what a luxury it was.

'I haven't finished yet,' he told her.

There was more? What? Surely it wasn't possible for things to be any worse?

'Before he died, Carlo appointed me as his sons' legal guardian.'

It was a joke. A cruel deliberate attempt to frighten her. Payback time with a vengeance. But of course it couldn't be true.

'What's wrong?' she heard Gabriel demanding softly when he caught her swift indrawn breath and the shocked disbelief she was trying to hide. 'Surely Carlo told you that he intended to appoint me as their legal family guardian in accordance with traditional Sardinian law?'

He knew, of course, that Carlo had done no such thing because his cousin had told him so himself.

'It is for the best,' Carlo had whispered painfully to Gabriel. 'Even though I know Sasha won't see it that way at first.'

She certainly didn't, Gabriel recognised. Her eyes were wild with disbelief as she shook her head in denial.

This couldn't be happening, Sasha thought frantically. This was the nightmare to end all nightmares. The ultimate betrayal. A knife-sharp edge of fear sliced into her heart and paralysed her defences.

'No!' she told him, shock bleeding the colour from her face, clenching her hands into small, anguished fists. 'No. I don't believe you.'

'My lawyers have all the necessary papers.'

This wasn't some kind of malicious joke, Sasha recognised numbly. This was real. Her head was aching, bursting with unanswerable questions. She was too distraught to maintain the protective distance of remote disinterest.

'I don't understand… Why would Carlo do something like that? Why?'

Gabriel shrugged, a small movement of powerfully strong shoulders. Sickeningly for a second the scene in front of her swung crazily out of focus and she was seeing another, younger Gabriel, sea water sluicing from the bare tanned strength of those same shoulders as he hauled himself up out of the ocean onto the deck of his yacht, his body naked and unashamedly ready for her, just as hers had been equally ready for him.

And she had always been ready for him. Ready, eager, wanting. Hungry for the intimacy of any sexual act that would bring him closer to her and keep him there. She had had no inhibitions, and she suspected he would not have allowed her to have any. With their privacy guaranteed she had thought nothing of shrugging on one of his shirts and wearing nothing else, as turned on by the knowledge that beneath it she was openly available to his touch as she knew he had been. As a lover he had opened her eyes to a whole new world of pleasure, and he had imprinted that pleasure on her body in such a way that she knew she would never be able to forget it. There had been long hours when he had held her on their bed and caressed and kissed his way over every inch of her—the curve of her throat, the tender flesh inside her arm, her fingers. If she closed her eyes she knew she would almost be able to feel the slow wet curl of his tongue as he drew slow patterns of almost unendurable erotic stimulation along the whole length of her.

Aroused to a fever pitch, she would invariably forget his command to remain still and reach for him, arching her back, spreading her legs, moaning with raw delight when he carefully held apart the outer lips of her sex and stroked his tongue-tip the full length of it. Her orgasm would begin before he entered her, her body welcoming his fierce thrusts even while deep down inside herself a part of her ached to feel him there without the barrier of the condoms he'd always insisted on using.

Abruptly Sasha realised the danger of what she was doing. *No!* Her silent tortured denial reverberated inside her skull. What was happening to her? How could he be making her remember that now?

'Isn't it obvious?' she could hear Gabriel saying coolly. 'Carlo knew the state his financial and business affairs were in. He told me himself that he wanted to do everything he could to protect his sons and their future. Obviously by making me their guardian he believed he would be morally compelling me to provide for them financially.'

'No, he wouldn't do that,' Sasha protested. But even as she said the words she knew that she was deceiving herself. It was exactly the sort of thing Carlo would have done—albeit for the best of motives. Carlo had had such a deep-rooted sense of family. He had been proud of being a Calbrini, proud too that the twins would bear that name. He had cared about her, and he had protected her from the pain of loving Gabriel and being rejected by him, but the boys had Calbrini blood in their veins, and in the end that had mattered more to him than her.

Sasha was trying hard to remain strong, to focus on what Gabriel was saying instead of slipping back into the past, but the memories Gabriel was evoking had a dangerously strong hold on her and were making her feel frighteningly weak. How could it be that just standing here with him could awaken the kind of erotic thoughts she had truly believed she had left behind in her past?

'To provide for them financially,' Gabriel repeated, adding as smoothly as though he were sliding a knife up through her ribs and straight into her heart, 'and to protect them from their mother.'

It took several seconds for her brain to absorb what he was saying, and then several more for her to react to the cruel injustice of his words. 'They don't need to be protected from me, and neither do they need you.'

'Carlo obviously didn't agree with you, and neither will the law. I am their guardian. They are my wards. That was their father's dying wish.'

'But I am their mother.'

'The kind of mother who some might say they would be better off not having.'

'You have no right to say that. You know nothing about my relationship with my sons.'

'I know you. You went to Carlo because he was prepared to give you what I would not. Now he is dead, and sooner rather than later you will be looking for another man to take his place. Obviously Carlo feared that should you remarry your new husband might not have Carlo's sons' best interests at heart, and he wanted to protect them.'

'I would never marry a man unless I thought he would love them as though they were his own.'

'Wouldn't you?'

Sasha suspected she knew what he was thinking. 'You still haven't forgiven your mother, have you? Well, I am not her, Gabriel. I love my sons—'

'Enough! This has nothing to do with my mother.'

Sasha wasn't going to argue with him. What was the point? It would be like trying to break down granite with her bare hands. But she knew that she was right. Gabriel measured women by the yardstick of his mother's failure to be a mother to him, and he condemned them all along with her. He wanted to believe that all women were capable of abandoning their children for money because he needed to believe it; because not to do so meant accepting that his own mother had left him because of some failure within himself to merit her maternal love. He spoke his beliefs as though they were a truth written in stone, and Sasha knew that inside his head, in what passed for his heart, they were. In his eyes she was already condemned and would remain condemned. What he believed could not be changed, because he did not want it to be changed.

She had learned so much on her own sometimes difficult and painful journey to maturity and acceptance of her own past. And most of all she had learned that it was impossible to make another person's journey of self-knowledge and healing for them.

Gabriel had decided a long time ago to sacrifice the ability to love and be loved in exchange for the protection of a bitter pride that would not allow him to see her sex as motivated by anything other than the most callous form of self-interest.

Carlo might have believed he was doing what was right, but Sasha wished he had not brought Gabriel back into her life—and more importantly into the lives of her sons. They meant everything to her. There was nothing she would not do to protect them, no sacrifice she would not make.

'You didn't have to agree to Carlo's request,' she forced herself to point out. 'Why did you? My sons mean nothing to you.'

Gabriel could hear the hostility in her voice. He looked towards the two boys. Sasha was right, of course; they meant nothing to him beyond the Calbrini blood in their veins. His initial reaction when Carlo had told him his intention had been to refuse. Why should he burden himself with the responsibility of his cousin's sons, especially when he knew what their mother was? It was obvious what Carlo was trying to do. He was bankrupt and in debt, his sons were too young to fend for themselves, and their mother could not be relied on to protect them; she would sell herself to the first man who could afford her. All this must have gone through Carlo's mind as it would have done his own. So Carlo had turned to him, on his sons' behalf, knowing that morally Gabriel could not and would not reject the claim of their shared Calbrini blood.

Since then, however, Gabriel had had more time to reflect on the situation. He had reasoned to himself that in accepting the role of guardian to Carlo's sons he could spare himself the necessity of producing heirs of his own with all the potential legal pitfalls that could entail. Carlo's sons were Calbrinis. He had decided that he would spend some time with Carlo's sons to evaluate for himself whether or not they were worthy of raising as his own heirs. If they were, then as their guardian he would raise them exactly as he would have done his own sons, to become the heirs his vast empire and wealth required. As for Sasha…

He could feel the burn inside his body like that of an old unhealed wound. Their shared history was a page of his life he had never been able to remove. The women who had gone before her, like those who had come after, had never managed to leave the imprint on his senses that she had. She was a payment owed to him in the balance sheet of his life. Fate was now giving him the opportunity to salve his wounded pride.

Once he had collected the capital and interest on her debt to him, once he had reversed the past and forced her into a position where *he* would be the one to walk away from her—for nothing else would salve his pride—then he would make it plain that there was no place for her in the new lives of her sons, and certainly not in his. Gabriel did not envisage any real problems. He knew Sasha. She was a hedonist and a sensualist, driven by sexual and financial greed. He was not foolish enough to think that he could simply trick her into doing what he wanted. The minute she guessed what he was planning she would cling to the boys, determined not to let go of her passport to his wealth. He would have to be subtle and thorough.

And ultimately, if she refused to relinquish her claim to her sons…?

If she was foolish enough to do that then she would soon realise her mistake.

'No, but they meant a great deal to Carlo.' Gabriel answered Sasha's question coolly. 'And my word means a great deal to me. Since I have given him my word that I will act in all ways towards them as though they were my own, that is exactly what I intend to do.'

'What?' His own? The shock of what Gabriel had said rocked Sasha back on her heels. Why hadn't she anticipated this? She knew how much Carlo had loved the boys, but she knew too how deep his Sardinian roots went, and how important his family and its honour were to him. If only Carlo had told her what he was planning she could have done something, anything—whatever it would have taken. Pleaded, begged, demanded that he didn't do this to her. He had known how Gabriel felt about her, how much he despised her. And he had known too...

She took a deep breath. She hadn't thought about any of this in years. She hadn't allowed herself to— not once since she had slipped from Gabriel's bed in the pale light of a false dawn while Gabriel slept, unaware of her intentions. She had taken nothing with her when she left the yacht—not the expensive clothes he had bought her, nor the jewellery—only her passport. And enough money to get the hotel where Carlo was staying, to give herself and her future into his keeping. She had been eighteen then, and Carlo had been in his mid-sixties. Small wonder that a month later, when he had married her, the officials had thought he was her elderly father. She had not cared, though. All she had cared about was that now she was safe.

She could see Gabriel looking at the boys, and she reacted immediately to what her maternal instincts translated as a threat, reaching for his arm, wanting to stop him from going to them. But before she could touch him Gabriel swung around, his own grip on her wrist making her wince. His body was tensed like that of a hunter, a *predator*, waiting for her to try to escape so that he could punish her. A shudder of recognition ripped through her belly as she was subjected to the once-familiar signs of her own body's arousal. How could this be happening? It was over ten years since Gabriel had last touched her. The twins' birth had flooded her senses and emotions with an intensity of a different kind of love that had obliterated all she had once felt for Gabriel. Or so she had told herself.

How could one touch do this to her? How could *he* make her feel like this—her lower belly hollow with anticipation, her legs trembling, sweat springing up along her hair line and adrenalin forcing its way along her veins? It was a trick of her own imagination, that was all, she tried to reassure herself. She did not want or desire him. How could she? But the ache of longing inside her was intensifying and drowning out rational thought. Arousal and anger, desire and dislike, all the sweet, savage sexual alchemy of their shared past swept back over her.

She had, she remembered, felt like this the first time she had seen him. Only then the liquid heat erupting inside her body had not been shadowed by either pain or knowledge. The physical ache of her longing for him had seduced her before he had even touched her, and when he had touched her… She closed her eyes, not wanting to remember but it was too late. Inside her head she could hear her own voice as she cried out to him, caught up in the grip of her own unbearable pleasure, her eyes wide open with the awed shock of it while he leaned over her in the shadowy coolness of the yacht's main cabin, watching her as the expert touch of his fingers brought her to orgasm. Her first orgasm. He had waited until its shuddering hold on her body had eased before giving her the look of hooded triumph that would become so familiar to her and saying laconically, 'Perhaps now would be a good time to tell me your name?'

She opened her eyes abruptly. Her face burned now at the memory of her own behaviour then. She had only been seventeen, she reminded herself shakily. A child whose head had been stuffed with daydreams. Still, she had felt she knew all there was to know. She was now twenty-eight, a woman who knew enough to realize how dangerous her past had been, and how lucky she was to have escaped from it, and from Gabriel. She was free of that now. Of that and of him, and of all that he had made her feel and want.

She could feel Gabriel looking at her, focusing on her, the intensity of his concentrated gaze making her tremble. He couldn't guess what she had been thinking, what she had been reliving. She was far too mature now to betray herself to him. Nevertheless, the dull ache inside her was refusing to subside and, as though she had no control over it whatsoever, she could feel her gaze being drawn to his body, to his throat, and the vee of sun-warmed flesh exposed by the neck of his polo shirt. Beneath it his torso would be ridged with muscle, the darkness of his body hair arrowing downwards over the tautness of his belly. Her gaze followed the downward arrowing of her thoughts, coming to rest where her hand and her lips had once rested so intimately and so pleasurably. She could still remember the hard sleekness of male flesh over rigid muscle, its smooth supple movement beneath her eager touch...

What was she *doing*? Frantically she pushed back the memories. She wanted badly to swallow, to wet the nervous dryness of her lips, but she was afraid of doing so in case...in case what? In case Gabriel guessed what she had been remembering and subjected her to the kind of savagely sexual possession she had once found so exciting? Here, with her sons less than ten yards away?

'Let go of me,' she breathed, trying to pull her wrist free.

'Are you sure that is what you really want? Once you begged me for my touch. Remember?'

She couldn't help it. She shuddered violently.

'Ah, yes. I see that you do,' he taunted her as he released her. Her flesh felt cold without his next to it. Cold and bereft. She mustn't let herself think like that.

'Let me warn you, Sasha, just in case you have forgotten. I know exactly what you are.' He studied her body with a contemptuous and knowing sexual inspection that made her want to hit him.

'I am the twins' mother, and that is the only way you will ever know me from now on, Gabriel,' she fired back at him. Were those words for his benefit, or for her own? He released her arm so quickly she almost lost her balance. She looked at him. His back was turned towards her. She shuddered. How could she ever have been so foolish as to have loved him? But she had. Desperately, wholly and completely, hungering for him to return her feelings, believing that she could trade sex for love. What a fool she had been. But she wasn't that fool any longer.

## CHAPTER THREE

STILL GRIPPED BY shock, Sasha watched Gabriel turn towards the boys. She couldn't get her head around the enormity of what Carlo had done. But they were different from other men, these Sardinian men. They lived by a different code; theirs was a paternalistic society, and the belief in their right to order the lives of their families absolute.

When Carlo had told her about Gabriel's mother she had seen that he did not share her shock that Gabriel's father should seek to force his daughter into a marriage of his choosing.

'No wonder she ran away,' she had commented.

Carlo had frowned at her and shaken his head. 'She was fortunate that her father forgave her and that he was powerful enough to persuade Luigi to marry her despite the humiliation she had forced on him.'

'But to make her marry a man she did not love—'

'It was his right as her father.'

'And forcing her to abandon Gabriel, her baby? You can't believe that was right, Carlo.'

'Not right, no, but Giorgio was a proud man and the head of our family. The purity of the Calbrini bloodline was a matter of honour to him, and to accept as his grandson a child whose blood—'

'But in the end he had to accept Gabriel, didn't he?'

Carlo had inclined his head, as though in acceptance of her argument, but Sasha had known that in his heart he was as old-fashioned and traditional as Gabriel's grandfather. She suspected that he had only told her the story of Gabriel's birth because, despite what Gabriel had done to her, Carlo had still felt he had a duty to stand by his second cousin. He might have offered her the protection of his money and his name, but he had still been a Calbrini. And so were her sons. Carlo had never forgotten that, and neither must she—although for very different reasons.

Gabriel was still watching her sons.

'There isn't any point in me introducing you to them. After all, you are hardly likely to be playing a hands-on role in their lives, are you?' she challenged him.

'On the contrary. I intend to make my duties as their guardian a priority—which is why I am here. Who knows how badly they may have been damaged by the circumstances of their life?'

He had answered without even looking at her.

'They miss Carlo, but his death has not damaged them…'

Gabriel swung round to face her.

'The damage to which I refer is not that caused by the death of their father but rather by the life of their mother.'

A terrible cold stillness had her in its grip.

'You have no right to say that.'

'I have every right. They are my wards. It is my moral and legal duty to protect them.'

'From me? I am their *mother*!' Her hands were curled so tightly her nails bit into her flesh.

He turned slowly to face her, the golden eagle eyes as flat as polished stones.

'You may be their mother, but you are also a woman who craves the lifestyle only a very rich man can provide. When such a man pays you for the use of your body he will not want his enjoyment of that body to be interrupted by the needs of a pair of nine-year-old boys. In the eyes of most courts such a mother would be considered derelict in her maternal duty and not worthy of the name.'

She could almost feel the acid burn of his bitterness.

'Just because your own mother abandoned you—'

'You will not speak of her.'

Sasha had never felt more angry, nor more afraid.

'I have decided that it is in the best interests of my wards that they remain here, on the island that was their father's home, while I consider what is best for their future.'

'That is not your right.'

Sasha was afraid, and fighting hard not to show it, Gabriel recognised. The pulse in her throat was fluttering like a trapped bird struggling to be free. He could almost feel the waves of panic and fear beating up through her body. He could certainly see the shocked outrage in her eyes.

'They are my sons,' Sasha insisted fiercely. '*My* sons.'

'And my legal wards now, under traditional Sardinian law. This is a patriarchal society, as you well know.'

Sasha was shaking her head. 'You can't do this. I won't let you.'

'You can't stop me.' He gave her a cold smile. 'You cannot afford to go to court. You have no money. Carlo is dead, and you need to find another man to support you. A man who, like Carlo, is blind to the reality of what you are. Don't bother denying it,' he told her harshly before she could protest. 'After all, we both know, don't we, that you are accustomed to selling yourself to whichever man will pay the most? After all, that is why you came to me…and why you left me. Isn't it?'

He had tossed the question at her almost casually, but Sasha wasn't deceived. Nothing Gabriel ever did was done casually or without purpose. Even knowing that, she couldn't stop herself from betraying her own agitation as she told him quickly, 'That was all a mistake.'

'Yes—your mistake,' he agreed.

'No, that wasn't…' she began, and then stopped. 'It was a long time ago.' What was she *doing*? She had no need to explain herself to him, and every need to protect herself from the contempt he had always felt for her. Gabriel was dangerous, he always had been and he always would be, and she now had the two best reasons in the world not to re-enact her own past like a moth drawn to the flame that would ultimately destroy it.

'Not that long ago. It's only just over ten years ago since I picked you up off the street where your previous lover had left you. Remember? You told me that you'd been offered the starring role in a porno movie mogul's latest skinflick, but you'd star in a private one for me instead. Your words, not mine!' He was walking away from her now and heading for her sons. 'The she-leopard does not change her spots.'

'Where are you going?' she demanded frantically, even though she already knew the answer. The smile he gave her made her bite down hard into her bottom lip to stop herself from shuddering in open dread.

'I am going to introduce myself to my wards,' Gabriel answered her softly.

For several precious seconds Sasha was too caught up in her own emotions and the past Gabriel had evoked to move, but somehow she managed to break free of them to run after him, calling out fiercely, 'Leave them alone! Don't you dare touch my children.'

Entering a new decade had added to her beauty rather than taken from it, Gabriel admitted reluctantly as he watched her speed towards him. Her breasts were rising and falling with emotion and exertion beneath the thin covering of her dress when she finally reached him. It caught him off guard to look at her and feel the familiar hunger grip his body. She had always had good breasts—firm-fleshed and erotically real, warm and pliable to the touch, the skin tasting of woman and sunshine and sex, her dark brown nipples always greedily eager for the attention of his fingers and his lips. In his mind's eye he could still see her, virtually naked on the private deck of his yacht, her head thrown back so that the sea breeze could tousle her hair, her lips curved into a smile of wanton, intensely sensual pleasure as she offered herself up to him.

Now, as then—although for different reasons—she was standing immediately in front of him, between him and her children in fact, so that it was impossible for him not to look directly at her. Motherhood had given her breasts a softer fullness that suited her, but it didn't seem to have taken away the narrowness of her waist, nor the sensuality of a body that was made for sexual pleasure. A body he had once known as intimately as he knew his own—perhaps more so. As a lover Sasha had had an incomparable blend of fierce sexual passion and a feminine ability to lose herself and give herself so completely in the act of sex that it had felt as if she was handing every bit of herself over to him for their mutual pleasure. But of course he had been far from the only man to enjoy Sasha's sexuality, and he certainly hadn't been the first to pay for it—if not in money, then certainly in kind, with the lifestyle of a rich man's mistress. She had as good as admitted that to him the night he had picked her up, if not actually out of the gutter, then certainly heading towards it.

He frowned darkly, angered by the power she still had to occupy his thoughts, even though he assured himself it was no longer with the white-hot overwhelming desire for her that had once burned inside his brain as well as his body. She had got under his skin and left an ache he could still feel ten years later, even if the savage heat of the need that had once threatened to consume him had ultimately burned out. Burned itself out, or been ruthlessly stamped out by him? What did it matter which? He had known from the first time he had taken her to bed that the intensity of his hunger for her was not something he wanted in his life. If he had aided in its destruction then he had acted wisely, out of self preservation. What he was feeling now was simply an echo of a long-dead feeling.

But not so dead that the embers didn't smoulder with the heat of his desire for compensation. It had been bad enough that she had walked out on him for Carlo. But the fact that Carlo had fathered two sons on her and taken pride in them had struck painfully at the carefully guarded wound left by the misery of Gabriel's own childhood.

For him—a man who had received neither love, compassion nor kindness—to be given the responsibility of protecting the childhood of these children was either an act of great foolhardiness or great trust. It had certainly been an act of moral desperation. Not that Gabriel would ever punish two innocent young lives for the sins of their mother—not after the way he himself had suffered.

He had received word that Carlo had died a matter of hours after he had seen him. Alone, without Sasha at his side, because she had been shopping.

Sasha. He didn't want to think about the past they had shared, but it refused to be thrust away. Inside his head he could see her clearly as she had been the night he had first seen her. Her hair longer than it was now, inexpertly streaked and slightly tangled in the warm evening breeze. She had been wearing a cheap short skirt and a top that had revealed more of her breasts than it concealed, making her look every inch exactly what she was as she stood on the roadside in St Tropez. He wouldn't even have contemplated stopping if she hadn't virtually thrown herself in front of his car. Pretty, available, hungry girls like Sasha were ten a penny in St Tropez in the season, going from lover to lover, climbing upwards while they could towards their ultimate trophy of a man foolish enough and rich enough to offer them more than a night's sex in return for a thick wad of euros. Sasha, he remembered, had been carrying a large straw basket which, she had told him with a small shrug, contained all her belongings.

'I had to leave quickly, so I just brought what I could,' she had told him disarmingly, when she had by some sleight of hand managed to get herself into the passenger seat of his Ferrari without him actually having invited her to do so.

That had been in May. From the little she had told him about herself he'd gathered that the man she had left had been part of the detritus swirling around in the wake of Cannes Film Festival—a 'producer' looking for young flesh to satisfy his own jaded appetite and those of the debased human beings he made his skinflicks for. But Gabriel hadn't wanted to waste time listening to her talk when there were so many far more pleasurable uses for those soft full lips of hers. There was a practical streak to Sasha, as there was to all successful courtesans. She had quickly worked out that having to satisfy only one man would be a far more cost-effective way of using her body than risking being passed hand to hand by the producer and his friends.

Oh, yes, she was very practical. Within a year she had made plans to move onwards and upwards—not just into another man's bed, but more profitably into his whole life. As his wife. And that man had been his own second cousin Carlo—a man old enough to be *his* father, never mind hers. It had been unthinkable that she would leave Gabriel; he was the one who controlled their relationship, not her. He paid the bills and called the tune; she was his for however long he desired her to be. But she had walked out on him, leaving behind an unpaid debt to his pride.

A debt for which fate was now giving him the opportunity to claim payment in full.

Sasha saw the familiar cruel smile curl down the edges of Gabriel's mouth. How many times had he taunted her with that smile before giving in to her pleas and satisfying the aching wanting that he himself had aroused within her flesh?

She had thought when she had met Gabriel that she knew all there was to know about sex and her own body. The truth was she had known nothing whatsoever about pleasure, and too much about need.

When Carlo had offered her an escape route from Gabriel and from the life she had lived before him, she had told herself that the only way to save herself was to seize it with both hands and never look back. And that was exactly what she had done.

But, while she might never have consciously looked back, in her dreams she had gone back so many times, and in such dreadful pain. She shuddered, blinking fiercely. In the years since her sons' conception she had taught herself to walk tall and to be proud for them, and for herself. She would never deny her past, but she believed she had learned from it, *grown* from it, and when the time came and her sons asked she would not lie to them about it.

For now, though, they were too young to be exposed to and tainted by her mistakes, and she would fight with everything she had to protect them from that and to keep them safe. The only way Gabriel would ever take them from her would be by taking her life first and then stepping over her lifeless body to get them, she told herself fiercely.

'I'm not going anywhere without my sons.'

'And they will be staying here. With me.'

'With you? In Sardinia? Where? You don't live here yourself,' she reminded him.

'I didn't, it's true, but now that I own the hotel I intend to turn it back into a private home. The boys will live here when they are not at school, so that they can grow up in their father's culture, his old home.'

On the surface it was both a sensible and a compassionate plan, but compassion was an emotion that simply didn't get under Gabriel's defensive radar. There was something he wasn't telling her. Some hidden agenda motivating him that he was keeping to himself. She looked quickly at her sons, her heart thudding with apprehension. It was easy to see their Calbrini heritage in their looks, even if they were too young to have developed the predatory Sardinian profile shared by both Carlo and Gabriel. Carlo had always said proudly that they were true Calbrinis, and he had promised her...

Her fingers curled tightly into her palms. Carlo had been a man of honour, she reassured herself. He would not have broken the promise he had made her before their birth.

'The boys are due back at school in London in September,' she told Gabriel warningly.

'It is only July. They have the whole summer to enjoy being here, and to get used to my role in their lives.'

'You're planning to spend the summer here?'

'Why not? Sardinia is my home, after all. It makes

sense for me to be here to supervise the turning back of the hotel into a private home, and to spend time getting to know my wards.'

She lifted her chin.

'You do realise that I shall be here with them?'

'Hoping to make time to slip away to Port Cervo and find someone to take Carlo's place? Another rich old man to sell yourself to? Or perhaps this time you're hoping for a rich young one? Don't get your hopes up too high, will you, Sasha? You're getting older, and you've got a lot of competition. Plus, not every man wants to be burdened with another man's sons. But then, of course, I was forgetting—that problem is easily solved, isn't it? You'll just put them in boarding school and go off and live your own life without them, like you did when Carlo was dying.'

'You have no right—' Sasha began, but it was too late.

Gabriel was ignoring her, stepping past her to walk determinedly towards the boys. She started to run over the slippery rocks, instinctively wanting to put herself between him and her sons, wincing as she slipped and the corner of one of the sharp rocks scraped against her bare leg, piercing the flesh. As though they sensed her anxiety, the boys had stopped playing to watch the two adults approaching them. Both of them now immediately hurried over to Sasha and stood one on other either side of her in a way that would normally have made her smile almost ruefully because of its instinctive maleness. The boys were totally identical, so much so that even she was sometimes almost deceived when they played tricks on people and pretended to change places. There were subtle differences between them, though, that only a mother could see,

She looked magnificent, Gabriel admitted. A tigress guarding her young, ignoring the blood trickling down her leg and the broken strap of her flimsy footwear.

Out of nowhere, raw, primitive and unwanted emotions savaged him.

Sardinia's family hierarchies and patriarchs had long memories, and the history of the island was filled with tales of revenge and bitterness waged between warring families. He came from those people who truly believed in the rule of an eye for an eye, even though in these modern times they paid lip service to modern laws, and that ancestral history rose up inside him now. He had believed that Sasha was *his*, and that she would remain his until he no longer had any use for her. That he had been the one who controlled their relationship, and through it *her*. It had been the primary unwritten law that governed their relationship. But she had broken that law, and in doing so she had offended his pride.

He could never forget what his mother had done to him, and how she had chosen to reject his claim on her. As he had grown to manhood he had told himself that he would not have his power or his emotional security challenged or threatened by any woman. In those relationships with women he chose to have *he* would always be the one who ended them. He *had* planned to end his relationship with Sasha. But she had walked out on him before he could. And, worse, she had walked out into the arms of another man. His cousin! Oh, yes, Sasha owed him—and he intended to drink his fill of his chosen cup of revenge.

## CHAPTER FOUR

SASHA WASN'T GOING to be parted from her sons, not for a minute—even if that meant she had to stay here with Gabriel, Sasha told herself fiercely. But thankfully it wouldn't be for long. Not even Gabriel could hold back the start of the new school year. Which reminded her... She looked down at the rings on her fingers. Thanks to her diligence and determination she now had the satisfying credentials of a degree and an MBA. And thanks to Carlo's generosity the sale of her jewellery should give her enough to buy a small house in London close to the boys' school, pay their school fees and put some money in the bank for a rainy day.

'Come,' Gabriel demanded autocratically, holding his hand out towards the nearest boy.

Sasha could feel Sam looking up at her questioningly.

It would be so easy to turn them against Gabriel, and to fill their pliable minds with thoughts of bitterness and resentment, to drip poison into them so that they became filled with hatred and fear for the man their father had appointed as their guardian. But, no matter what she felt personally, she could not do that to them. She would not damage them in that kind of way. They came before everything and everyone else, in her life and in her heart.

Forcing herself to smile, she gave Sam and then Nico a small gentle push towards Gabriel.

'Your father has appointed Gabriel to be your guardian, and that means that we can stay here in Sardinia for the rest of the summer,' she told them as lightly as she could.

It was better to keep things simple and easy for them to accept and understand. They both loved Sardinia, and why shouldn't they? This country was, after all, a big part of them and their family history. They had spent every summer here since their birth.

IT FELT ODD to receive the formal handshakes of these two miniature representations of his own family genes mingled with those of their mother instead of embracing them in true Sardinian fashion, Gabriel acknowledged. But then their father had been an elderly father, very much of the old school, and part educated in England himself, so naturally their manners reflected that.

'What are we to call you?' Sam asked shyly.

'Gabriel is the second cousin of your father,' Sasha explained quickly, not willing to give Gabriel the opportunity to take control even in this small matter. 'So perhaps you should call him Cousin Gabriel?'

'Cousin Gabriel.' Sam rolled the words around his tongue. He was both the more serious and at times the more reckless of the two boys, whereas Nico tended to follow his twin's lead. 'I like it,' he announced judiciously.

'Good. I am glad that you do,' Gabriel told him cordially, neatly taking charge of the conversation. 'I used to call your father Cousin Carlo when I first knew him.'

Oh, very clever, Sasha acknowledged, as she saw the way her sons were starting to relax and move closer to him, like to like, male to male, the boys drawn instinctively towards this new figure in their lives.

Carlo had loved them deeply, but when he had become ill two energetic youngsters had been too much for him to cope with other than for a few minutes at a time. So she had set herself up as buffer between her sons and her husband, wanting to protect both from pain—emotional pain on the part of her sons, and physical pain on the part of her frail husband.

'Can we do some fishing this afternoon?' Nico asked her eagerly.

Fishing was a new passion, and most days the three of them spent time sitting on the rocks, waiting for fish to bite on the lines Sasha had taught the boys how to bait.

But it was Gabriel who answered, before she could, saying calmly, 'There are some matters I need to discuss with your mother, so we must return to the hotel. But perhaps this afternoon you can show me the best place to fish.'

He was seducing her sons every bit as easily as he had once seduced her, Sasha recognized, as the twins danced up and down with delight, eagerly falling into step beside Gabriel and abandoning her as they all made their way back to the hotel.

'Can you play football?' she could hear Nico asking Gabriel with eager shyness.

Immediately Gabriel stopped walking and turned to

look down at the small earnest-looking face turned up towards his own. 'Do fish swim?' he teased Nico, adding with a small shrug, 'I'm Italian, aren't I?'

'Sam supports Chelsea, but AC Milan is my team.' Nico beamed.

'I support Chelsea because half of us is English,' Sam informed Gabriel seriously. 'So it's only fair, isn't it?'

Her sons were so engrossed in talking about football with Gabriel that she might as well not be here, Sasha decided with a sharp pang.

'You need to get that leg cleaned up.' They had reached the hotel, and Gabriel's terse instruction brought Sasha's lips together in an usually tight line.

'Oh, please.' Her voice dripped sarcasm. 'Don't try to pretend you're concerned. The compassionate act doesn't suit you, Gabriel, and besides, we both know that you have no compassion for the female sex in general, and me in particular.'

She turned to look at her sons, who had been lagging behind but who had now caught up with them. 'Boys, go and get cleaned up, please, and then down to the kitchen for lunch.'

Sasha believed in nurturing her sons with loving but firm boundaries. She upheld the importance of good manners, but this, in her opinion, was a double-lane highway. If she expected her sons to behave politely, and to understand the importance of good manners, they deserved to be on the receiving end of them themselves. So far—backed up, thankfully, by the same kind of attitude in their school—they were developing a happy mixture of automatic pleases and thank-yous accompanied by natural boyish high spirits and occasional forgetfulness.

'You're a fine one to talk about concern,' Gabriel said as soon as the boys had raced upstairs, out of their hearing. 'You may be clever enough not to employ full-time care for those two—Carlo would never have agreed to that, as we both know—but you obviously make sure you aren't left with *too* much responsibility for their day-to-day care.'

'Just because they asked you a few questions about football, that hardly makes me an uncaring or uninvolved mother,' Sasha told him scornfully.

'That wasn't what I meant. I was referring to the fact that you are sending them down to the kitchen to eat while you, no doubt, will enjoy your lunch somewhere a little more elegant and without their presence. If you were left to your own devices you would probably also import a lover—possibly the same one you were seen dining with in New York.'

Sasha stared at him in outraged fury. She was too angry to even think about responding to him. She owed him nothing. Less than nothing. And she wasn't going to give any kind of legitimacy to his accusations by bothering to defend herself from them. Why should she?

'It's a pity there isn't something you could take for that perverted and warped sense of reality of yours, Gabriel. And, for your information, whoever you were paying to spy on me didn't deserve their fee. If they had done their work properly then they would have known that the only man I spent any time with when I was in New York was the specialist oncologist I had gone to see. You see, unlike you, I didn't want to sit around waiting for Carlo to die when there was the remotest chance that there could be some drug or treatment that might have given him some extra time,' she told him contemptuously, before turning on her heel and following her sons upstairs.

He didn't let her get very far, his fingers manacling her wrist and yanking her round to face him before she had climbed more than a couple of stairs.

'Very effective—or at least it would have been if I did not know you so well. Has it occurred to you that Carlo could have been ready to die? That he might even have preferred to die peacefully in his own bed rather than have his life eked out for a few months, days or weeks, so that you could continue to feed off him? While he was alive he was your passport to the life you had always wanted, the life you sold your body to get. He was besotted by you and you knew it—so much so that he begged me to lend him more money at any rate I cared to name just so he could satisfy your greed.'

'That's not true!'

Her face was as white as the marble hallway and its curling flight of stairs. Her eyes had filled with tears. They clouded her vision, making Gabriel's features shimmer and break up. 'It was Carlo's pride that made him go on borrowing, not me. I didn't even know what he was doing.'

'Liar.'

He was still holding her wrist, and as she looked down at him she was abruptly reminded of another time and another set of marble stairs on which she had stood and looked down into his face—laughed down,

in fact, with delight and teasing provocation. The stairs
had been in an exclusive atelier, where he had taken
her to try on the dress that she had been modelling for
him, layers of black silk chiffon that sighed and whispered against her skin as she walked. She had leaned
towards him, she remembered, not caring that the silk
was slipping from her, in truth delighting in the fact that
his gaze was caressing her semi-naked body, and that
his hand was cupping her bare breast. She had still believed then that it just wasn't possible for him to mean it
when he said that love and emotion had no place in his
life. She had been so crazily in love with him that she
had believed the sheer force of her love for him would
make him love her back. Then.

But this was now. Separated from the past by the
ocean of tears she had cried, and the protective wall she
had thrown up around herself. That wall was impene-
trable, reinforced with the bitterness of reality and the
strength of her hatred, bonded together with her tears.

'I hate you so much,' she told him fiercely, her emotions darkening her eyes. She could feel the blistering hiss of Gabriel's exhaled breath against her skin
as his own anger overwhelmed him and he jerked her
towards him.

She had been standing awkwardly on the stair,
caught in mid-step, and his angry movement made her
overbalance and lurch into him. 'So you say. But my bet
is that you would still go to bed with me—for a price.'

The pain inside her was instant and savage, making
her recoil and fight to escape it, her nostrils flaring and
the smooth muscles of her throat tightening her skin.

'You were the one who taught me to separate my

emotions from my body, to treat sex as a physical activity with no connection to any kind of emotional feelings. So yes, I dare say if I wanted to have sex with you I could detach myself enough from my emotional loathing of you as a person to enable me to do so,' she agreed thinly. 'But I do not want to, and neither do I need to use my body as currency.'

'Why? Have you found another man to replace Carlo before he is even cold in his grave?' What was that pain slicing and ripping at his guts? He didn't want her; he had stopped wanting her when she had started her unsuccessful bid for a more permanent role in his life. He could hear her voice now, soft with false emotion as she told him, 'I love you, Gabriel, and I know that you love me, even if you refuse to say the words.'

'You know wrong, then,' he had answered, and had meant it. 'I do not love anyone. The ability and the desire to love was kicked and beaten out of me by foster parents. The same foster parents who claimed to love me when they discovered that I'd become financially successful. You say you love me, but what you really mean is that you want me to keep you permanently in my life because I am rich and you are poor. What you love is what I give you.'

'That isn't true,' she had protested. But of course he had known better than to believe her.

He looked at her now as she told him fiercely, 'No. Unlike you, Gabriel, I've moved on from my past.' She lifted her head proudly. 'I have a degree now, and an MBA. I'm fully qualified to get a job that pays me enough to support myself and my sons.' She only prayed that would be true.

Gabriel had to fight against the shock of feeling that was gripping him. Why the hell should he be so angry and resentful at the thought of her working to support herself and being independent of him?

'You can't deceive me, Sasha, with your pseudo-maternal act,' he retaliated. 'Were you the mother you are trying to pretend to be, do you think for one moment that Carlo would have felt it necessary to appoint me as his sons' guardian? It's obvious that in the end he recognised exactly what you are, and that he wanted to protect them.'

Sasha had raised her hand before she could rationalise what she was doing, but just as swiftly he reacted to her action, clipping her arms to her sides. Before she could guess what he intended to do he was suddenly dragging her into his arms and kissing her in angry punishment. The pressure of his mouth ground down on her own, bruising the softness of her lips as she fought against his domination. But it was her retaliatory savage nip at his bottom lip that drew the blood she could taste on her tongue. He thrust her away so roughly that she almost fell, his eyes as dark as murder as he wiped the back of his hand across his split lip.

'Bitch,' he said brutally, before he turned and strode back down the stairs, leaving her standing watching him whilst her belly churned with ice and fire, fear and need, hatred and… And what? The opposite of hatred was love, and she did not love him. She raised the back of her hand to her eyes, shocked to see that it came away wet with tears.

PART OF THE charm of the hotel was that it was in many ways still very much a private house, Sasha admitted as she stood in the bedroom of the top-floor private suite that Carlo had always insisted was not to be treated as part of the hotel or occupied by anyone else.

Below this, the next floor contained another large suite and three smaller ones, with the rest of the bedrooms contained in what had once been the stable block of the house. The reception rooms were decorated and furnished as though they were rooms in a private home, and a large conservatory had been added to the rear of the house to provide a dining room that opened out onto a terrace, beyond which was the swimming pool. It would be easy enough for a man with Gabriel's wealth to turn it back into a private home. And it would certainly be more comfortable than the semi-fortress in the mountains that had been his grandfather's home.

She and Carlo had occupied separate bedrooms throughout their marriage. Hers looked out to sea, and was decorated in a palette of soft, barely-there blues and aquas and natural fabrics. She needed to speak to Maria about lunch. She picked up the telephone receiver.

Her call completed, she slipped off her linen dress and went into her bathroom to clean the cut on her leg. The time she had spent outside with the boys was giving her body a soft tan that was driving away the pallor caused by so many hours spent at Carlo's bedside. She barely glanced at her own reflection, though. Her head had begun to ache with the tension and pressure of all the morning had brought.

Why, *why* had Carlo done this? He must have known what it would do to her. He had always promised her that he would never…

But of course she knew why he had done it. It had

been his way of providing for Sam and Nico. And for her? Had he really thought she would allow Gabriel to support her? Had he believed that Gabriel would? Who knew what thoughts might have filled the head of a dying man.

Automatically she cleaned the small cut, but her mind wasn't really on what she was doing. There was a faint smear of dried blood on her dress, so she went into her dressing room and removed a pair of jeans and a tee shirt from the closet. She would have liked to have a shower before she put them on, but the boys would be hungry.

Downstairs in the kitchen, the boys and Maria, who came in to cook for them when they were in residence, were gathered around a large, well-worn and equally well-scrubbed kitchen table.

'Look, Mum, Maria is going to make a cake with these eggs from Flossie and Bessie,' Sam announced proudly.

Flossie and Bessie were the boys' bantam hens—another cornerstone of Sasha's determination to bring up her sons in a very specific way. This particular cornerstone involved active participation in becoming aware of what good food was, where it came from, and how it should be cooked.

'We're going to make chocolate brownies—but after lunch.'

'Good choice,' an unexpected male voice announced easily—unexpected and, far as she was concerned, very definitely unwanted. Involuntarily her gaze flew to his mouth. His lip had stopped bleeding but it was obviously swollen. 'Chocolate brownies are one of my favourites.'

What was happening to her? Why couldn't she make herself stop looking at his mouth? If she didn't, he would notice, and then... Could Maria and the boys feel her tension, and with it the antipathy and distrust with which she and Gabriel were filling the homey room? It appalled her that she should be reacting to him like this. She was twenty-eight now, for heaven's sake, not seventeen and vulnerable to being totally overwhelmed by his sexuality and her own immaturity.

But there was no mistaking the hot flare of her immediate arousal. It might be hidden within her body, but she could not hide from it. Anger, rejection, panic flowed through her veins like red hot lava. Why was this happening? She had lived ten whole years without him. Years during which she had been happy and secure, years during which she had privately celebrated her own freedom from the destructive emotions and needs that had tied her to him—the hungers she hadn't been able to control but he had, using them to hold her in thrall to him. There had been nothing she would not have done to please him, no pleasure more intense for her than the pleasure of pleasing him. But this ache in her body now was an unwanted reminder that, just as he had known how to compel and arouse her, he had also known how to please and satisfy her. The sex between them had been all-consuming and almost compulsive. How could one man have the power to affect her like this? It shouldn't be possible.

She tried to focus on the table in front of her. Good food should be eaten with a good digestion, and that required contentment. Already her appetite was betraying just how anxious and on edge Gabriel's presence made her feel.

What was he doing down here in the kitchen? She had already telephoned Maria to alert her to the fact that they had an unexpected guest for lunch, only to learn that Gabriel had already been to the kitchen to introduce himself to her and to explain that he would be staying.

The hotel had been officially closed from the date of Carlo's death and after the subsequent discovery of how close to bankruptcy his finances were. The Michelin-starred chef, like the imposing *maître d'* and the elegant receptionist, had left for a more secure job, and only a skeleton staff which included Maria and certain members of her family remained at the hotel.

Sasha spoke swiftly to Maria, switching automatically to the local dialect as she asked her if Gabriel had ordered lunch. Gabriel, who was fluent in several languages, had always spoken with her in English, just as he had done earlier down on the beach. He was doing so again now.

'Maria offered to serve me my lunch on the terrace, but when I discovered she was alone down here in the kitchen I told her that she need not put herself to so much trouble. She is, after all, no longer young, and the terrace is a good walk away.'

Sasha could hear the curt disapproval in his voice and knew immediately that it was directed at her.

'Actually, *I* will be the one serving you lunch, not Maria,' she corrected him. She wasn't going to tell him that it would also have fallen to her to make lunch for him as well—not because Maria was incapable of doing so, but because, contrary to what Gabriel seemed to think, she did not need him to point out to her that the elderly woman's rheumatism made it difficult and uncomfortable for her to take on too many tasks. Maria and her husband, and their extended family, were dependent on the hotel not just for their wages but also for the roof over their heads, and Sasha was already dipping into her own small reserves of cash to ensure that they did not suffer any hardship. Not that she intended to tell Gabriel any of this. Right now, what she wanted more than anything else was to have him out of her life or, failing that, at least out of the kitchen. Unable to risk looking directly at him, she told him dismissively, 'I'm sure you can find your way back to the terrace.'

'Where are you going to eat?'

A stomach-churning mixture of rejection and unstoppable, dangerous excitement held her rigid. He wasn't going to suggest that she ate with him, reprising the night they had met, was he? It was like being picked up and dropped bodily from a great height into a seething cauldron of frighteningly powerful emotions. Emotions that rightfully belonged in the past and had no place here, she tried to remind herself.

'Mum always eats down here in the kitchen with us,' Sam answered Gabriel helpfully, his youthful voice a small, still, cool rescuing hand of reality and sanity.

'As you know, the hotel is closed.' Of course he knew. He knew everything there was to know about the current state of the business because he now owned it.

She still couldn't risk looking directly at him. He, of course, was used to the very best of everything, and a chef on standby twenty-four-seven. 'The boys and I eat very simply. You'd be better off going into Port Cervo. There are plenty of restaurants there.'

'What are you having to eat?' Gabriel asked the boys, ignoring her.

'Fish,' Sam answered, adding enthusiastically, 'We chose it ourselves at the market this morning. Mum hates it when they are still flapping, but that is how you can tell they have just been landed. Pietro told us that,' he informed Gabriel importantly. 'Sometimes he even lets us go out onto his boat and see them in the net. We can ask him if you can come too if you like,' he added generously.

Just standing listening to her sons, just watching them, filled Sasha with a fiercely proud aching well of love. Tears pricked at the backs of her eyes, but she blinked them away. Boy children did not like 'soppy' displays of maternal emotion.

'Do you suppose there will be enough fish for me?' she could hear Gabriel asking Sam, treating him as an equal and not as a child—which, of course, was bound to appeal to her sons and make Gabriel instantly acceptable, she acknowledged grimly. And he knew it too. She could see that from the look he was giving her over the boys' heads. It was one of open triumph.

'If you prefer meat to fish we have some local lamb. It will take slightly longer to cook,' she told him woodenly, deliberately looking slightly past him instead of directly at him, 'but I can recommend it. We serve it in a kebab with locally grown peppers, onions and mushrooms, on a bed of wild rice. It's a local recipe—'

'I grew up here,' Gabriel cut in, and reminded her

grimly. 'As you very well know. I'll have the fish,' he told her curtly.

'Mum is teaching us how to fillet it,' Nico said gravely.

'You're planning to raise two chefs?' Gabriel asked her softly, in a slightly unkind voice.

'No, I'm raising two sons to be independent and as aware of their environment and the pleasure of the simple, good things this life provides as they can,' Sasha corrected him fiercely. '*My* sons—'

'And *my* wards,' he interrupted her softly—and threateningly, Sasha recognised as small shiver ran down her spine.

Her relationship with her sons was not what he had expected, Gabriel admitted as he watched her. *She* was not what he had expected. He had anticipated a surface show of overdone pseudo-maternal concern, such as he was used to seeing from many of the wives of his peers. Women who used their children as accessories for celebrity photo opportunities and then handed them over to others to do the real hands-on caring the minute the cameras were no longer there. But, no matter how much he might wish to do so, he couldn't pretend that he hadn't seen the love in her eyes whenever Sasha looked at the twins.

He knew, of course, that the discovery that she was virtually penniless had severely curtailed Sasha's ability to live the life Carlo had given her, but he had assumed that, while her lifestyle had necessarily changed, she herself wouldn't have done so. The woman he was watching now, though, seemed perfectly at home in this kitchen environment and perfectly at ease in her role as a hands-on mother.

He looked round the comfortable, homey room, at the confident smiling faces of the two boys who were now his responsibility. He had been scarcely even allowed to enter the kitchen of his foster parents' farmhouse. It had not possessed the warmth and cleanliness, the security he could see and sense in this room. Like him, it had been dirty and neglected, tainted with the wretchedness of emotional poverty and fear. Because here in this room there was love?

Love? Automatically he lifted his hand to press his fingertips against the dull ache beneath his breastbone. He didn't believe in love. Love did not exist. And if it didn't exist then the fact that as a child he had not been given any didn't matter and couldn't hurt him. This was his private and unacknowledged inner mantra.

IN THE END they all had the fish, and all ate together at the kitchen table. Not that Sasha managed to do much eating. Although she had tried to position herself so that she wouldn't have to see Gabriel, she was still nerve-wrenchingly conscious of him. If he had insisted on eating with them just to torment her, he was certainly succeeding.

She could still remember the first meal they had eaten together. It had been on board his yacht, where he had taken her after he had picked her up in St Tropez. Then she had not had any trouble eating. She hadn't had a decent meal in days and had been so hungry. He had raised his eyebrows slightly when she had cleaned her plate within seconds, looking from it to her face, and then to her body.

She had thought she had been so very clever. She had been watching him all week, fantasising about him, weaving idiotic daydreams around him consisting of hopelessly implausible Cinderella themes and happy-ever-afters, in the way that only a seventeen-year-old desperately hungry for love could. She had seen him on the waterfront and had naïvely assumed that he was crewing for one of the huge yachts filling the small harbour. Having seen him striding briskly past the cafés dressed in jeans and a tee shirt, it had simply not occurred to her that he might own one. He had been the kind of man a girl like her could only dream about— tall, dark and impossibly handsome, the kind of man who had all it took to sweep a girl off her feet and carry her off with him into his life. The truth was that she had fantasised herself into being more than half in love with him before she had even spoken to him.

And she had been so very desperate for love. Her mother had died giving birth to her, and her father had been advised to have her fostered. She had been four years old when he had remarried, and although he and his new wife had attempted to make her welcome in their lives, her great need for love had led to problems—especially when her stepmother had become pregnant. She had been taken back into care and had remained there until she was sixteen, craving love but too institutionalised to know how to fit into a normal family framework.

Social Services had helped her to find a job and accommodation, but the kindly shop owners she had worked for had understandably been wary and embarrassed when she had tried to push her way into their family, desperately wanting them to be the mother and father to her that she had never had. She had received counselling after that, for her 'inappropriate attachment issues', but what good was counselling when all she'd wanted was to be loved?

Her social workers had found her another job—in a supermarket this time—and when she and six other girls had had a small win on the Lottery it had been decided that they would have a holiday in St Tropez.

It had been one of the other girls, well endowed and twenty to Sasha's seventeen, who had struck up the acquaintanceship with the seedy 'film director' who had leeringly suggested that he feature the girls in one of his movies, claiming that he was in Cannes for the Film Festival.

An argument had raged hotly between those girls who'd wanted no truck with what they termed 'a sleazy porno merchant' and the smaller number who'd wanted fame at any price, and Sasha had found herself in the position of being pressured by Doreen, the pneumatic blonde, to join her in pornstar fame.

While the girls had been arguing amongst themselves, Sasha had been busy daydreaming about Gabriel, weaving a fantasy life for them both in which he fell head over heels in love with her and they lived happily ever after. Although, of course, she hadn't even known his name at that stage.

Now she knew that the fantasies she had created for herself as she was growing up—first that of being part of a close-knit family with loving parents, and then her desire for Gabriel to fall in love with her—had been her way of trying to give herself the love she had not received as a child. In her daydreams she could create her world as she yearned for it to be. But in reality that was impossible. No real relationship could have carried the burdensome weight of her expectations.

The night before the girls had been due to fly back to the UK, Sasha had seized her chance to bring herself to Gabriel's attention. By what self-destructive instinct had she homed in on a man who was as emotionally damaged as she was herself? Theirs had always been a relationship doomed to failure—if you could use the word 'relationship' to describe what they had shared. Theirs had been a dangerously compulsive sexual addiction to one another coupled with an equally dangerous hunger for emotional dependency on her part and an ingrained rejection of emotional intimacy on Gabriel's. If she had deliberately set out to do so she could not have found someone less able to meet her expectations. A wiser person would have seen that. But all she had seen was the fantasy she had created.

On that first night she had truly believed that the most challenging element of her daydream future had been finding the bravado to step in front of his car with assumed studied nonchalance, mimicking the more worldly-wise girls. Miraculously, it had worked. She had inveigled her way into his car and from there to his bed. But what she hadn't known then was that there was no access from there to his heart…

The boys had finished their lunch and were clamouring to go back outside, bringing Sasha back to the present.

TODAY HAD TO have been just about the longest and worst day of her life, Sasha reflected tiredly, several hours later. The boys were now in bed, but, drained of physical and mental energy, Sasha felt too emotionally wired to sleep. But sleep she must. The boys were always awake early.

Gabriel had gone up to the suite he had claimed hours ago, saying brusquely that he had some work he needed to do and telling the boys that he would see them in the morning. It shocked her how easily he could tell them apart—something that Carlo had never been able to do.

Gabriel. She still didn't want to believe that this had happened, that he was here, she admitted as she made her way from the bathroom to her waiting bed.

GABRIEL HALF WOKE up in the darkness of the unfamiliar room, so disorientated between past and present that before he could stop himself he was automatically reaching out, expecting Sasha to be there, his hand already cupping to take the warm, soft weight of her breast and rub his thumb-tip over her nipple in the caress she had told him so many times she could not resist. He had never known a woman so sexually sensitive to his touch, so immediately and uncontrollably responsive and aroused by him. But then he had also never known another time when he himself had been so equally and eagerly sexually charged. There had been times when his hunger for her had actually led him to analyse the feasibility of dismissing the yacht's crew and sailing it himself, simply so that he could have the convenience of taking Sasha wherever and whenever he wanted.

She had baulked a little at first when he had suggested she wear one of his shirts over the erotically designed swimwear he had bought her instead of its matching cover-ups. But when he had told her softly and explicitly that beneath the protective cover up of his shirt he wanted her naked and ready for him, the look on her face had been one of open excitement rather than rejection.

Gabriel wasn't the type to be turned on by the thought of others witnessing their intimacy—quite the contrary—but it had become necessary for him to know that she was there, and that he could help himself to the sweetest of all fruits without hindrance. Unlike in his youth, when the basic necessities of life had been withheld from him.

He had enjoyed knowing that all it took to bring the tide of aroused colour surging up under her skin was to slide his hand beneath the hem of the shirt and stroke his way up her naked thigh. Long before his fingers had discreetly parted the soft closure of the tender outer lips of her sex she would be leaning into him, her eyes closing, her body trembling violently with the urgency of her need. There had been times when it had satisfied him more to watch her orgasm against his stroking fingers and know how completely enslaved she was by her desire for him than it had to feel his own body reaching its climax within hers. Sometimes. But his own flesh hadn't been able to go very long without hungering for the firm slide of her muscles as they gripped and caressed, and urged him deeper into her, so deep sometimes that the act of possessing her felt as if he was making her a part of himself.

Gabriel frowned when he realised that he couldn't feel the softness of Sasha's flesh at an easy arm's length from his possession. Beneath his hand the bed felt cold and empty.

Abruptly he was fully awake and even more fully aware. He cursed himself beneath his breath, and his face burned with angry determination. His pride would not be satisfied until he had brought Sasha to the point where she was begging him to take her; when nothing mattered to her other than his possession of her; when *he* was the one to walk away from her.

It was years since he had woken in the night like this, and the only reason he could be doing so now, he reasoned, was because his subconscious sensed he was close to punishing Sasha for what she had done. That was all. Nothing else. How could there be anything else?

He moved to the middle of the bed and determinedly closed his eyes. Only when his pride had been satisfied would he be able to properly address the issue of his duty toward Carlo's sons, and the need to protect them from the damage that having Sasha for a mother must be inflicting on them.

## CHAPTER FIVE

A PATH LED DOWN from the house to the beach, and as he stood at the top of it Gabriel could see Sasha and her sons walking along the shore. They hadn't seen him as yet, giving him the opportunity to study them at leisure. The early-morning sun was warming the sand and glittering on the sea. Every now and again either Sasha or one of the boys paused to crouch down and pick up a shell or a pebble.

Sasha looked more like a girl than a woman, in a T-shirt, with a pair of binoculars slung round her neck, and cut-off jeans, her hair caught back off her face in a band. He could hear the sound of their conversation but not what they were saying. Occasional bursts of laughter indicated that they were all enjoying themselves. Sasha looked out to sea and said something to the boys, lifting the binoculars to her eyes and then crouching down beside them. Nico—somehow Gabriel knew without knowing how or why he knew that it *was* Nico—leaned against her, putting his arm round her and his head on her shoulder while Sam stood on her other side. As Gabriel watched she handed the binoculars to Sam and then to Nico. Gabriel shielded his eyes with his hand and looked out to sea himself. In the distance he could just about make out the shape of a small

school of dolphins. Sasha had always been entranced
by the creatures, he remembered.

Nico was handing the binoculars back to her. She
kissed him on the top of his head as she took them from
him, one arm wrapped firmly around Sam, the other
around Nico.

There was a pain in his gut, a familiar dull ache
that suddenly flared into a hot, stabbing sensation.
As a child he had never known the tenderness of any
woman's maternal embrace, never mind that of his own
mother. Kicks and curses had been his lot, followed by
the harsh pride of a grandfather who had tolerated him
because he'd had no choice.

Down on the beach, Sasha gave her sons a final hug
and then released them. These early-morning walks
were a part of their traditional holiday ritual, made especially pleasurable this morning thanks to the sight-
ing of the dolphins.

She was just straightening up when Sam called out
excitedly, 'There's Cousin Gabriel!' and began to race
across the sand towards him, followed by Nico.

Sam reached Gabriel first, flinging himself against
him. There was no need for her to worry that her sons
might object to Gabriel's presence in their lives, she
acknowledged. Nico was now clinging to him as well,
and their faces were turned up toward Gabriel's as they
chattered non-stop, telling him about their walk and the
excitement of seeing the dolphins.

'I'm going to write about seeing them in my life
book,' Nico announced.

'So am I in mine,' Sam insisted, not to be outdone.

'You could do some research on them first,' Sasha

suggested. 'Perhaps we'll be able to find some pictures on the Internet you can paste into your books.'

'I've already written in mine about Gabriel being our guardian,' Nico told Sasha. 'Perhaps I should put a photograph of him in my life book as well.'

'What's a life book?' Gabriel asked.

'It's a form of diary,' Sasha answered him distantly. 'The boys have kept a life book right from when they could first write. They put in their good memories—'

'And when we feel sad as well, like when Dad died," Sam piped up. 'Race you to the house, Nico,' Sam called out to his brother.

On the face of it, Sasha was everything a good mother should be, Gabriel acknowledged. Involved with her children, concerned for them, protective of them, but at the same time encouraging them to grow towards independence. On the face of it. But the truth was that she was no more than a good actress who had played her part for so long it was almost real. He knew that.

With the boys gone, Sasha kept her distance from Gabriel. Her whole body ached with anxious tension, as though she was constantly holding her breath and tensing her muscles. She had barely slept the last three nights, since Gabriel had arrived, and she knew that her nervous system was running on empty with fear-induced adrenalin.

The twins had run on ahead of them, eager for their breakfast. Automatically Sasha increased her own walking pace, so that she could catch up with them, deliberately keeping her gaze focused on the two boys as she started to walk past Gabriel.

'You're wasting your time—you know that, don't

you? You can't fool me, Sasha. I know you far too well. I know what motivates you and what drives you.'

Gabriel's low-voiced assertion was just loud enough for only her to hear, Sasha recognised. Her heart had started to thump in an unsteady, almost sickeningly heavy beat. How *could* he know about the sexual effect he was having on her? Not even the fun of her walk along the beach with the boys had had the power to silence the hammering pulse of need that had invaded her body. How was it possible for her to feel like this? She had truly believed that the long weeks she had spent after leaving him, too sick with physical and emotional longing for him to do more than gratefully allow Carlo to take care of her as though she were an invalid, had burned away that part of her that was so vulnerable to him and inoculated her against him for ever. But what if she was wrong? What if, like a drug addict or an alcoholic, she could never truly claim to be free of her old addiction to him?

She *was* free of it, she told herself fiercely. She had learned the difference between the destructive nature of the unhealthy physical and emotional need that had driven her relationship with Gabriel and the life-enhancing qualities that comprised a healthy relationship. And she still wanted him physically? *No!*

'You may think you know me, Gabriel,' she retorted, as calmly as she could. 'But the girl you knew no longer exists. Carlo gave me—'

'Carlo gave you what?' She winced at the savage tone of his voice. 'Sexual pleasure? Sexual satisfaction? Did he make you moan in hot pleasure when he touched you with his old hands, when he filled you with his withered flesh, Sasha? Or did you close your eyes and think about his money and his ring on your finger? Did he give you *this*?' he demanded.

And then, shockingly, his fingers were digging into the soft flesh of her waist as he pulled her towards him, one hand immediately securing her flaying fists behind her back while the other slid through her hair, holding her so that she could not even turn her head to avoid the dark possession of his kiss.

The boys had disappeared inside the house, and the rhythmic sound of the waves surging against the shore mingled with the beat of her own blood surging through her veins. She was surrounded by an assault against her senses she couldn't withstand: the familiar scent of Gabriel's skin; the living, breathing male reality of him as he held her; the way her own body instantly accommodated the intimate thrust of his leg between her own; the sensation of her breasts swelling with arousal as his tongue thrust against hers in a slow, erotic dance of sensual pleasure that stripped her defences from her. Already her body was anticipating the touch of his hand. Already the ache deep inside her had become a sharply tight pang of longing.

A seagull mewed in the sky above them and immediately Gabriel released her.

'You may think you can deceive me by acting the devoted widow, Sasha, but you can't. I can see right through your little act.' Gabriel was breathing heavily, his chest rising and falling unsteadily as he spoke. Sasha focused on its movement as she struggled to make sense of what that just happened.

She badly wanted to be sick. Her stomach was churn-

ing with nausea and a guilt that was pushing her to
hit back at him, to hurt him as he had done her. She
lifted her head and looked at him, her eyes dark with
emotion. 'Do you know something, Gabriel?' she told
him shakily. 'I actually feel sorry for you. You think
you're so strong, but in reality you are pitifully damaged. You can't comprehend that it's possible for a
person to change because *you* can't change. You can't
comprehend that it's possible for love and respect to
exist within a relationship because *you* have never experienced them. All you can do is mirror the pain of
your childhood and reflect it back to others. Thanks to
Carlo, I have learned how to be emotionally healthy.
That was his gift to me, and the most precious gift I
have to give my sons. I've changed. I'm not the girl you
knew any longer.'

Keeping her head held high, Sasha walked past him
and into the house.

Gabriel could feel the inner explosion of his own
anger in the ice-cold shards of fury that splintered
through him. So Sasha pitied him, did she? Well, very
soon now she was going to realise that she should have
saved her precious pity for herself—because she was
going to need it. He could feel the savage pulse of the
tumult of emotions surging through him.

How dared she, a woman who had lived as she had
done, accuse him of being damaged? And as for her
having changed—that was impossible. But for some
reason an image had lodged itself inside his mind of the
way she had held her sons as the three of them watched
the dolphins, and it refused to be deleted. Whatever she
might have been, wasn't it the truth that she was now

a woman with two sons whom she loved with an intensity that he could almost feel, never mind see? But if he allowed himself to accept that he was misjudging Sasha, then what might that lead to? Pain? Regret? The admission that he had lost something irreplaceable, something infinitely precious?

That could not be allowed to happen. No matter what the evidence to the contrary, he had to go on believing that Sasha was not to be trusted or believed, that she was just putting on an act. He could not forget that she had come to him from another man, from other *men,* saying openly that she preferred what he had to offer her. And she had left him for exactly the same reason. He owed it to Carlo and to Carlo's sons to be there for them against the day she chose to change again, and trade in her love for them for a new love with someone else.

No matter what she might say, he did not trust her. Sooner rather than later she was going to start looking for another rich and foolish man to take over Carlo's role in her life. She could act the doting mother all she liked now, but that couldn't alter the fact that she had already put the boys into boarding school once to suit her own needs, so she could be free to jet off to New York. How could she be the loving mother she was so successfully portraying and have done that? Especially when their father had been dying and they must have needed her more than ever? It wasn't possible.

TWO HOURS LATER Gabriel looked up from his computer and out of the window of the room in the main guest suite he was using as a temporary office. The demands of his business were such that it should not have been possible for any thoughts of Sasha to surface, but somehow they had done so. For all her assumed anger and contempt, he had still felt her body's unmistakable response to him.

Had she taken lovers during her marriage to Carlo? That feeling gripping him surely wasn't really pain; it was simply anger on his cousin's behalf. When Sasha had walked out on him he had refused to think about her or what she might be doing, but now, living in such physical proximity to her, that wasn't possible. Her presence filled the house so that even when she wasn't physically visible he could feel her around him.

He looked at his computer. Several e-mails had just come through, including one from his PA in Florence whom he had instructed to find a scholarly tutor capable of evaluating the boys' strengths and weaknesses so that he could make a decision as to their future. He certainly wasn't going to allow Sasha to send them to boarding school. And one from an architect capable of turning the hotel back into a private house. He owned properties all over the world, but neither they nor his yacht were the right environment for a pair of nine-year-olds.

Quickly he opened and read the e-mails, and then instructed his PA to have the two men at the top of the list flown out to Sardinia so that he could interview them.

Sasha, of course, would not like what he was planning to do. She would no doubt much prefer to live at his expense in the kind of environment she most enjoyed: the kind of environment that went with designer shops and exclusive restaurants. No doubt she thought she had the upper hand, and that because he was allowing her to remain here in Sardinia at his expense he would continue to do so.

But there was no way he was going to underwrite her lifestyle. Even if she had easily been the best lay he had ever had. The very best. So good that no one else had ever come close to matching the intensity of the sexual chemistry they had shared. Not that he had originally planned to have sex with her the evening he had picked her up. But she had made it so obvious that she was up for it. And a quick glance at her tanned bare arms had reassured him that, unlike so many of the girls who hung out in crowded places like St Tropez in the season, her flesh showed no telltale needle marks. Nor, so far as he had been able to tell, had she been drinking.

So he had taken her back to his yacht, watching with cynical amusement as she affected round-eyed awe and excitement, squeaking breathlessly, 'You mean that it's *yours*?' For all the world as though that wasn't the main reason why she had targeted him in the first place.

Gabriel did not normally allow himself to be caught by girls like her—pretty, cheap, available, throw-away girls, used and then discarded by the men who came there. He considered himself to be above that. The women he bedded were older and more professional— more skilled, too, at concealing what their profession was. But she had jumped out of the car, and without intending to he had ended up inviting her on board the yacht. Her smile had illuminated her whole face. She had no doubt heard that men liked women who were eager or grateful, and had decided to become both.

'So what are you doing in St Tropez?' he asked her. Not that he didn't know, of course.

'I came with some friends,' she replied.

For 'friends' he mentally substituted the word 'men', but he humoured her by enquiring innocently, 'Won't they be wondering where you are?'

'Not really,' she said promptly. 'They aren't exactly friends. More just people I know.'

'Like the film director?' he suggested dulcetly.

He saw immediately that she didn't like that question. She played with the handle of her basket and refused to look at him.

'He isn't important now.'

Now *what*? Now that she thought she had found a better deal?

'But he'll be wondering where you are?' he persisted.

'I told him I wasn't interested.'

Just as the look in her eyes as she lifted her head and gazed at him told him that she was interested in him.

He stood up, about to summon one of the crew to escort her off the yacht. He was bored with St Tropez, and had already told the captain they would be leaving in the morning for Italy and the Amalfi coast. But instead, and to his own bemusement, he heard himself asking her if she wanted something to eat.

She ate quickly and hungrily, but she left the champagne he had instructed the steward to pour for her. When she had finished, he asked her if she would like to 'freshen up'. She frowned and looked confused, before bursting out breathlessly, 'Oh you mean you're going to go to bed with me?'

Had he meant that? If so, her gaucheness almost

made him change his mind. He was used to women so-
phisticated enough to understand the rules of the game
and play by them. But, on the other hand, they would
not have looked at him as she was doing, with open
delight and eager anticipation. No doubt because she
was thinking of the money she was about to earn, he
derided himself.

Down below, in the owner's suite of the yacht, he
watched, leaning against the closed door to his stateroom, while she stood in the middle of the carpet and
spun around, her eyes shining as she stared at the luxury surrounding her.

'I can't believe that this is really on a boat,' she exclaimed.

'It's not,' he corrected her dryly. 'This is not a boat,
it's a yacht. And the bathroom is through there.'

As she started to walk towards the door he had indicated, still clutching her unwieldy straw basket, he told
her impatiently, 'You can leave your bag here.'

'It's got my passport in it, and my plane ticket home.'

'Well, they'll be perfectly safe here.'

She put the basket down on one of the stateroom's
silk-upholstered chairs, the basket's shabbiness incon-
gruous against the chair's luxury.

He gave her a handful of minutes before following
her into the bathroom. She was standing in the shower
with her back to him. She was thin, but still shapely,
with a narrow waist and softly curved hips, and long,
slender legs. She had obviously washed her hair, the
water making it look darker, softening the brashness
of its blonde streaks. It tumbled down her back, and
soap slid silkily over her naked body, caressing the

smooth perfection of her skin. And then she turned around and saw him, and the slow ache that that had been building from his first sight of her suddenly ignited into hard urgency.

He could barely remember removing his own clothes, or stepping into the shower with her, but he could remember the feel of her slick wet flesh beneath his hands. He could remember too what it had done to him to see her shudder with open sensual pleasure when he cupped her breasts and then played slowly with her erect tight nipples. She hadn't hidden anything from him, letting him feel and hear her immediate arousal in a way that had been uniquely sensual.

He hadn't kissed her at first. He rarely kissed his lovers on the mouth unless they demanded it; for him it was an overrated pleasure. He preferred the visual erotic stimulation of sight and touch, and watching the reactions chase one another across Sasha's face as he had stroked and caressed her naked body had been erotic. Not just her face but her whole body had registered her willingness to show him her sexual vulnerability to him. At first he had wondered if she might be faking her reaction, but he'd known that the flush of arousal staining her skin couldn't be faked.

But what had finally shattered his own control had been the way in which she had shuddered so intensely when he'd slid his hand down over her hip and stroked his fingertips from it to her pubic bone that she might almost have been on the verge of orgasm.

Then he had kissed her. Driven to do so by something deep inside himself he hadn't been able to ignore, a deep kiss, a possessing kiss, that had taken her mouth and held it whilst she'd shuddered and lain against him. He remembered how he had then lifted her hands to his own body, telling her thickly, 'My turn now.'

She had looked at him with dazed, awed eyes, before eagerly starting to massage the creamy foam against his chest with trembling hands. When the water from the shower had sluiced the suds downwards she had taken him by surprise, leaning forward and kissing his throat, and then stringing kisses along his collarbone while her hands soaped lower, causing his belly to tighten in fierce anticipation.

What he had not anticipated, though, was the soft questing touch of her lips against his nipple. Just thinking about it now was enough to make his whole body stiffen with the same confusion that he had felt then.

'I am the one who should be doing that to you.' He had stopped her, cupping her face in his hands. In response she had said nothing, merely dropping on her knees in front of him before slowly and carefully taking him into her mouth, her action piercing him with the most intense sexual pleasure he had ever known.

He hadn't understood the intensity of his response to her then, and he didn't now. Something in the soft stroke of her lips, something in the way she had touched him and looked at him, had taken him to a different level of arousal. He had picked her up and carried her to the bed, and before the water had dried from her skin he had brought her to orgasm with the touch of his hand, delaying his own completion to have the erotic pleasure of witnessing hers.

## CHAPTER SIX

SHE WASN'T EVEN going to think about Gabriel, never mind start analyzing and brooding over that disturbing interlude on the beach path, Sasha assured herself. And then immediately destroyed her own defence system by asking herself angrily why she was so afraid to call that kiss a kiss that she had to refer to it as an 'interlude'. So Gabriel had kissed her. All that proved was exactly what she already knew—that the line she had drawn under their relationship when she had walked out on him had somehow developed a gap wide enough to allow him the power to arouse her.

She put down her hairbrush. She could see her reflection in the bedroom mirror. She was wearing the diamond earstuds that, along with the cheap plastic bangles the boys had carefully chosen and wrapped for her themselves last Christmas, were the only things that really meant something to her. Carlo had given them to her shortly after they had learned she was expecting twins. A pre-birth gift from them and their father, he had told her lovingly. She had tried to protest that at nearly two carats of flawless diamond each they were far too expensive, but Carlo had overruled her, insisting that diamond earstuds were essential for an Italian woman.

And then, when the twins had been born, both weighing in at well over eight pounds, he had told her triumphantly that to have given her anything less than two carats per earring would have been an insult to their sons.

As she shook her head at her own memories the earrings flashed white fire back at her in the mirror. She shouldn't be sitting here, wasting time. She had an important appointment in Port Cervo before lunch. As for Gabriel—once September came and the boys were back at school she wouldn't have to see him again for months.

But that was still nearly six weeks away, and after fewer than three days in his company she was already struggling to suppress her physical ache for him.

For him? How did she know that he was the cause of her sexual longing? She was twenty-eight and she had lived a celibate life since the twins' conception. A celibate life as a married woman. There had been plenty of men who had made it more than plain that they would have enjoyed helping her to break her marriage vows, but she had simply not had the need. It had been burned out of her for ever. Or so she had believed. It could simply be coincidence that Gabriel's presence was making her feel like this. Another man might have exactly the same effect on her as he did.

The trouble was, she didn't have another man to check out that theory. Of course the other way to find out was to give in to what her body was demanding and… And what? Ask Gabriel to take her to bed? Oh, yes, he would love her to do that, wouldn't he, and confirm his beliefs about her?

She picked up her hairbrush, but then put it down again.

She had known from his acid comments when she was with him that Gabriel's own childhood had been an unhappy one. He had told her that his mother had abandoned him, and how his grandfather had treated him, but aside from feeling that this gave them something in common Sasha hadn't thought to delve deeper into his past for the very simple reason that she felt so protective of her own.

She had had to work and grow through her own past before she'd had enough self-knowledge and empathy to ask Carlo more about Gabriel's.

She had been shocked by what Carlo had told her, but while it had helped her understand why Gabriel had rejected the love she had wanted to give him, she had also recognised that it needed more than another person's love to heal Gabriel's emotional wounds. It needed his own love for himself. No amount of money or success could buy him that, and no one could give it to him either.

But, even knowing what did, she still couldn't help feeling compassionate pity for the child Gabriel had been. Tears blurred her eyes now, just thinking about the neglect he had suffered—he had only been a baby, totally dependent on his mother, when she had abandoned him at her father's insistence so that she could go back to the life she missed. But he wasn't a helpless baby now. He was a very dangerous man, and she would be a fool not to remember that.

'WHERE ARE YOU GOING?'

Sasha froze in mid-step on the stairs, her colour rising as she stared up at Gabriel, who was watching her from the landing above. She hadn't heard the door to his suite open, and now she was standing there feeling like a naughty schoolgirl caught out in some forbidden act.

'Why do you want to know?' she countered.

Gabriel's assessing gaze slid smoothly over her. She was quite obviously dressed to go out somewhere. His gaze sharpened, a feeling he didn't want to own tightening his muscles. Why the hell should he care what she did or who she did it with? It was her sons that were his concern.

'If you're planning to take the boys with you—'

'I'm not.' Sasha stopped him. She had already arranged for Maria's daughter Isabella to keep an eye on them for her. Isabella had two daughters of her own, about the same age as the twins, and Sasha knew she could trust her to keep them firmly in view and out of trouble or danger.

'No, I thought not,' Gabriel agreed. 'So much for the doting mother act.'

Sasha could feel her temper rising. 'I am going out on business—not that it is any business of yours—and that is why I am not taking the boys.'

'I wouldn't have allowed you to take them anyway,' Gabriel told her smoothly. 'I've arranged to interview a tutor for them later this afternoon, and naturally he will want to speak to them.'

Sasha opened her mouth and then closed it again as she tried to put the fiery tumult of angry objections fighting for expression inside her head into some kind of logical order.

'You don't have the right to forbid me to take my

sons anywhere,' she finally managed. 'Neither do they need a tutor. They're on holiday.'

She had seen the results of children being hot-housed by over-ambitious parents. She wanted her sons to fulfil their academic potential, of course, but she also wanted them to grow up knowing the freedoms and joys of childhood.

'They are my wards, and as such surely even you can see that in order to fulfil my responsibilities towards them I need to know more about them.'

'You could do that by being with them and talking to them, listening to them,' she said scornfully. 'They are children, Gabriel, not some new business acquisition you've bought. You can't understand how they work simply by reading a report someone else has prepared. Like…like some kind of balance sheet. What will you do if your report says that they aren't clever enough to allow you to maximise your investment? Offload them to someone else?'

'Don't be ridiculous. You always were over-emotional.'

Over-emotional! 'You are talking about my sons,' Sasha reminded him hotly. 'Not some…' She shook her head. What was the point of arguing with Gabriel like this? There weren't the words to make him understand how she felt because he himself was so incapable of feeling anything.

'You can't do this, Gabriel,' she said firmly instead. 'I won't let you. And what about the boys themselves? How do you think they are going to feel?'

'You make it sound as though they are going to be subjected to some kind of torture, when in fact you have already subjected them to pretty much the same thing yourself.'

'What?'

'They sat an entrance exam for their preparatory school, surely?'

Sasha nibbled her bottom lip. They had, of course, and with typical male confidence they had revelled in the chance to boast to her afterwards about how clever they had been.

'Professor Fennini is an extremely highly qualified educationalist, with many years' experience in his field.'

Sasha gave Gabriel a blistering look. 'You said you were interviewing a potential tutor,' she said curtly.

'If necessary he will tutor the boys, but naturally initially I want him to assess them.'

'There you go again,' Sasha exploded. 'They are children, Gabriel. *Children*. I appreciate that you never had a proper childhood—'

'Which is why I intend to make sure that my heirs are receiving everything they need to equip them.'

Sasha discovered that she needed to cling to the banister for support. Her heart was pounding nauseatingly fast, and the shock felt as if icy cold water had been poured into her veins

'Your *heirs*?' she managed to mumble. 'What…what do you mean?'

'Isn't it obvious? I mean that since Carlo's sons are my natural heirs, I would like to have some idea of how well equipped they are going to be as adults to take on that responsibility.'

The relief that surged through her was almost as physically debilitating as her fear had been.

'So I was right. This isn't just some tutor you're talking about. Well, neither you nor he are going to subject my sons to any kind of psychological tests. Has it even occurred to you that they may not *want* to be involved in your business, Gabriel? There's nothing to stop you having children of your own, you know.'

'No, there isn't, and that had been my intention. But it seems to me that since Carlo's sons are already here, and related to me by blood, it makes sense for them to be my heirs. And as for psychological tests, you are letting your imagination run away with you. The professor will simply talk with them for a little while, and then I will talk with him. And there is one thing you can be sure of: my wards will *not* be packed off to a boarding school.'

Sasha could feel the despair rising inside her. But there was no way she was going to be forced into explaining her actions to Gabriel, and no way was she going to beg for his understanding and support. Suppressing her instinct to defend herself, she said instead, 'So when is this professor supposed to be arriving?'

'After lunch. And, contrary to what you seem to think, his assessment of them is as much for their benefit as mine.'

'I'll be back by then. He is not to so much as ask them a single question unless I am there,' Sasha warned him fiercely.

She desperately needed some time to herself, to think. She still felt slightly sick and light-headed. Without another word she hurried downstairs, and then went out into the garden, where Sam and Nico were busily engaged in showing Maria's granddaughters how good they were at standing on their heads.

'*Ayeii,* boy children!' Maria's daughter laughed, but her eyes were soft with approval and affection as she watched.

Boy children, indeed, Sasha agreed, before thanking Isabella for keeping an eye on them for her and making her way around to the front of the house and the small, serviceable car Carlo had bought for her use.

It wouldn't take her long to drive into Port Cervo, the elegant resort on the Smerealda cost, with its beautiful harbour and exclusive hotels. She hoped she had dressed appropriately for the occasion. At this time of year the harbour at Port Cervo would be filled with expensive yachts, and immaculately elegant designer-clad women would be strolling its streets and shopping in its exclusive boutiques. For the purpose of her business it was important that she looked as though she was still part of that world.

Gabriel watched her leave from an upper storey window and frowned. She was wearing a taupe-coloured linen dress similar in style to the one she had been wearing the day he had arrived. A gold bracelet glinted on her wrist; large dark sunglasses with tortoiseshell frames shielded her eyes. As she slid into the driving seat of the car, he could see the natural pink gleam of her toenails in sandals that showed off the delicacy of her ankles and feet.

In the still heat of the late morning he felt as though he could almost smell the warmth of her scent. The whole house echoed subtly with it—in rooms through which she had passed and, earlier this morning, on the boys' hair, as though she had bent to kiss their heads. It was everywhere except for the rooms he had claimed for himself.

There could be only one place she was going dressed like that. And only one reason. His mouth hardened. She could give herself to as many men as she wished— once she had repaid her debt to him.

SASHA PARKED HER car and then made her way through the elegant streets to her destination, hesitating only momentarily outside, before pressing the bell and waiting for the door to open.

The owner of the shop himself came forward to greet her, sweeping her into an elegant private office.

'Would you care for some coffee?' he asked.

Sasha shook her head and opened her handbag. When she had telephoned him earlier she had explained the purpose of her visit, to save herself any potential embarrassment. From his lack of any surprise she had guessed that he had heard about Carlo's financial problems. Placing her bag on the table in front of her, she removed the boxes she had placed so carefully inside it, opening them one by one: the necklace of diamonds and emeralds and the matching earrings Carlo had given her on their first wedding anniversary; the Cartier ring with its emerald-cut diamonds which she knew had cost over a quarter of a million euros; the huge solitaire that was her engagement ring; the yellow diamond ring surrounded by white diamonds that he had given her the Christmas before last.

Finally she reached for her diamond earstuds, and for the first time her fingers trembled.

'How much can you give me for everything?' she asked the jeweller quietly.

He picked up a magnifying glass and started to study each item carefully. It was over half an hour before he spoke, and when he did the amount he told her he was prepared to offer her for her jewellery made her shake with relief.

It was, she suspected, nowhere near what Carlo had paid for it, but it was still enough to put a roof over their heads, and if she was careful there should be enough to pay the boys' school fees. They liked their school, and she didn't want to move them if she could avoid it.

She gave a small, terse nod of her head, her eyes widening in surprise as the jeweller pushed her solitaire earrings back across the table to her.

'I have made the calculation without including these,' he told her quietly. 'You should keep them. I am sure it is what your late husband would have wished.'

Sasha had to bite her lip to stop it from trembling. She was so overcome with emotion that it took her several seconds to put the earrings back on.

Ten minutes later she had left the jewellers and was walking purposefully into the bank, the cheque for the sale of her jewellery in her handbag.

Carlo had been kind and generous, but he had been old-fashioned as well. Sasha had never had any real money of her own. Carlo had deemed it unnecessary. She'd had an allowance and a credit card, the bills for which had been sent to him, but that was all. It felt strange to be paying such a large amount into her account. Strange, but empowering. Now she and the boys were not beholden to Gabriel. She could, if she wished, book them seats on the first flight back to London. But her sons would be disappointed to have their summer holiday cut short, she admitted, and for their sakes she would endure Gabriel's company—and his charity—for a few more weeks.

But once the boys were safely back at school…

She had it all planned out. She would rent somewhere at first, close enough to the school for her to take the boys there in the morning and collect them in the afternoon. And hopefully she would find a job quickly. Later, she would look for a small property to buy. They would not be rich, but they would manage. And her sons would be happy—she intended to make sure of that.

Now it was time for her to go back to the house—and Gabriel. Sasha closed her eyes and wished for strength. She had never imagined their paths would cross again—Gabriel and Carlo were related to one another, but they had rarely met, and she had made it plain to Carlo that she didn't want to have any contact with Gabriel. And she had certainly never suspected, not even in her darkest nightmares, that when she did see him again she would feel the way she was feeling right now.

She was almost tempted to do what he had already accused her of doing and take a lover—any lover—just to prove to herself that it was the long years without sex coupled with his presence, reactivating her memories of the sex they had had making her lie awake at night longing for him. Not Gabriel himself. Her sexual experience was limited; maybe her body had stored memories of a pleasure far in excess of that which they had actually shared. And maybe if she could show her body that it would stop tormenting her so much. Perhaps she ought to put *that* theory to the test. Sasha stopped walking and stared unseeingly before her. That was a crazy idea. Crazy and dangerous.

## CHAPTER SEVEN

'YOUR SONS ARE very fortunate in their mother,' Professor Fennini told Sasha with a warm smile. He had arrived earlier in the afternoon, shortly after the lunch which she had made following her own return from Port Cervo. And, despite her original determination to dislike him, Sasha had to admit that he had completely won her over—and not because of his flattering remarks about her parenting. The boys had taken to him immediately, and Sasha had quickly recognised how skilled he was at dealing with children and teaching them.

He had spent most of the afternoon not so much observing but joining in with the boys' activities, his questions so subtle that Sasha's maternal anxieties were quickly eased.

'I believe that school holidays should be treated as downtime for them. I don't want them hot-housed and pushed from activity to activity. I want them to learn how to learn for themselves, and how to live and enjoy life.'

'That is very obvious from the way you interact with them,' the Professor told her with another approving smile. 'I hope I have put to rest your fears regarding the term they had to board at their school,' he continued, and Sasha tensed.

She had been relieved to have the opportunity to bring this up privately with him, and she had been even more relieved when he had assured her that from his conversation with them it was quite plain to him that, if anything, the boys had rather enjoyed the novelty of being boarders and that they had certainly not suffered because of it, but she did not want her vulnerability and fear laid bare for Gabriel to see. However, there was nothing she could say now, with Gabriel standing there with her, to warn the Professor that she would prefer him to change the subject.

'Gabriel had told me of his own concerns with regard to that situation,' the Professor explained. 'It is entirely understandable that you should both have raised this issue with me, but I do assure you, Sasha, that in view of the fact that their father was dying and you were attempting to get the best medical care you could for him, you really had no other alternative. I have heard of the professor you went to see in New York. He has achieved some remarkable results with his innovative cancer care.'

'Yes. I had hoped… But, as he explained to me, Carlo's condition was too advanced for him to be able to do anything. With hindsight it would have been better if I'd stayed with Carlo.'

'You did what you believed to be in his best interests,' the Professor reassured her. 'And, as for the twins, it was far better for them to be living amongst their friends and in an emotionally familiar and secure environment than to witness the trauma of what was happening at home. I suspect there must have been many times when you wished you had them with you, for the comfort that would have given you,' he said in a kind voice.

It was hard for her to force back the tears threatening to fill her eyes. This was the first time that anyone had recognised how much she had longed for someone to lean on when Carlo had been dying.

'Yes, there were,' she admitted huskily. 'But I didn't want to turn them into an emotional support system for myself.'

'I do not see you as the kind of mother who would ever do that to her children,' the Professor said warmly. 'We can all see how well balanced and happy they are. As I was saying to Gabriel earlier,' he continued, 'since it is his wish that the boys are encouraged to take an interest in the way international politics and business interact, it would be a good idea to build on their natural interest in the environment and history, which you have already encouraged.' He was a tall man, with an earnest manner and the slightly stooped stance of an academic, and it was impossible for Sasha not to respond to his warmth and enthusiasm.

The boys were playing outside, within view of the window of the room Gabriel had turned into his office, and Sasha watched them while she waited for the Professor to finish his coffee and tell them his observations. From the noise they were making the imaginary game the boys were playing obviously involved some kind of motor racing.

She didn't see Gabriel move to stand at her side and look down at the boys with her, but she immediately sensed that he was there. She desperately wanted to move and put more distance between them, but she was too close to the window. And he was too close to her.

'I believe they are practising for Formula One.' The Professor sounded grave, but when Sasha looked at him she could see that his eyes were twinkling. 'They told me that Nico is to design the car and Sam will drive it.'

'Ferrari had better look to its laurels, then,' Gabriel said dryly.

'It is good that you have allowed them to retain the closeness of their twinship and yet at the same time encouraged them to develop their individual and different skills,' the Professor told Sasha.

'Nico is the thinker and Sam the doer,' Gabriel said abruptly.

Sasha stared at him, unable to conceal the shock it had given her to hear him describe the twins' personalities so accurately after having virtually only just met them. It made her more uneasy than she wanted to admit that he could distinguish the physical differences between them so easily, but *this*. He had always been an insightful person, of course, just so long as it wasn't *her* behaviour he was analysing. Right now, though, she was far more concerned about her sons than she was about herself.

Gabriel saw the swift, shocked look Sasha was giving him.

'What's wrong?' he demanded tersely.

'You've picked up on the differences between Sam and Nico very quickly,' she admitted reluctantly.

Gabriel gave a dismissive shrug. He didn't totally understand himself why he found it so easy to differentiate between the two boys, nor why he knew it was necessary to communicate with them in slightly different ways. He did know, though, that at some deep level they touched a part of him that he hadn't even realised he possessed. He had always had good instincts where people were concerned, he acknowledged, and he had always been able to stand back and judge their behaviour analytically. Like he had Sasha's? The Professor's revelations about her reason for boarding the twins at school had been too reasonable for him to dismiss. And no one could have faked the emotion he had just seen her trying to suppress.

He could almost feel the shift in mental focus within himself, forcing him to admit the possibility that he had deliberately chosen to view the facts from a warped angle to suit his own needs. Right now his conscience was making its feelings plain, and demanding some honest answers to some harsh questions. He *did* have to acknowledge that Sasha was a good mother, didn't he?

He would acknowledge nothing, he told himself savagely. The fierce surge of pain that came with thinking about Sasha gripped him. Out of the corner of his eye he could see the Professor moving closer to Sasha as he talked to her. Immediately Gabriel moved too, stepping close beside her.

Sasha tensed. What did he think she was going to do? Tell Professor Fennini that she wouldn't give permission for her sons to be tutored? Unlike Gabriel, she was flexible enough to change her mind. As the Professor had already said, the boys were at the stage where they were like greedy sponges, eager to soak up ideas and information and to learn new skills, provided they were delivered in the right way. She could see that with the Professor they would be. And she would be there to monitor what was going on so that she could step in if she felt it necessary.

Gabriel was obscuring her view of the boys so she stepped away, her jaw tensing slightly when she saw his mouth harden.

'I was particularly intrigued by the boys' life books,' the Professor was saying. 'It is a concept I have seen used very effectively to help troubled children, but I must admit I had not thought to use it to provide a record of a happy childhood.'

Sasha gave a small shrug. She wasn't going to tell the Professor about her own childhood, or explain that it was through her therapy that she had learned about creating life books.

'Originally I wanted to encourage the boys to keep diaries,' she explained. 'And the life books seemed a natural step. They are more interactive and fun for them. We agreed they could have private sections for their private thoughts, and open sections for what we do together.'

Gabriel listened in silence. Professor Fennini's praise for Sasha's parenting underlined everything he had already seen for himself. So why was he finding it so hard to let go of his preconceived and now unsustainable belief that she was not a good mother? Was it perhaps because *he* wanted to be part of the twins' lives? And part of Sasha's—a woman who had walked out on him? Somewhere deep inside the most private and vulnerable part of him a long-buried fear was pushing painfully through the protective layers of denial. What if the blame for Sasha leaving him lay not with her, but with him?

THAT DEEPLY BURIED doubt, once exposed, was something Gabriel couldn't ignore. Long after the Professor had shaken hands with him and told him enthusiastically that he was looking forward to starting work with the twins the following week, and Sasha had made it clear that she intended to spend what was left of the day with her sons, Gabriel discovered that he kept returning to the question, like a man with an aching tooth, probing the sore place even though it increased his pain.

Inside his head he kept comparing the twins' childhood with his own; not, he recognised with a stab of shocked bewilderment, a material comparison, but a comparison of the love they received which he had not. Memories he had never allowed himself to acknowledge surfaced: images of himself as a child, holding out his arms to his foster mother only to retreat in bewilderment and misery when she responded with harsh words and stinging blows. He could hear his grandfather telling him how bitterly he resented him for being his only heir, that corrosive pride rasping in his voice. His grandfather had made no secret of the bitterness he felt towards him, Gabriel remembered.

'COUSIN GABRIEL…' THERE was a distinctly wheedling note in Sam's voice that caused Gabriel to give him a rueful look. 'Me and Nico were just thinking that if Mum were to ask you what we wanted for our birthday next week, you could tell her that we need proper grown-up bikes.'

It took Gabriel several seconds to properly take in what Sam was saying. 'Your birthday is next week?' he demanded. He made a swift mental calculation. Next week... That meant Sasha had conceived the twins while she had still been living with him. And that meant that she had betrayed him with Carlo when they had still been lovers. He could feel the savagery of his anger boiling up inside him, and threatening to overwhelm him.

Sam nodded his head enthusiastically, oblivious to the effect of his words. 'We'll be ten,' he told Gabriel proudly.

'Mum says that we can't have proper bikes until we're eleven,' Nico reminded his twin, but Gabriel was oblivious to the warning looks Sam was giving Nico. He needed to see Sasha and he needed to see her *now*. Leaving the two boys, he strode downstairs and found her in the living room, looking over some of the materials left by Professor Fennini.

'I want a word with you,' he told her grimly.

Sasha was tempted to tell him that she certainly did not want any words with him, but he had already manacled her arm in an almost painful grip and was forcing her upstairs to his suite.

'What are you doing, Gabriel?' she protested. 'You can't just manhandle me as though you own me. I won't have it. And where are the boys—'

'The boys are fine.' He paused and found he needed to take a deep breath before he could say, 'Sam has just told me that it's their birthday next week.'

Sasha could feel the trickle of now familiar icy-cold fear seeping into her bloodstream. She would have given anything to shake her head and say no but of course she couldn't.

'Yes, that's right,' she said instead.

'So they were conceived in December?'

Her heart jumped into her throat, her panic threatening to choke her. 'I…they…there were complications, and in the end they were delivered early.' She sidestepped his question.

'How early? Not, I take it, three months early?' he suggested sarcastically.

Sash could feel her face starting to burn.

'They were conceived while you were still with me, weren't they?' Gabriel demanded flatly.

There was no escape. She had been dreading this for so long that in some ways she was relived that it could no longer be avoided.

'Answer me, damn you, Sasha. They were conceived while you were with me, *weren't they*?' Gabriel repeated harshly. His fingers were still clamped round her arm, and as he spoke he gave her a small, almost rough shake.

Sasha was familiar with the icy coldness of his angry contempt, but she had never seen him gripped by this kind of fury before. She felt helpless against it, and very vulnerable, but she knew she couldn't conceal the truth from him any longer.

'Yes,' she admitted, bowing her head and waiting for the inevitable accusation she knew must come. Carlo had warned her this might happen, but she had told him she wouldn't let it, that she would make sure she kept the greatest distance possible between Gabriel and herself to ensure it didn't. And, foolishly, she had even begun to feel that she was safe, and that Gabriel would never challenge her deception.

'You were seeing Carlo behind my back—sleeping with him while you were sharing my bed, giving yourself to him when I thought you were only giving yourself to me. You were pregnant by him, but still claiming to love me!' Gabriel couldn't contain the savagery of what he was feeling. It had been bad enough that she had actually walked out on him without a word, but this newly discovered betrayal was more than he could endure.

Sasha looked at him uncomprehendingly.

'Don't look at me like that—as though you don't understand what I'm saying,' Gabriel raged. 'You know perfectly well! You were sharing Carlo's bed at the same time as you were sharing mine. You let him get you pregnant while you were sleeping with me. How long had it been going on? How long were you letting him sleep with you while I believed—'

'It wasn't like that!' Sasha protested sickly.

'You're lying. Of course it was like that.' Gabriel rubbed his hand over his eyes, as though it physically sickened him to look at her. 'Didn't you care about the risk you were taking, having unprotected sex with him?'

'It wasn't planned. It was an accident…a mistake!'

'You can say that again. Did Carlo know that you were telling me that you loved me when you must have known you were carrying his bastards?'

Sasha raised her hand, but Gabriel caught hold of

it, forcing it back down to her side. 'Why tell me you loved me? Or can I guess…?'

'Why not? You seem to be determined to guess at everything else,' Sasha said fiercely.

'There's no guesswork involved in subtracting nine months from a year,' he told her bluntly. 'I suppose you didn't want to leave me until you were sure of Carlo. And of course knowing you were carrying his child was bound to clinch the deal for him. An old man with no children, no heir, and there you were, offering him not one but two.'

'I didn't know it was twins then—'

'Mum, Maria's here…'

Quickly Sasha pulled herself free of Gabriel's grip as she heard Sam's voice from outside the room.

SASHA LOOKED TOWARDS the window, where the moonlight was spilling into the darkness of her bedroom. Her heart was thudding heavily and she could feel the dampness of tears on her eyelashes and face. She had been dreaming about Gabriel with such intensity that even now she was awake it was still with her.

Her nervous system could only withstand so many attacks. When Gabriel had confronted her about the boys' birthdays, she had thought…

She and Carlo had lived very quietly for the first two years of their marriage, in Carlo's apartment in New York. They hadn't made any public announcement about the birth of the twins; the Calbrini family, while extensive, wasn't close knit, and no one had ever queried the exact date of the boys' birth.

Until now.

She was wide awake now, her thoughts haunted not just by the present but also by the past.

She and Gabriel had already been enjoying the sunshine of the Caribbean island of St Lucia for several weeks on board Gabriel's yacht when Carlo had arrived, to check out a hotel he was thinking of buying. A chance meeting at a harbourside restaurant had led to Gabriel introducing her to his second cousin, and Sasha had immediately sensed the genuine kindness in the older man.

She and Gabriel had been together for over a year, and it had both frustrated and upset her that while sexually Gabriel was the most perfect lover she could ever imagine, emotionally he still held her at a distance.

'Why do you never say that you love me?' she could remember blurting out during their first Christmas together. They had been in Paris at the time, and he had taken her out and bought her the most ridiculously expensive designer clothes, plus some equally expensive and very erotic underwear.

'Because I don't,' he had replied calmly.

They had been in bed in their suite at the Georges V, and Sasha could still remember the huge cold lump that had formed inside her body and the pain that had accompanied it.

'But you must,' she had protested desperately. 'You *must,* Gabriel. You *have* to love me.' She had burst into tears, but, far from comforting her, Gabriel had simply pushed back the bedclothes and got out of bed.

'I don't do emotional scenes, Sasha,' he had told her coolly. 'I don't love you because I don't consider that love exists. Be grateful for what we have, because believe me, there are any number of women who would gladly change places with you.' He had pulled on his clothes, and then added callously, 'I'm going out now. When I come back, I don't want to be greeted by any more of this stupidity.'

She hadn't been able to believe he could be so brutal. They had been together for months, and naïvely she had convinced herself that it was just a matter of time before he told her that he loved her. After all, he had known she loved him. She had always been telling him so, and he had never tired of having sex with her. He had spent money on her, and time with her, and in her mind she had transmuted these into the emotional bond her own neediness craved. Within half an hour she had stopped crying and convinced herself that he hadn't meant what he'd said, that as a man he was simply reluctant to admit his feelings for her.

That had been what she had told herself in Paris, and that had been what she was still telling herself months later in the Caribbean. He did love her; she was sure of it. Otherwise why would he still want to make love to her? And he *had* wanted to make love to her; there had been no doubt about that. Sexually Gabriel had not only never tired of her, he never seemed to feel he had had enough of her. She had woken in the mornings to the feel of his hands on her body, sleepily squirming in delicious pleasure beneath their roving touch, and she had fallen asleep late at night with her body soft and boneless with sexual satisfaction.

They had had a simple routine on board the yacht. More often than not Gabriel would work in the morning, and then spend the lazy heat of the Caribbean afternoons making love to her—and not always in bed. Gabriel had been an imaginative and adventurous lover, who enjoyed drawn-out, sensually erotic love-play.

She couldn't remember now when she had first been on her own with Carlo. It might have been during one of those solitary mornings when she had left the yacht to wander round the Caribbean port's expensive shops. She could remember, though, that she had quickly fallen into the habit of meeting Carlo for morning coffee, and how flattered she had been when he had suggested that she might like to see the hotel he was planning to buy.

Soon she had started confiding in him about her feelings for Gabriel, and he had told her the dreadful story of Gabriel's childhood.

'Oh, but that will bring us even closer together,' Sasha had breathed, pink-cheeked with sympathy and fellow feeling. 'I was dreadfully unhappy when I was growing up too. Poor Gabriel.'

Carlo, she remembered, had done his best to explain to her that the trauma of Gabriel's childhood had not affected him in the same way as hers had her, but she hadn't taken in what he was saying, because it wasn't what she wanted to hear.

Instead she had clung to her belief that Gabriel loved her.

She had even relayed that belief to Gabriel himself, the day before her eighteenth birthday. She had been dropping hints about her birthday to him for weeks, and finally, when they'd been in bed together that afternoon, her body still quivering in the aftermath of her pleasure, Gabriel had smoothed his hand over her stomach, causing her to tense with almost unbearable anticipation.

'So come on, then. You've dropped enough hints about this birthday of yours—what exactly is it you want?' he had demanded lazily.

She could still picture the scene all these years later: the sunlight-dappled shadows of the main cabin with its luxurious furnishings, the huge bed, its sheets tangled and pushed out of the way, Gabriel's naked body, muscled and firm-fleshed, tanned from the Caribbean sun, the familiar look of male arousal darkening his eyes. He had leaned towards her, capturing her nipple between his thumb and forefinger and teasing it so expertly that she'd writhed with renewed longing.

'I want you,' she had told him emotionally. 'I want you and your love, Gabriel, and I want us to be together for always. And—'

But before she could say any more he had released her and pushed himself away from her, getting up off the bed, his face tightening with open anger.

'What kind of game is this, Sasha?' he had demanded.

'I don't know what you mean,' she had answered him, truthfully. 'It isn't a game. I love you, Gabriel. And now that Carlo has told me about what happened when you were a child, that brings us even closer—'

She hadn't been allowed to go any further. He had leaned across the bed and roughly dragged her to her feet.

'Closer? What is all this, Sasha? The only way I want to be *close to you*, as you call it, is when I'm having sex with you. All this rubbish about love doesn't cut it with me. You know that—or you should do by now.'

She had never seen him so angry, and she had started to tremble, suddenly shocked out of her rosy fantasy into the cold sharpness of reality. But somehow she hadn't been able to stop herself from begging.

'You don't mean that. You've got to love me, Gabriel, you've *got* to.' She had been filled with panic and fear, clinging to him and sobbing, when he forcibly removed her hands from his body. 'Tell me you love me, Gabriel...'

'*I* haven't *got* to do anything, Sasha. The onus in this relationship is on you to please me. That's the way it is—you play and I pay. Look, you're a fantastic lay,' he had continued, 'and I know I'm not the first man to have told you that. We're having a good time together, and we can continue to have a good time together, but I don't want to hear another word about love.'

Something inside her had sickened and withered when she had heard those words, but stubbornly she had ignored her own pain to protest unsteadily, 'But you must want to get married and...and have children. We would have such beautiful children, Gabriel.'

She could still see the look in his eyes as he had stared at her and said, flatly and emotionlessly, 'Children are the last thing I want, and I certainly don't want them with a woman like you.' He had left her then, and she had lain in bed, too numb to move and too afraid to let herself think.

They had gone out for dinner that evening, and she had still been in shock. She had hardly eaten anything, but she had opened her gift and dutifully admired the

Cartier watch Gabriel had given her. When they had left the restaurant, he had taken hold of her in the darkness of the street, pushing aside the thin straps of her dress so that he could mould his hand around the naked warmth of her breast, caressing it with aroused urgency and kissing her so fiercely that her lips had felt slightly bruised. But she hadn't been able to feel anything. She had still been too numb, almost distanced, from what was happening.

They had gone back to the yacht and he had almost torn the clothes off her body in his need to possess her, pushing her against the door of his cabin the moment they were inside and pulling down the top of her dress, holding her hands captive behind her back, his mouth hot against her naked flesh.

He had taken her quickly, but, typically, not before speedily stretching a condom over his erection, then almost viscerally thrusting deeply into her, and coming almost immediately.

'Enjoy what we have Sasha,' he had said, still breathing heavily. 'Because I certainly intend to. This is all there is for us, and it's all there ever will be. It's called sex. Not love, sex. But you know as well as I do that you can't live without it, and you can't live without me.' His voice had held a note of undisguised triumph.

Standing silently within the circle of his arms, Sasha had known what she had to do.

It had been three o'clock in the morning when she had walked into the foyer of the hotel where Carlo was staying. At first the receptionist had refused to telephone him, but in the end she had given in.

'He says you're to go up,' she had told Sasha grudgingly.

Carlo had obviously been in bed. He'd opened the door to her wearing a monogrammed silk dressing gown, looking every inch the elderly man that he was. The contrast between him and Gabriel could not have been more cruelly underlined. Gabriel slept nude; he was a man at the height of his sexual power. There, in the harsh overhead light, Sasha saw how old Carlo was—even older than she had thought.

'I've left Gabriel,' she had said, and burst into tears.

Carlo had led her over to a chair and persuaded her to sit down. Then, quietly and compassionately, he had asked her gently, 'You're pregnant, aren't you?'

## CHAPTER EIGHT

SASHA THREW BACK the bedcovers and got out of bed. She knew she wouldn't be able to get back to sleep now, and even with the curtains closed she could see the first pale glimmer of the coming day.

It was five o'clock in the morning, and by rights she ought to be asleep, not standing here in one of the respectable nightshirts motherhood had taught her to wear, letting her emotions be ripped to pieces on the sharks' teeth of a decade-old pain.

She had broken down completely when Carlo had guessed her secret, as much because he had seen so easily what Gabriel had not as at his genuine compassion.

'I wanted him to say he loved me but he wouldn't,' she had sobbed. 'All he wants from me is sex. He doesn't care about me at all.'

The romantic happy-ever-after fantasy she had created so lovingly had not so much crashed down around her as simply evaporated in the blast of Gabriel's reaction to her pleading.

And, although she hadn't been able to say so to Carlo, a man almost old enough to be her grandfather, tonight, for the first time when Gabriel had touched her, instead of feeling desire she had felt numb despair. He didn't love her and he never would. But she had still clung tenaciously to her own need.

'Do you think he will change his mind?' she had hiccupped tearfully. 'Maybe you could speak to him for me, Carlo?'

'You want me to tell him about the baby?' he had asked, adding meaningfully, 'You must remember, Sasha, that he may not react as you would wish. He may even insist that he does not want this child and that you should…'

That was the moment when she had taken her first faltering step towards maturity, Sasha reflected. That heartbeat of time when she had placed her hand protectively on her still-flat belly and put aside her own need, recognising instead the harsh truth Carlo had just shown her and reacting to it.

'No.' She had shaken her head. 'Gabriel must never know.'

Carlo had been wonderful then, taking care of everything, chartering a private plane, marrying her before she could refuse, and insisting that it was best for everyone if he did. He was, after all, related to her child by blood. He had no children of his own, he was a rich man who would have loved to be a father, and her marriage to him would be in name only.

She could not be Gabriel's lover and the mother of his child, she had warned herself when she had felt her courage faltering. And she would never inflict the misery of her own childhood on her child. This baby was going to have all the love she could give it—all the love its father had rejected.

Fortunately, for the twins' sake, the expensive and

highly qualified New York doctor whose professional services Carlo had insisted she should have had been wise enough to recognise that she had a problem. The counselling she had received both prior to and after the twins' birth had helped her to understand that the wrong kind of love could be as damaging to a child as none at all. And that, in her opinion, had been Carlo's greatest gift to them all.

By the time the twins were taking their first unsteady steps and walking unaided she too had been taking her own first emotional steps forward unaided. They had learned and grown together, she and the twins. Her love for them had healed her.

Carlo had always treated the boys as his. Everyone had. No one had ever remotely suggested that Carlo might not have fathered them. Especially not Gabriel. Carlo had told her how Gabriel had said that he was a fool to have married her. This had led to a gulf between the two men, much to Sasha's private relief. She hadn't wanted Gabriel in their lives because she hadn't felt she could trust herself around him.

The last thing she had expected to happen when Carlo was dying was that he would send for Gabriel and entrust the twins' future to him. It filled her with a mixture of anxiety and acceptance to see how easily and naturally Gabriel related to the twins, and she had thought when he'd challenged her about their birthday that he had finally guessed the truth. She had been holding her breath ever since he had arrived in Sardinia, waiting for him to look at the boys and see his own features in theirs. Her heart turned over in slow torture every time she saw him talking to them, and then again when she saw the way they looked back at him, so innocently, ready to love him even without knowing who he was.

But the fact that he was their father had obviously never even crossed his mind. The deception he believed he had uncovered was so implausible compared with the simplicity of the truth that if it had been another couple she suspected it would have made her laugh in disbelief. How could he not see that the twins were his? How could he possibly think she, or indeed any woman, could want to go from his bed, the bed of a man at his sexual height, to the bed of a man like Carlo, elderly and sexually withered? For an intelligent man Gabriel was being remarkably blind to the truth. Yes, she knew that Gabriel had always worn protection, and he would not have expected her to get pregnant, but since when had it been a fail-safe barrier to conception? Especially with a man as sexually active as Gabriel had been with her. Didn't he even question that it might be possible, knowing how much she had loved him, that the twins were his? That she had gone to Carlo in order to protect them and herself, not to exchange his body for Carlo's? Obviously not. And of course she knew why. It was because of his childhood. Because it hadn't occurred to him that he might *want* to be the twins' father.

Sasha didn't even realise she was crying until she felt the damp splash of her tears falling onto the back of her hands as she gripped the polished wood of the window.

They were his heirs, and that was enough for Gabriel. In fact that was all he wanted them to be. He felt no emotion for them, just as he didn't for her. Although that wasn't quite true, she acknowledged. He *did* feel some emotion for her: anger, contempt, bitterness, and most of all a driving need to punish her for leaving him.

So what did she feel for him? She didn't think she had the strength to let herself answer that question. Her head had begun to ache.

The sky was lightening by the minute. Sasha opened the shutters and looked out. The air smelled clean and fresh. A walk along the beach might help to clear her head. It was too early for anyone else to be up, and the beach was private enough for her to walk there safely in her nightshirt, which after all covered her to mid-thigh.

Ten minutes later she was on the shore. There was something deliciously pagan and yet somehow child-like about walking barefoot along a sandy beach, Sasha thought. She paused to watch the waves curl and fret along the shore as they welcomed the first rays of the sun.

WHAT THE HELL was happening to him? There was no point trying to sleep now, Gabriel admitted grimly. And there was no point lying here tormenting himself with images of Sasha and Carlo. How could he not have known what she was doing? How could he not have sensed it, felt it every time he had touched her? He had thought she owed him a debt for walking out on him, but he had had no idea of just how great her betrayal had been. She had been pregnant with another's man's child and he hadn't even known. She had been having sex with Carlo at the same time as she was sleeping with him, and such was her skill at deceit that he had never once suspected. She had taken him for a complete fool, using him while she waited for Carlo to offer her what she really wanted.

There was an explosion of sensation in the centre of his body, a physical pain that roiled like tongues of fire, and stabbed him with deadly sharp knives.

Somewhere in the savage turmoil of his thoughts a small voice questioned how he could recognise that it was his emotions that were causing him so much pain. He didn't do emotions. Especially not where a woman like Sasha was concerned. His relationship with Sasha had merely been sexual. He felt the way he did because she had shared with someone else the sexual favours that should have been exclusively his, he told himself; that was all. He had been keeping her, and because of that surely he had had every right to expect the exclusive use of her body.

He realised suddenly that the strange noise he could hear inside his head was the sound of him grinding his own teeth. Had she enjoyed deceiving him? Had she held that pleasure to her when he was holding her? Had she lain in his arms, planning her future with Carlo? His head felt as though it was about to burst, and there was a tight feeling inside his chest; his eyes felt raw and gritty and his throat ached. He couldn't understand what was happening to him, or why, but he knew he couldn't lie here and be tormented by it any longer. He threw back the bedclothes and pulled on a pair of cut-offs.

A walk along the beach might help him calm down.

GABRIEL SAW SASHA before she saw him. She was standing staring out to sea, the early-morning breeze flattening the thin fabric of her nightshirt against her body.

He could see her outline as clearly as though she was naked: the soft swell of her breasts contrasting with the stiff hardness of her nipples; the narrowness of her waist and the curve of her hips; the hollow indentation of her spine followed by the rounded shape of her buttocks, the thin cotton pressed against the cleft between them just as it was drawn tautly over the mound of her pubic bone.

Inside his head old images were forming, battering down his defences. Another time and another beach, as deserted as this one. Sasha standing there, naked apart from a sunhat, dipping a small fishing net into one of the rock pools, so engrossed in what she was doing that she hadn't heard him approaching her from behind until he had pulled her back into his body and then stroked his hands over her, her breasts, her belly, the inside of her thighs, over and over again until she was moaning with longing. He could still remember the slick warmth of her wetness between the silky-smooth flesh of the pouting lips no longer concealing her sex but eagerly opening to his touch. She had moved against him, as urgently eager for him as he was for her, leaning forward over the rock in front of her. He had taken her there and then, holding her hips as he thrust deep into the hot satin heat of her welcoming flesh and felt her muscles tighten greedily around him.

The erection pressed against the fabric of his cut-offs was caused by the past, not the present, Gabriel reasoned. Sasha had no power to arouse him now unless he chose to allow her to.

Suddenly Sasha turned her head and saw him. For a

second she simply stared at him, and then abruptly she turned on her heel and started to run.

Gabriel's reaction was instinctive and immediate. Sasha could hear the fierce pounding of his feet on the sand above the shocked thud of her own heartbeat. He was closing the distance between them but she still ran on, driven by the instinct of the prey to escape from the hunter.

He caught her just when the breath had started to rasp in her throat, grabbing hold of her arm and swinging her round to face him so hard that she almost lost her footing.

She could hardly breathe, and her heart was thumping erratically. She was still in shock, Sasha recognised. Her chest hurt too much for her to be able to speak. She tried to pull her arm out of Gabriel's grip, and when he refused to let her go and pulled her closer to him she lifted her free hand, intending to push him away. But the minute it came in contact with the bare warmth of his flesh her whole body was seized with a tremor she couldn't control. She gave an involuntary gasp of despair, her eyes widening. And then Gabriel's head was blotting out the light and he was kissing her with a savage passion that swept her back in time. Helplessly she closed her eyes and gave herself up to it, returning the angry fury of his kiss with her own pain, letting him take and punish her mouth while she dug her nails into the smooth flesh of his back in mute response to their mutual hostility and helpless need.

The part of her that was still capable of thought knew that he resented his desire for her as much as she did hers for him. But it wasn't enough to stop him from shaping her body with his hands as though he was re-possessing it, and it wasn't enough to stop her from responding to him.

From out of nowhere, between them they had un-leashed something they were both powerless to control, Sasha recognised dizzily. It was rushing through her veins, surging past her defences in a tumult of hot, ur-gent desire that pounded through her body.

It had been so long since she had felt like this. Too long. Sensations formed semi-conscious thoughts in-side her head, instructing her body. She shuddered and moaned, arching her throat for the hot, familiar slide of Gabriel's mouth against her sensitive flesh. Each second was filled with a building intensity of aching torment. She could feel the familiar heaviness in her lower body, the slow, certain softening and opening of the thick-fleshed lips of her sex, and the urge to part her legs and lean into Gabriel so that he could feel for himself how ready she was for him. She moaned deep in her throat, a sound between a purr and a growl of fe-male pleasure, when she felt the hard jut of his erection pressing into her. Automatically her hand dropped to-wards his groin, her fingertips pressing eagerly against the bulge straining against the fabric of his cut-offs. She had just enough sanity to be aware that they were out of sight of the house, protected from view by the rocks enclosing them, but she wasn't sure she would have cared if they hadn't been, Sasha realised, as Gabriel caressed her nipple through the fabric of her nightshirt.

'Gabriel…' Her need whimpered through her fran-tic gasp of his name and her body arched into his. She tugged impatiently at the waist of his cut-offs, sliding

down the zip and closing her eyes in aching pleasure as
she slipped her hand inside and discovered that he was
naked beneath them. She stroked the tips of her fingers
along his rigid length in breathless pleasure.

'Wait.'

The harsh command jolted her into an anguished
silent protest.

Watching her, Gabriel shook his head and reached
for the hem of her nightshirt. Sasha's eyes widened,
the breath locking in her throat. And then she nodded
and lifted her arms, so that he could pull the nightshirt
free of her body.

Before she could drop her arms his mouth was on her
naked breasts, tasting their familiar scented warmth, his
teeth tugging erotically at the dark thrust of one nipple
in the way she remembered whilst his hand cupped and
caressed her other breast.

It was more pleasure than she could bear. It made
her cry out aloud and rake her nails down his back as
she moaned his name. Already she could feel the once
familiar rhythmic force building up inside her body.

There was no need for her to say anything, or for Gabriel to ask. They seemed to move together as though
their movements were pre-orchestrated.

Gabriel leaned down and lifted her bodily against
himself. As she wrapped her legs around him he could
feel the sharp grittiness of the sand from her feet rubbing abrasively against his skin, a reminder that intense
pleasure needed to be edged with the sting of pain.

Maybe that was why he felt this overpowering need
for her now. Because without her his life had been bland
and dull. Maybe he needed the pain to really feel. Un-

connected thoughts flashed through his head and were dismissed as Sasha wrapped her arms tightly around his neck. Bracing himself against the smooth wall of rock behind him, Gabriel thrust hotly into her.

Immediately her head dropped back, a low moan of pleasure dragging from her throat as he thrust deeper into the tight heat of the muscles holding him skin to skin so perfectly that they might have been his own.

It had always been like this with her, always, and that knowledge had haunted his dreams and savaged his pride. No other woman had ever made him feel like this. No other woman had made him want like this, driving him to break through the barrier that separated them into two different human beings. But it was only now, in the sexual extremis of his desire, that he was allowing himself to admit that to himself.

He had forgotten just how intense the pleasure of being with Sasha like this was. How could he have lived so long without it, without her?

Sasha wrapped herself as tightly around Gabriel as she could, savouring each wonderfully familiar thrust of his body. Her muscles clung to him, drawing him deeper, and she strained against him, wanting to possess all of him and be possessed by all of him. Her senses were flooded with an erotic stimulation and need that brought emotional tears to her eyes. She matched the movements of his body, taking and returning every rhythmic pulse. She pressed her lips to the base of his throat, caressing his sweat-slick skin, its taste sharp, salty and familiar.

She heard him cry out her name, and then she was

gasping and shuddering wildly as she felt the first fierce spasm of her own orgasm.

WORDLESSLY GABRIEL RELEASED Sasha, drawing great gulps of air into his straining chest. It must be lack of oxygen that was causing him to tremble from head to foot like a boy who had just had his first woman, he told himself dizzily.

Sasha couldn't believe what she had done. Her whole body was trembling so much she could hardly stand. She felt oddly weak, and yet at the same time filled with a heady sense of triumph and satisfaction.

She looked up at Gabriel.

'You owed me that,' he told her grimly, breathing hard. 'That and more.'

The rising sun dazzled her, making her turn away from its glittering light. She could see her nightshirt lying on the sand. She picked it up and pulled it on. She felt as though she was existing in some kind of void—something akin to the emotional equivalent of the golden hour after a major accident, when the victim was so traumatised that the body failed to recognise the severity of its injuries.

Without saying a word to Gabriel she started to walk back to the house.

## CHAPTER NINE

FORTUNATELY it was still too early for anyone else to be up, because by the time Sasha had finally reached the sanctuary of her bedroom she was trembling with shock.

She sank down onto her bed, tears pricking her eyes. What on earth had come over her? She had behaved like…like a woman who hadn't had sex for ten years. Or like a woman who had yearned for ten years to be with the only man she could ever love.

GABRIEL STOOD BENEATH the hot spray of the shower, washing Sasha's scent from his skin. Something had happened to him out there on the beach, something so precious and so illuminating that deep inside himself he wanted to reach out and hold the memory of it safe for ever. It made him want to reach out to Sasha with tenderness; it made him want to hold her for ever. But it also made him afraid. It had the potential to threaten everything he believed, everything he had built his life on.

He made himself focus on the reality of the situation: while he might not have planned what had happened on the beach, it proved that he was right about Sasha. It proved that she was no more loyal to Carlo than she had been to him. So where was the moral euphoria he should be feeling? The sense of righteousness and triumph? Why was he feeling more like an ex-addict who had suddenly and fatally been exposed to his favourite drug of choice and discovered that its pleasure was even more potent than he had remembered?

Just once, just one more time, so that this time he would be the one to walk away from her and leave her aching. That was what he had told himself, but already he knew it wasn't going to be like that. Already he was thinking about the next time…and the next. Already he was thinking about waking up in the night and reaching out to find her there next to him. Already he was filled with emotions that—

*Emotions?* But he didn't have emotions—especially not for Sasha. The huge discrepancy between what he had told himself to think and what was actually happening to him held him still as unwanted self-knowledge trickled through the gaps in the barriers he had thrown up, slowly but inexorably gathering force. The pain he had always denied he could feel was already squeezing his heart. On the beach, holding Sasha, completing the circle of human intimacy with her in that small, quiet moment of supreme peace after the intensity of his climax, a thought as soft as a drifting feather had brushed against his heart, telling him that here, in this private moment of time with Sasha, lay the greatest happiness he could ever know.

THERE WERE UNFAMILIAR aches in her body that weren't caused by having spent the last three hours keeping her muscles under rigid control while she walked round the house with Gabriel and his architect as he inspected it with a view to returning it to a private home.

Now the three of them were standing outside, and the architect was delivering his opinion.

'I don't see any major problems,' he was telling Gabriel enthusiastically. 'I must say,' he added approvingly to Sasha, 'that when you originally converted the house into a hotel your architect did an excellent job of retaining its original features.'

Sasha had to force herself to at least appear to be giving her attention to what he was saying. Not because she wasn't interested. Architecture and interior décor and design were her passions, but right now she was still feeling the fall-out from this morning's very different passion. While her body might be aching with sensual lassitude, her head could hardly contain the thumping force of her mental self-flagellation. It was no use to keep on saying to herself, How could you? She had, and now she had to live with the consequences of what she had done. And right now, she acknowledged, the most unbearable of all those consequences was the way that standing anywhere within a five-yard radius of Gabriel was causing her body to go into a frenzy of sexual lust.

She would have given anything to refuse his suggestion that she join him and the architect on their inspection of the house, but her pride wouldn't let her. So now she was suffering the outcome of that pride as every nerve-ending bombarded her body with messages that were dangerously and explicitly erotic. Gabriel might be dressed now, in buff-coloured chinos and a soft white linen shirt, but all she could see in her mind's eye was his naked body, and it produced a sheeny dew of perspiration on her she was mortally afraid must carry the female scent of her desire for him.

She had kept as much distance between them as she could, standing to one side of him to keep him out of her line of vision, making sure she walked next to the architect and not Gabriel, but she was still acutely aware of him.

'One thing I would like incorporated into the grounds is a hard surface circuit for the boys.'

'For your sons' bikes and skateboards, you mean?' the architect asked. 'A good idea.'

Sasha sucked in her breath, waiting for Gabriel to correct him and tell him that Sam and Nico were not his sons but his wards, but the architect was already speaking again, telling them ruefully, 'My own sons complain that there is nowhere for them to enjoy those things since my wife says that the city traffic makes it too dangerous for them to use the roads. I must say I envy you this wonderful location you have here. You are close enough to Port Cervo to be able to enjoy its facilities without being too close, plus you have this magnificent stretch of private beach.'

'The land has been in the Calbrini family for many generations,' Gabriel told him, while Sasha writhed in inner torment as she remembered what use they had put the privacy of that beach to only this morning.

The architect was looking towards his hire car, obviously ready to leave. Sasha exhaled in relief and said a quick goodbye to him before making her escape, unaware of the way Gabriel turned to watch her walk away from them.

She found the boys on the terrace, talking excitedly

to Professor Fennini about the afternoon trip they were going to make exploring some of the island's historical sites. Even without turning around she knew that Gabriel had followed her onto the terrace.

Her hands were shaking so hard as she poured herself a glass of water from the jug that some of it spilled onto the table. In her desperation to put as much distance between Gabriel and herself she tried to step past him too quickly and missed her step. She would have collided with one of the wrought-iron chairs if Gabriel hadn't reached out and covered the metal with his hand, so that she bumped into his fingers instead.

She couldn't move. She couldn't do anything. Her body greedily soaked up the forbidden pleasure of physical contact with his. Her hand was trembling so badly she could hardly hold her glass of water, and she could see the boys looking at her. What must they be thinking? They were too young to understand what was happening to her, of course. But her face started to burn with maternal guilt.

'Mum, why don't you wear your rings any more?' Nico asked her curiously.

Her initial relief was quickly followed by fresh tension. She looked down at her left hand, bare of everything apart from her thin wedding band.

'The car is here, boys, it is time for us to leave,' the Professor announced jovially.

Sasha went with them to the front of the house, where the driver was waiting with the air-conditioned Mercedes Gabriel had hired to take them to the places the Professor wanted them to see, and gave each of the boys a quick hug and a brief kiss.

Gabriel was saying something to the Professor, and Sasha took advantage of their conversation to go back into the house. Her head was aching with the pressure of her distracted thoughts. She was still in shock from this morning, unable to truly reconcile what she had done with the reality of her true relationship with Gabriel. Gabriel despised her. He was hostile towards her, he had a grudge against her, and yet even knowing that she had still allowed him...

*Allowed* him? What had happened that morning hadn't happened as the result of any kind of conscious decision. Like a furious storm coming out nowhere, it had been beyond human control.

'Sasha.'

She stiffened, tempted to turn and run from him, as she had done this morning. It wasn't just her face but her whole body that was burning now.

She forced herself to turn around and look at him.

'You never answered Nico,' he said. 'Why aren't you wearing your rings?'

She took a deep breath. 'Because I've sold them,' she told him evenly. 'My jewellery was the only asset that was mine, so I took it into Port Cervo and sold it. When the boys go back to school I intend to use the money to buy a home for the three of us in London. Contrary to what you may think, Gabriel, I do not want to live at your expense.'

'You sold your jewellery?' An icy shock of angry fear sheeted through Gabriel. If she had money then she would not need him. And he needed her to need him, Gabriel suddenly recognised.

'Yes.' Sasha gave him a steady look. 'The boys need

a proper settled home. They are my sons, and there isn't anything I wouldn't do to give them that, Gabriel.'

'You could have—'

'What?' she challenged him. 'Asked you for help?' As she had once asked him for his love? 'I think we both know what your reaction to that would have been, don't we? I've got rather a bad headache, and I'm not in the mood for this conversation, Gabriel. What I choose to do with my jewellery is my own affair and no one else's.' She turned on her heel and headed for the stairs.

FOR SOME UNFATHOMABLE reason Gabriel felt as though someone had just dropped a leaden weight into his chest cavity.

Sasha was walking upstairs, and for a second he was tempted to go after her and demand to know how she could reconcile her love for her sons with what she had done to him. She had, after all, told him that she loved him. She had begged him to return that love. He could still remember the intensity of the confusion and anger she had aroused in him, the strength of his desire to reject what she was saying. Yet at the same time her words had pierced him with an unfamiliar sensation— pain, even if at the time he had refused to acknowledge it. Now that long-buried memory surfaced.

His throat felt tight and his heart was hammering painfully against his ribs—because of Sasha? Because she was a mother who loved her sons? Was he *jealous* of that love?

It was like receiving a sickening sledgehammer blow out of nowhere, against which he had no defences.

One of the first things his grandfather had done

when he had taken Gabriel to live with him had been
to show him the diamond and ruby necklace he had
given to Gabriel's mother when she had returned home.

'This is what she sold you for,' he had taunted Gabriel, before complaining bitterly, 'She should have
married the husband I chose for her in the first place,
then maybe I would have the grandson the Calbrini
name deserves, instead of a misbegotten nothing like
you.'

After his grandfather's death Gabriel had destroyed
the portrait of his mother wearing the rubies she had
valued so much more than him, and he had locked the
necklace itself away in the Calbrini family bank vault.

This time spent here with Sasha should have reinforced everything he thought and believed about her
and her sex. It should have given him the satisfaction
of a due debt paid. But instead it had thrown up such
huge inconsistencies in the logic of his own thinking
that he couldn't ignore them any more.

There was one thing that he could do, though. He
walked out of the house and got into his car. He knew
Port Cervo well enough to guess which jeweller Sasha
would have visited.

The owner of the shop was reluctant to tell him at
first how much he had given Sasha, but in the end Gabriel got his way. Gabriel wrote him a cheque, to which
he added a substantial extra sum for 'inconvenience'
and, having recovered Sasha's jewellery, made his way
back to his car.

SASHA HADN'T BEEN lying about her headache. The soft
roar of the Mercedes telling her that Gabriel had gone

out and that she had the house to herself made her sigh shakily with relief. No need to pretend now. No need to protect herself or worry about what she might reveal for a few precious hours.

She stripped off her clothes and stepped under the shower, welcoming the cool mist of water on her tense, hot skin.

This morning on the beach…

Stop it, she warned herself. Don't think about that. But she wanted to. She wanted to think about it and relive it and relish every second of it, secretly hoarding it away…

She switched off the shower and reached for a towel, wrapping it around herself before padding into her bedroom. This hunger possessing her didn't mean anything, she tried to reassure herself. It was just a physical appetite, that was all… The needy girl who had been so desperate for Gabriel's love had gone. And the woman who had taken her place didn't need his love.

She had her sons, her self respect, a new life in front of her. What she did not need was to be dragged back into the past, to be reclaimed by a damaging relationship. Gabriel hadn't changed; he had made that obvious. He didn't want to change. He had built his whole life on the foundation stone of his mother's desertion, and without that foundation…. The reality was that he wanted to despise her, Sasha acknowledged. As powerful as the sexual attraction between them was, it was built on darkness and bitterness, and that made it destructive and damaging for both of them.

She took two painkillers, and closed the shutters to block out the sunlight before crawling into her bed.

Tears filled her eyes and slid down her face. They weren't just caused by the pain of her headache, she admitted, although why on earth she should cry for Gabriel, as well as herself, she couldn't understand.

THE HOUSE WAS empty and silent. A sensation like a huge fist gripping and crushing his heart filled Gabriel's chest. Like an image on a screen, he saw himself striding through the darkness of the main cabin of his yacht, calling out irritably to Sasha, wanting to know why she wasn't in his bed.

But this time she could hardly have left with Carlo. His cousin was dead, after all, and the small car Sasha drove was parked outside. It was adrenalin-fuelled anger that was making his pulse race and his stomach muscles knot, Gabriel told himself. He checked the downstairs rooms and found them empty, then moved towards the stairs.

THE SOUND OF the Mercedes's engine purring past her window woke Sasha from her brief sleep. Gabriel was back. She pushed back the bedclothes, relieved to discover that her headache had eased. She heard Gabriel rapping on the main door to her suite, calling out her name impatiently.

'Yes, I'm here. I won't be a minute,' she called back, abandoning her attempt to get dressed when she heard him come in and cross the wooden floor to the suite's private sitting room. In another minute he would be in her bedroom. Panicking slightly, she reached for a fresh towel and wrapped it around her body, calling out to him, 'Don't come in, Gabriel, I'm not dressed.'

But it was too late. He'd already pushed open the bedroom door and was standing in the middle of the room, frowning darkly at her.

'What's going on?' he demanded sharply.

Sasha frowned. His eyes were searching the room as though he was a jealous lover, expecting to find a rival. Her imagination was playing tricks on her, she decided.

'Why are the shutters closed?'

'I had a headache, so I decided to go to bed for an hour,' Sasha told him.

'On your own?'

Sasha stared at him. What on earth had got into him? Surely he didn't seriously believe that she had a lover hidden away in here?

'I had a headache,' she repeated. 'Going to bed to get rid of it is something that people do, Gabriel.'

His mouth compressed, and suddenly Sasha could almost smell the past: the sleepy afternoon air of the yacht's cabin scented with the sensuality of their sex. She could feel the heat crawling over her skin. Without a word, just by looking at her, Gabriel had taken her back to that time.

'*You* may still go to bed in the afternoon for sex,' she told him fiercely. 'But I most certainly do not.' Did she sound as though she wanted to? Was she unconsciously giving him an unsubtle message that she wanted him? 'What did you want me for?' she asked him. 'I'd like to get dressed; the boys will be back soon.'

He put down the large square package he was carrying and looked at his watch. 'They won't be back for another two or three hours yet,' he said, before picking up the package and holding it out to her.

'What…what is it?' she asked him warily.

'Why do you not open it and see?' He walked across the room to the door, but instead of going through it he closed it and turned around. 'Open it, Sasha,' he repeated coolly.

As soon as she had removed the outer wrapping paper and lifted the lid of the box inside it, to see the familiar name on the tissue paper, she knew. Her hands trembled as she removed the tissue, her mouth tightening when she found the small individual jewellers' boxes beneath it. She opened the top box, a wave of anger surging through her when she saw the familiar diamond ring. Snapping the box shut, she looked up at Gabriel.

'You'd better check that it's all there,' he told her curtly.

'What is this, Gabriel?' she demanded, ignoring his command, and somehow managing to keep her voice from cracking with anger.

'It's your jewellery. What does it look like?'

'No, it isn't.' Sasha shook her head, cramming the lid back on top of the box and thrusting it away from her. 'I sold my jewellery.'

'And I bought it back for you.'

'You had no right! Do you realise what you've done? How much did you pay for it? More than I sold it for, I'm sure.' His silence gave her the answer. An angry flush burned her face. 'How dare you do this to me, Gabriel? The reason I sold the jewellery was so I could provide a home for my sons and myself, so that we could have our independence from you. You had no right—'

'I had *every* right.' Gabriel stopped her, furious him-self. Didn't she realise how lucky she was? How gener-ous he was being? Or how controlling? an inner voice suggested. How determined to keep her in debt to you? He silenced the small, self-mocking voice. 'I have the Calbrini name to think of. How do you think it looks to have you selling the jewellery Carlo gave you?'

'Not as gossip-worthy as you buying it back,' Sasha said bitingly. 'Everyone knows that Carlo died virtu-ally bankrupt. I had nothing to be ashamed of in sell-ing my jewellery, Gabriel. But now thanks to you—'

'Thanks to me, what?' he demanded dangerously.

'Do you really need me to tell you? Why did you buy it back, Gabriel? So that it would make me feel indebted to you? Grateful to you? So that you would have control over me? By buying the jewellery back you're forcing me to pay for it again, and to be left in debt for whatever extra you handed over to the jeweller. You've stolen my freedom from me, Gabriel,' she told him, white-faced with anger. 'Just like your grandfa-ther stole your mother's freedom. But I'm not her, and I won't be bought or bullied, and I won't be forced to live in perpetual debt to you.'

She was shaking from head to foot as the true reali-sation of what he had done to her began to sink in. She picked up the box and thrust it towards him. 'Here—take it. I don't want it. And I don't want you. I won't let you force me into playing the role you've chosen for me, Gabriel. I'm not your mother. I'm me.'

'At least my mother didn't sleep around and share her favours with two men at the same time. You're right. You aren't her. You're a—'

It was too much for Sasha's self-control. The anger inside her boiled over. She raised her hand and slapped him across his face—hard. Immediately Gabriel dropped the box and grabbed hold of her.

Sick with shock and shame, Sasha shivered with self-disgust. This was what happened when Gabriel invaded her life. He brought with him memories from her past that aroused the kind of emotions she wasn't equipped to withstand. Even now, with anger and shame swirling through her, she still wanted him, she admitted. She had to put some distance between them.

'Gabriel, let me go,' she begged, twisting and turning in his grip, forgetting that all she was wearing was a towel. It slipped off at exactly the moment Gabriel lost his self-control and picked her up bodily to stop her struggling.

Sasha sucked in an unsteady breath as she saw the look in his eyes when his hands encountered naked flesh instead of the towel.

A thick, dangerous silence gripped the room.

'Gabriel,' Sasha pleaded again, but it was too late. He was already kicking the towel and the contents of the cardboard box out of the way and carrying her over to the bed.

'You're right,' he told her thickly. 'You are in debt to me, and I intend to claim full payment—right here and now.'

# CHAPTER TEN

HELPLESSLY, SASHA LOOKED back at him as her original anger transmuted into a sharp thrill of longing, and the hand she had lifted to push him away curled round his neck to urge him down towards her.

This, of course, was why she had needed to keep a distance between them. Because when she was near him all she could think of was how much she ached for him.

The seventeen-year-old who had gazed at Gabriel and created a fantasy world of love to enclose the two of them had had no awareness of the reality of what she would feel for him. Sex to her had been something that went hand-in-hand with love, was a mere by-product of it. She had been totally unaware of its compulsive urgency and energy, its ferocity and intensity. She had had no idea that this was how she would come to feel. That girl was not to blame for what she, as a woman, was feeling now, Sasha recognised.

She closed her eyes and ran her hands feverishly over Gabriel's torso, avidly relearning its shape, tugging buttons free of buttonholes as he kissed her, plunging her straight down into the depths of her own desire to that place where there was no reason, only the voices of her senses, whispering to her to hurry, to take what she could while she could, while there was still time.

She pushed his shirt off his shoulders, her eyes open now, as she watched him shrug it off completely, her body following his as he moved back to unfasten his belt. She leaned forward, tracing the line of his collarbone with her finger tip and then following it with small, slow kisses, breathing in the raw male scent of him as she stroked and kissed her way down his body. She was completely lost in the world of her own longing.

His belt was unfastened, his hands on the waistband of his chinos. Sasha lifted her hands and placed them against his chest, pushing him flat on the bed and then replacing his hands on his waistband with her own.

Slowly and carefully, inch by inch, kiss by kiss, she eased down his zip, relishing the sensual pleasure of slowly exposing to her touch and her gaze the plain of his belly crossed by the neat line of dark hair. She circled his navel with the tip of her tongue and then lifted her head to look, solemn-eyed, where the neat line of dark hair started to thicken. Beneath her hand, through the fabric of his chinos, she could feel his erection. A pulse quickened in her own body. She tugged impatiently at his chinos, exhaling in fierce relief when he responded to her need and stood up to remove the rest of his clothes.

On the beach there hadn't been time for her to look at him properly, but now she could. Her heart lifted and lurched against her ribs, her nipples tightening as white-hot desire—a woman's desire, not a girl's—shot through her. This too was something she hadn't known at seventeen. This fierce desire, stripped bare of the sweetness of fantasy, this real woman's need for an equally real man in the most elemental way there was. At seventeen all she had really wanted and craved from him was emotional love. Now, here, in this bed, she was fully prepared to sacrifice love for the physical satisfaction he could give her, Sasha decided fiercely. She was a woman now, with a woman's right to indulge her own sexuality and need. What had happened between them on the beach had turned the key on ten years' worth of sexual denial and repression.

But she couldn't afford this kind of self-indulgence, a warning inner voice reminded her. She was not free to do so. She was a mother, as well as a woman: a mother who needed to think first of her sons and not herself. Gabriel was their guardian, and she couldn't give him the weapons to corrupt their innocent belief in her.

As though he had guessed what she was thinking, and already sensed her withdrawal, Gabriel reached for her, telling her fiercely, 'It's too late for second thoughts now, Sasha. I mean to claim what's rightfully mine. And I intend to show you just what you gave up when you walked out on me.'

The softness of his voice, so loaded with sensual promise, made her tremble with longing. He was stroking her skin with the lightest of touches, the merest brush of his fingertips against her flesh, which suddenly burned for so much more. It was as though he was deliberately teasing her body, Sasha recognised, as he kissed her mouth lightly and then withdrew from her, only to repeat the brief kiss again and again, whilst the teasing, trailing movement of his fingertips against her skin became a form of slow torment.

Desperate for more than he was giving her, she tried to hold him closer. But he simply closed his hands round her upper arms and kept her still while he kissed her throat and then her shoulders, so briefly that she had to hold her breath so as not to miss the sensation.

'You want me,' he whispered to her. 'Don't you?'

All she could do was let the convulsions of open pleasure that seized her body give him his answer, and then moan against the liquid heat of her reward when his lips skimmed her breast, moving closer to her nipple. It was impossible to stop her body from straining eagerly towards him, or her hand, miraculously freed from imprisonment, from cupping the back of his head to urge him closer. The slow, erotic pull of his lips on the hard peak of her breast had always had the power to turn her belly liquid with erotic delight. But her memory had failed to provide a true record of the intensity, Sasha recognised weakly, when the teasing sensation of Gabriel's tongue-tip circling her eager flesh became the heat of his mouth closing on it. Pangs of pleasure so intense that they made her cry out seized her, gave her over to wave after wave of surging arousal. It flooded her and possessed her, picking her up and carrying her with it.

Without her saying a word, Gabriel found the soft wetness his touch had made ready for him. The feel of his fingers against her sex drove her desire higher, her whole body arching up to the heat of his mouth to the caress of his fingertip circling the swollen ache of the source of her female pleasure.

For a few seconds it was enough. But her body held memories of other, deeper pleasures, and it demanded that the circling fingertip become a slow, deliberate stroke over the whole length of her outer sex. Not just once, but over and over again, until she was grinding her hips and her teeth in frustration, then reaching up to grip hold of Gabriel in her need to feel him fill the waiting emptiness inside her.

'You want me?' He had moved back a little from her to position himself between her legs.

Sasha nodded her head and watched him, waiting, holding her breath as longing flooded her body.

His hands were on her hips. He was bending his head over her body, lowering it, his breath warming her belly.

Sasha drew in a defensive breath and tensed her body against an intimacy she didn't think she could survive. This wasn't what she had expected, or wanted. It was too intimate, too personal, too liable to strip her of all her defences and leave her exposed to him.

But it was too late to stop him. Gabriel's tongue-tip was already delicately stroking between the swollen pads of flesh that had opened as if in sensual offering, causing a rush of hot, shocked delight to invade her.

His tongue brushed slowly over the pulsing swell of aroused flesh it was seeking. Sasha tried, but failed to hold back her cry of pleasure. It radiated out from the place where the slow brushstrokes had become a sensually rhythmic slide. She could feel the swift assent to her climax coiling tightly inside her. It was too late now to escape. Her back arched of its own accord, her toes curling tightly as the feeling inside her soared towards its cataclysmic point of explosion. She felt Gabriel move, his weight settling against her, his heat between her thighs as he lifted her hips and thrust powerfully into her.

For the space of several strokes her body trembled on the edge of release, her muscles greedy for the sensation of his movement within them. And then the deep, gripping spasms of pleasure took over, possessing her completely as he drove through them to take her even higher. She could feel the sudden hot spill of his own climax with its added frisson of extra sensuality, and then the intensity was dying, leaving her lying defenceless and dependent on the support of Gabriel's arms in its retreating tide.

For a long time it was impossible for her to speak. All she could do was lie there, listening as the harsh sound of Gabriel's breathing softened, and accept the spasmodic aftershocks still galvanising her body.

Finally Gabriel released her and moved away from her. 'You have thrown in my face all those things Carlo gave, but we both know that he never gave you what I just have.'

His words reached her as though they had dropped like stones into deep water from a great height, disappearing from view but leaving behind them echoes of their existence that would last for ever.

'There's more to life and living than sex, Gabriel.'

'You can say that now,' he mocked her. 'But ten minutes ago—'

'I can't change the past, but I can control my future,' Sasha retaliated. 'I won't be used as your sexual plaything, Gabriel. I have my sons to consider. No amount of pleasure in bed with you can come anywhere near being worth compromising my relationship with them.'

'You say that now. But we both know that I can make you change your mind.'

Sasha closed her eyes, not wanting to watch as he gathered up his clothes, not wanting to know when he left her. But of course she did.

## CHAPTER ELEVEN

HE HAD DONE what he had promised himself he would do. He had forced Sasha to admit that no other man could make her feel the way he could. So why wasn't he feeling elated? Why did his triumph feel so empty? Why was there this ache inside his chest? This driving need to see her smile at him with that same tender warmth with which she smiled at the twins?

Why had he allowed his need for her to overpower him to such an extent that he had had sex with her not once, but twice, without using any kind of protection? Why did he wake in the night longing for her closeness, wanting more than just the cry of her pleasure during sex?

But more of what? What exactly *did* he want from her? His heart knew the answer. His *heart*? He didn't have a heart; his mother had destroyed his emotions almost before they had been formed. He had never feared loving anyone because he had never believed he was able to love. So what, then, was this feeling that ached through him?

The truth was that Sasha was a woman any man would be a fool not to love.

Gabriel stared unseeingly at his computer screen, unable to understand where that thought had come from, and equally unable to reject the truth of it. The girl who he had once held in such bitter contempt for the damage she had done to his pride had become a woman worthy of anyone's respect, and she now had the power to inflict pain on something far more vulnerable than his pride.

Slowly, carefully, like a man lost in a tunnel without a light to guide him, Gabriel felt his way cautiously through the unknown territory of this new world of emotions he had suddenly entered, flinching when a careless movement brought him up against a sharp, painful discovery.

Was this what love was? This powerful combination of strength and weakness, of a need to have and a need to give, of wanting to protect as well as wanting to possess? When he thought back—really thought back—hadn't he felt those things for her all those years ago, even if he had denied both their existence and their meaning?

Love. He tasted the word, rolling it around his mouth, feeling its form and shape while inside his head an image of Sasha formed.

The sound of the twins' voices on the other side of the half-open door to his office broke into his thoughts.

'You ask him,' he could hear Sam saying.

'No, you ask him.' Nico was insistent.

A rueful smile tugged at his mouth as he guessed that the purpose of this unscheduled deputation was another attempt to get him on their side in the matter of their longed-for bicycles. Pushing back his chair, he got up and strolled over to the door, opening it and inviting them in.

The twins exchanged expressive looks, shuffling closer together in a way that was unintentionally endearing. They were still young enough to automatically seek the comfort of each other's physical presence, Gabriel realised as he closed the door and walked back to his chair. Having undergone some kind of radical transformation, he was now suddenly discovering that not only did he have a heart, but that it was vulnerable to the most unabashed and foolish kind of sentimentality.

'Right, so who is going to ask me whatever it is, then?' he invited.

Another eloquent exchanged look, followed by a sharp dig in Nico's ribs from Sam's elbow, seemed to decide the matter.

Nico shuffled forward a couple of inches. 'Me and Sam have been wondering if you're our real father.'

The simple question stunned Gabriel, and when he didn't answer, Nico continued in a kind voice, 'It's okay. Before Dad died he told me and Sam that he wasn't our real father.'

'Yes, but he did say, too, Nico, that he'd always be our dad and that he loved us very much,' Sam put in.

'I know that. But he didn't tell us who our real father was, did he?'

Sam, eager now to take over from Nico, gave him a scornful look.

'No, but that was because he said that one day, when we were old enough, Mum would explain it all to us, and that we weren't to tell her what he'd told us. He said that he was proud of us and that we were real Calbrinis,' Sam informed Gabriel importantly, before giving Nico another sharp nudge.

Dutifully, Nico fixed his earnest gaze on him. 'Well, me and Sam have been thinking, and we wondered…'

Gabriel watched as they exchanged more looks.

'We would really like if it you were our father,' Nico said in a rush.

'Yes, it would be really cool,' Sam agreed.

It took from the first thunderstruck realisation of what they had said to the change of his heartbeat to a sudden heavy thud of recognition for Gabriel to recognise that such a short span of time had the power to change his whole life. As though the hitherto secret combination of a complex locking mechanism had suddenly clicked into place, a series of doors opened inside his head, allowing the truth to walk freely through them.

Of course they were his. How could they not be? The wonder was not that they were, but that he had not recognised it before now.

He walked over to his sons and crouched down beside them. Their familiar features blurred slightly, causing him to blink.

'Do you really want me to be your father?' he asked. It was the first time in his life that he had thought of the emotional needs of others as something more important than what he himself might want.

The boys looked at one another and then at him, wide watermelon grins transforming their faces as they nodded their heads in unison.

'Yes.'

'We knew it was you—didn't we, Nico?' Sam said smugly.

'Yes. We both knew,' Nico told Gabriel gravely, before reaching out and tucking his hand around Gabriel's arm, leaning against him.

*This* was why Carlo had wanted him to be their guardian, Gabriel suddenly realised, emotion clogging his throat as he knelt there, with a child—a *son*—in each arm, hugging them both fiercely to him. No wonder he had felt so instantly at ease with them, so immediately determined to protect them. *This* was what Carlo had struggled to tell him, only to change his mind. Because he had feared that Gabriel might reject the truth?

'I think for the moment, until I've spoken to your mother, we should keep this to ourselves,' Gabriel told his sons.

'But not for too long,' Sam countered. 'Now that you're our father you'll be able to tell Mum that we can have bikes for our birthday.'

When had they thought that one up? Gabriel wondered wryly as he received a pair of happy, confident smiles. As male logic went, it seemed a reasonable exchange, but Gabriel doubted that Sasha would see it that way.

The boys went to join the Professor, sworn to secrecy and having happily assured Gabriel that they were glad he was their real father.

Against all the odds, they had the kind of sturdy emotional self-belief that he could only envy. No, not against all the odds, but because of their mother. Because *she* had given them something more precious and more valuable than any amount of money or material possessions. She had given them a mother and a father, the secure knowledge that they were loved and wanted, the loving firmness of boundaries they had been taught to respect, and most of all the emotional freedom to be themselves. Wasn't Sasha herself the most valuable gift life had given them?

And the most important gift life had given *him*?

Sasha. He needed to talk to her.

HE FOUND HER in the kitchen, emptying the dishwasher. She looked up when he walked in, and then looked away again quickly. He wanted to look at her and to go on looking at her, marvelling that her body had nurtured the lives of their sons, that she was responsible for the miracle of their existence. But not solely responsible, of course.

'The boys have just been to see me.'

'They're hoping you'll persuade me to let them have bikes for their birthday,' Sasha said.

'They wanted to know if I am their real father.'

The water jug she had been holding slipped from Sasha's grasp, smashing onto the tiles in a shower of broken glass.

The look on her face told Gabriel everything he needed to know.

'Carlo was their father,' she whispered, bending down to start picking up the broken glass.

'No—leave it. You'll cut yourself,' Gabriel warned, but it was too late. Blood was dripping from her palm, where a shard of glass had slipped in her shaking hands and cut the skin.

Sasha stared numbly at the bright red blood welling from the small cut. She felt oddly separated from what was happening, as though some huge force had shunted her sideways into a place where she could only observe herself at a distance.

'But he didn't father them. He told them that himself, Sasha, so there's no point denying it.'

This couldn't be happening. She looked down at the glass.

'This needs cleaning up,' she told him. 'I—'

'I'll do it. You come and sit down.'

How had she got here, to the kitchen chair? She watched blankly as Gabriel deftly swept up the broken glass and disposed of it.

'Now, let's have a look at that hand.' Docilely she let Gabriel lead her to the sink and run cold water over her palm, before removing the first aid kit from the cupboard and putting a protective dressing over the cut.

He took her back to the table and sat her down.

'The twins are my sons; we both know that. But what I don't know is why you didn't tell me at the time.'

Shock was relinquishing its numbing hold on her now. There would be time later to worry about the effect Carlo's revelation must have had on the twins, and to wonder exactly what he had told them and why. Right now she needed to make sure that Gabriel understood that her sons were *hers*, that they were nothing to do with him.

She took a deep, steadying breath. 'Do you really need to ask that question? I'd pleaded with you to love me, Gabriel. I'd been sick virtually very morning for weeks, and I had guessed why, even if I lied to you and told you it was food poisoning. I'd even given you the opportunity to say you wanted children. I'd done everything to give you a chance to guess the truth short of spelling it out for you.

'Carlo guessed, and he hardly knew me. Carlo understood how I felt, and how afraid I was. You'd already rejected me. What if you rejected the child I was carrying—or worse? When you told me you didn't want children it made me afraid. Not afraid for me, but afraid for them. I thought you might put pressure on me to terminate the pregnancy.' Sasha closed her eyes and swallowed. 'I was afraid that I'd give in, that I'd do whatever you wanted me to do simply because you wanted it.

'Carlo made it easy for me to make the right decision. It's because of Carlo, not you or me, that the twins are here today. It was Carlo who fathered them, Gabriel. Because he was the one who gave them a father's protection and love.'

Regret, shame, and most of all pain—Gabriel could feel them crawling along his veins.

'You should have told me.'

'Perhaps *you* should have known,' Sasha retorted levelly. 'I'll never know what I did to deserve Carlo. I'll never cease to be thankful for what he gave me. Sometimes I wonder if maybe fate sent him; not for me, but for the twins. But it doesn't really matter which of us he was here to rescue, because out of his generosity and his compassion he rescued us all. Without him I would either have given in and let you persuade me to terminate my pregnancy, or ended up on the street, where my sons would have grown up in even worse circumstances than my own. They say that it passes from generation to generation, don't they? That damaged children become damaging parents. I was so lucky to be given the chance to change that pattern.'

'You're over-dramatising,' Gabriel said. 'Okay, so I said I didn't want children. But if I'd been faced with the fact that you were already pregnant—'

'You say that now, Gabriel, but the truth is that neither of us were fit to be parents. I was little more than a needy child myself, clamouring for love from a man who couldn't give it. Having the children was my wake-up call. Thanks to Carlo, I was able to take advantage of the very best kind of help. I already loved my babies, but I had to learn to love myself. I had to learn to accept my past, but to leave it as my past and not bring it into the present with me. Carlo was so proud of the boys. True Calbrinis—that's what he always called them.'

The conversation wasn't taking the course Gabriel had expected or hoped for. Sasha seemed stubbornly determined to reject his attempts to forge a bond between them via their sons. The revelations which had so awed and impressed him apparently had no impact on her. Couldn't she see that he was a changed man? That he recognised the errors of his past and was now ready to make amends for them?

'They are my sons,' he told her firmly.

Sasha shook her head. 'No. Your sons, Gabriel, would be as damaged and as tainted by your childhood as you are yourself. An adult can't find salvation through a child. You have to give to them, not take from them.'

'I made mistakes, I admit that. But it's not too late…'

'It's not too late for what?' Sasha asked.

It's not too late for us, was what he wanted to say, but instead he said, 'I know you, Sasha—'

She stopped him immediately. 'No, you don't know me, Gabriel. You never did. To you I'm a cheap tart you picked up off the street, a piece of flesh to provide you with pleasure. You believed I'd two-timed you with Carlo. You thought—'

He had made mistakes, Gabriel knew that, but he wasn't solely to blame for that. Her accusations stung and made him react defensively. 'Do you blame me?' he demanded. 'The night we met you told me—'

Sasha gave him a weary look. What did it matter now what she told him? 'The night we met I was still a virgin. *That's* how little you know me, Gabriel.' She pushed back her chair and stood up unsteadily.

'That can't be true,' Gabriel protested. 'What about that porno film director? You implied—'

Sasha gave a mirthless smile. 'Oh, yes, I certainly implied—and he certainly existed. He tried to proposition one of the girls I was on holiday with. The truth is that I was very young and even more foolish. I wanted you to think I was sexy and desirable…I was too naïve to realise you'd simply think I was used and available.'

'I don't understand any of this. You claim you were a virgin, so why the hell did you go to bed with me? You must have known—'

'What? That all you wanted was a one-night stand?' Sasha shook her head. 'Gabriel, I was seventeen. I'd been in care since I was a child. I craved love. I thought it was the answer to everything. My prince would ride into my life and sweep me up into his arms and we'd live happily ever after. That was all I wanted—to be loved. To be in love.'

He could hear the derision in her voice at her own foolishness and somehow that hurt him—for her.

'The other girls were older than me. I'd only been included in the holiday because we all worked together. I got in their way, and on their nerves, so I spent most of my time on my own. I saw you the first day we arrived in St Tropez. You were walking past the café where I was having a cup of coffee. You fitted my mental template of hero perfectly. All it took was a handful of seconds to convince myself that it was love at first sight, and that you were the only man I could ever and would ever love.' She gave a small shrug. 'That's how my neediness expressed itself.

'I started hanging around the harbour, hoping I'd see you. And I did. Coming off the yacht. I thought you must work on it. It never occurred to me that you owned it.' She smiled sadly. 'Your money was never the draw for me, Gabriel, although of course you could never believe that. It scared me half to death when I realised just how wealthy you were, but by then it was too late. I was deeply in love. So much in love and so very hungry for you that even that first time what little pain there was was far outweighed by my pleasure.'

Gabriel closed his eyes. He could remember that first time and how good it had felt, how good *she* had felt, with the close sheath of her muscles gripping him tightly. He had put that down to her experience. He should have known… And perhaps deep inside he had known, but had preferred to pretend that he did not. Shame and an acute sense of loss tightened his throat.

'And of course I'd convinced myself that you returned my feelings,' Sasha continued lightly. 'Even
though you did everything possible to make it obvious
that you didn't. But what did I know? All I knew was
my own need. No one had ever loved me; I had no experience of what real love was. So predictably, I looked
for love where I was never going to find it. I set myself
the task of making myself good enough for you to reward me with your love. It's a common enough pattern.
The more you withheld your love, the harder I worked
to try to gain it.'

'I didn't know—'

'How could you? We never talked, we simply had
sex, and I made up my foolish fantasies. Even when
you did mention your mother and your grandfather,
it never occurred to me that those relationships had
to impact on ours. I simply thought how wonderful
it was that we had both had unhappy childhoods and
how it must bond us together. I convinced myself that
I had been given the opportunity to give you the love
you had never had. I agreed with you that your mother
was cruel and selfish. I couldn't reason then that she
might have been afraid and alone, that she might have
found herself in a marriage that wasn't working, and
that she might have been tricked by her father into returning home, only to discover too late that the price
of being rescued from an unwanted marriage was the
loss of her son.'

Sasha could see that Gabriel was frowning, and there
was a bleak look in his eyes. 'I'm not saying that's what
happened, Gabriel. I'm simply saying that there could
be other explanations than the one you were given.'

Gabriel wasn't looking convinced.

'Look, I'm not trying to rewrite your family history or defend your mother. But you were too young when your mother left to know what she felt or why she did it. All you know is what you were told by others.'

Sasha gave a small tired shrug. 'We can look back to our childhoods, see the pain there and blame our parents, and then we can look back to their childhoods and see that they were damaged too. But where does it end, Gabriel? How far back do we go in loading the blame? How much of our lives do we need to spend looking for answers in the past and blaming others for our present? I had to step away from my childhood and re-create myself as the person the twins needed me to be. It was the biggest turning point in the whole of my life.'

That wasn't entirely true. But Sasha wasn't about to tell Gabriel that even now he still held a grip on her heart that no amount of counselling or anything else could release.

'So you reinvented yourself and turned your whole life around by deciding that your childhood wasn't as bad as you remembered? Unfortunately I don't have your imagination.'

The love for Gabriel that she had tried so hard to tell herself was dead filled Sasha's heart. She ached to go to him and hold him, make whole and heal all the damaged places of his past. In her mind's eye she could see him as a child—alone, afraid, and unloved; *hurting*. Tears stung her eyes. She wanted to reach into the past and snatch Gabriel the child from it, so that she could give him love. But she knew that no amount of love from her could take away his bitterness. And she knew too that she couldn't risk that bitterness flowing from him into the lives of her sons.

'Nothing more to say?' Gabriel asked grimly. 'This kind of talk is all very well, Sasha, but you can't really expect me to believe it can alter reality. Forget the past. What we need to talk about now is the present, and our sons.'

Sasha looked away from him.

'What's wrong?' Gabriel demanded. 'Or can I guess? You'd have preferred it if I'd never learned the truth, wouldn't you? That I'd continued to believe that Carlo fathered them?'

'Yes,' Sasha admitted quietly.

'Thanks for that vote of confidence.'

'I'm thinking of the boys.'

'And what you're thinking is that I'm not good enough to be their father?' Gabriel said.

Sasha dipped her head. This was so difficult, and so painful. She could remember how she had felt when she had first realised she was pregnant, her sense of excited awe that *she* was having *Gabriel's* baby. She had felt as though she'd had the greatest gift on earth bestowed on her. The pregnancy had been accidental; she had been far too much the junior partner in their relationship to think of doing something like deliberately sabotaging Gabriel's contraception. The fact that she had conceived despite Gabriel's precautions had just made her feel that her pregnancy was extra special and meant to be. She had been delirious with joy, expecting with every early-morning bout of sickness to hear Gabriel announcing that he knew she was pregnant. She had even imagined the scene, right down to his words of love and reverence as he held her and told her how thrilled he was, how much he loved her. He would insist on marrying her immediately, of course, and they would live happily ever after with their adorable baby.

Only it hadn't worked like that. Now she knew that she must have had some inner instinct warning her of what was to come. Why else would she have lied when Gabriel had commented on her sickness, saying it was food poisoning? She might have believed she wanted him to guess she was pregnant, but something deep within her had made her keep it a secret.

She had been in her second month when she had begun to feel impatient with Gabriel's lack of insight, and she had started to drop heavy hints about babies. That was when Gabriel had told her bitingly that far too many people produced children they didn't want. And he had underlined his views with explicit descriptions of his own childhood.

Remembering that time now, she took a deep breath.

'I don't think that you are whole enough to be the father I want for them. I don't want them to suffer the repercussions of your childhood, Gabriel,' she told him quietly.

It hurt her physically to see the shock in his eyes and the way he battled to conceal it from her.

'You think I'd *hurt* them, physically abuse them?' he burst out.

Sasha shook her head. 'No,' she told him honestly. 'I lived with you for long enough to know that you wouldn't hurt them that way. But there are other ways of harming those we love.'

'So you *do* accept that I love them?'

Sasha smiled ruefully. From the moment they had set eyes on one another Gabriel and the twins had formed a united male bond that had given her more cause for guilty anxiety than she wanted to admit. If he'd known right from the start they were his children Gabriel couldn't have been more of a father during these few weeks they had all spent together. He possessed an instinctive perception of what would work for them and what wouldn't, and he treated them as individuals instead of lumping them together as 'the twins'. But most telling of all was the way in which he had immediately and instinctively been able to tell them apart. Something that until now only she had been able to do. Carlo had certainly never managed to work out which of them was which.

'Yes, I do accept that. But even love can be damaging, Gabriel. It's natural for us to want to give our own children the best of everything, emotionally and materially. But that isn't always a good thing.'

'You mean you think I'd overload them with too much love and money because I'd want to give them what I never had?'

'Tell me honestly that you haven't already mentally picked out top-of-the-range bicycles for them,' Sasha asked him dryly. She could tell from the way Gabriel avoided her gaze that she was right. 'It isn't that I don't believe you love them, Gabriel, or that I doubt for one minute that you'd want the very best of everything for them. It's… I've had to learn that sometimes the best thing you can do for them is to say no.'

'So you don't want me to be part of their lives because you think I'll spoil them?'

'You are *already* a part of their lives. You're their guardian and their father.'

'Sasha.' He reached across the table and took hold of her hand before she could stop him.

'I understand what you're saying, and, yes, I accept that being a father is going to involve me in a pretty steep learning curve. But what about the other side of the equation?'

'What other side?' Sasha asked woodenly. But she already knew. This was it. She was living her worst nightmare—and her most longed-for dream.

'You and I share a history that holds a lot of pain and anger. I know that. But it also holds our sons. I know that I've let the best thing in my life slip away from me because I was too blind to see what I had. We've already proved that sexually we're not so much compatible as combustible.' Gabriel paused, and the smouldering look in his eyes made Sasha's toes curl and her heart thump with remembered pleasure. 'The best gift any parent can give their child is surely the security of a loving home life. I'd like to give that to our sons.'

It might have taken him a long time to accept that he loved Sasha, but now that he had he didn't intend to waste any more of it. There was nothing he wanted to hold back from her now; not his love, not his admission that he had deliberately made himself think the worst of her, not his heartfelt apology for his mistakes—nothing! He wanted a clean conscience, a clean fresh start, a new beginning for them all, and a life in which he could show Sasha just how much she and their sons meant to him every single day.

'You mean you want the four of us to live together

as a family?' There was a note of caution in her voice he could fully understand.

'I want us to live together as a family—yes, Sasha. And I want you and I to live as husband and wife. I want to marry you, Sasha. I want our sons to grow up with us as their parents.'

Just for a few precious seconds Sasha allowed herself to dream and believe, to think the impossible. But only for a few seconds. Because she already knew what her answer had to be.

'No,' she told Gabriel quietly.

'No? Why not? What—?'

'It wouldn't work, Gabriel. I accept that sexually we…it works between us,' she agreed hurriedly, not wanting to linger on thoughts that could only add to the rebellion inside her, threatening to overturn her hard-won decision. 'But you and I… We both may love the boys, but let's not pretend that we love one another. Because we both know that we don't.'

They were the hardest words she had ever had to say. All the more so because they were a lie. No matter what she'd told herself during the intervening years, she knew herself too well now to be able to pretend that the way he made her feel was purely sexual. But she also knew that for her sons' sake she could not afford to love him—especially not via a public relationship and a commitment that could rebound on them.

In a dream world, a perfect world, this was where she would fling herself into his arms with cries of joy that they would live happily ever after. But reality wasn't like that. Reality could be harsh and unforgiving.

'On the contrary, I know nothing of the sort,' she

heard Gabriel saying softly. Her heart skipped a beat. Had he guessed that she still loved him? And if so… 'You may not love me any more, Sasha, but I do love you.'

If only she could let herself believe that. The thrill of hearing those words after so many years was threatening to sweep away all her doubts. But she mustn't let it.

'You say that now, Gabriel, but how can I believe it? How can you? Only days ago you believed that I was a bad mother, a woman who went from one man's bed to another's, a woman who was looking for a rich man to support her. Remember?'

Gabriel couldn't deny it. 'I said all those things, yes,' he said. 'And, yes, initially I was convinced that they were true. But it didn't take me very long to realise just how wrong I was, even if I was too stubborn to face up to it. I had to make myself believe them, Sasha, because my pride wouldn't let me admit how I really felt when you walked out on me that day. I'd sworn that I would never risk falling in love and I couldn't admit that I had. Besides, if you'd really wanted a wealthy man to seduce, you could have seduced me.' He smiled at her, to show that he was making a joke against himself. 'Perhaps a part of me was hoping that you would.'

Sasha didn't trust herself to say anything.

'Why didn't you tell me why you boarded the boys at their school?'

Could that really be pain she could hear in his voice? Now she *had* to speak. 'I didn't see the point. I didn't think you would believe me. It seemed to me that you were determined to think the worst of me.'

'You're right. I was. Hearing the Professor talk about

the good sense you'd shown felt like being kicked in the stomach. And if that wasn't enough to jolt me out of my stupidity then the shock of discovering that you had sold your jewellery certainly was. I recognise now that deep down I've loved you all along—'

Sasha shook her head and stopped him. 'That's easy enough to say, Gabriel. But it seems to me that you've discovered you love me far too quickly after you discovered the boys were yours.'

Gabriel admitted that she had every right to throw that accusation at him—even if it wasn't true. He was thrilled to know he was the twins' father. And it had given him a distinctly male sense of satisfaction to learn that he had been her first lover. But neither of those facts could have made him love her if he hadn't done so already. *He* knew that. But how could he explain to her the slow and very painful process by which he had come to recognise what his real feelings for her were when he was still struggling to analyse them for himself? This was all such new territory to him, uncharted and untested, and no captain ever set sail on a sea he knew nothing about. Not unless he was desperate. And right now that was exactly what he was.

'I loved you before that—' he began.

'I find that very hard to believe,' Sasha told him flatly. But I want to believe you, her heart was crying. I want to believe you more than I've wanted anything in my whole life. More than the twins' emotional security? If the answer was yes, then what kind of mother did that make her? A mother just like Gabriel believed his had been? If she gave in, and then he changed his mind and discovered that he didn't love her after all, how long would it be before he was accusing her of exactly that?

'I'm ready to do whatever it takes to prove it,' Gabriel continued.

'There isn't any point.'

'There is for me. You loved me once, and I believe—'

'That wasn't love. It was a teenager's fantasy,' Sasha lied.

'So you don't love me any more—but you still had sex with me.'

'It happens,' Sasha told him evenly.

'How often?'

He was still holding her hand, and she wondered if he had felt the sudden betraying tremor that ran through it.

'Meaning what?' she sidestepped.

'Meaning how often since you left me have you had sex with men you don't love?'

'Look, Gabriel, this won't get us anywhere. I fully accept that as the twins' father you have a role to play in their lives—'

'There hasn't been anyone, has there?' he said softly, overruling her attempt to change the subject. Oh, but he wanted so badly to take her in his arms and kiss her until she clung to him as she had done in bed. Something, some instinct he hadn't even known he had, was telling him that there hadn't been anyone else in the years they had been apart. And surely that had to mean something?

'I was a married woman, with two young children and a husband—a sick husband; that hardly left me any time to indulge in extra-marital sex,' Sasha pointed out.

'In other words, there hasn't been anyone?'

He didn't have to sound so damned pleased about it, Sasha thought angrily. 'So what? That doesn't mean I've spent the last ten years yearning for you!'

'Did I say it did? It does prove, though, surely, that we must have something going for us?'

This was getting out of hand. Another few minutes and she'd be drowning in the sea of counter-arguments he was throwing at her. 'So I indulged in a quick shag for old times' sake. That doesn't mean anything.'

'Now, I *know* you're lying.' Gabriel was actually laughing. 'And it wasn't just a shag. It was full-on, passionate, intimate lovemaking, and you know it.'

She couldn't take any more of this. Her defences were crumbling into nothing. 'It doesn't matter what you say or what I feel. Can't you see?' she said wildly. 'This isn't about us, Gabriel, it's about the boys. What if I gave in and agreed? And then what if a month—a year—ten years—down the line you got bored of playing happy families. What then? It's not as though I'm trying to deny you a role in the boys' lives. You are their father, and you are their guardian. You're free to form your own relationship with them. But not via my bed. I'm not doing anything that might lead to them becoming victims of a bitter broken home.'

'I could change your mind,' Gabriel warned her softly. 'I could take you in my arms right here and now and make you—'

'Make me what? Make me want you? Yes, you could do that. But it wouldn't make me change my mind.'

'Very well.' Sasha didn't know whether to be relieved or disappointed when he removed his hand from hers and stood up. 'I understand what you're saying.'

He was starting to turn away from her, and it took every ounce of will-power she possessed not to call him back and tell him how she really felt.

'But I give you fair warning, Sasha, I don't intend to give up. I intend to do whatever it takes to convince you that you and I and the boys have a future together as a family, and that you and I have a future together as husband and wife.'

'I can't stop you from wanting that,' Sasha said. 'But what I want is what's best for the boys. You implied that you would take them away from their school. I want them to stay. They're happy there, and they're doing well.'

Was she testing him? Gabriel wondered. If so, she was going to find that he meant every word he had said to her.

'You're their mother,' he told her firmly. 'I trust your judgement as to where their best interests lie. My own suggestion would be that they should be encouraged to incorporate an awareness of their Italian heritage into their lives.'

He was giving in and agreeing that the boys could stay at their school? 'But what about the Professor?' she reminded him. 'I thought—'

'His initial role was to assess the twins' educational needs. I'm sure he'll understand when we tell him that they are going to continue at their existing school. In fact, I'm sure he will thoroughly approve.'

'And because he approves you're happy to let them

stay there?' Sasha guessed. So much for thinking that Gabriel was giving in to her.

Immediately Gabriel shook his head. 'I don't need the Professor's expertise to tell me that the boys are happy at school and learning well. And, despite what you may think, I don't need an intermediary to tell me that they are well adjusted and well cared for.'

'I wasn't suggesting that you do.' Sasha tussled with her conscience, and then admitted reluctantly, 'You're very good with them, Gabriel. You understand them much better than Carlo did.' As if to make up for her weakness, she added fiercely, 'But when they go back to school I'm going back with them. I shall look for a job, and I intend to find somewhere to live close to the school and my work. That was why I sold my jewellery, so that I could do that.'

'Fine,' Gabriel agreed cordially.

Why wasn't he objecting, frowning…arguing with her, pleading with her to stay with him? And why was she disappointed that he wasn't?

'When do we leave?'

'We?' That wasn't joyful relief she was feeling—even if it felt remarkably like it.

'Of course. I meant what I said, Sasha. From now on where you and the twins go, I go. I don't care how long it takes, or what I have to do to make it happen. I am going to prove to you that we have a future together.'

'That's impossible.'

'Nothing's impossible.'

# CHAPTER TWELVE

SASHA SMILED AS she looked at the pretty Christmas tree decorating the sitting room of her small rented flat. It was Christmas Eve, the boys had already gone to bed, and once she had placed their stockings at the end of their beds she was going to do the same. It was gone ten, and tomorrow they were spending the day with Gabriel, at his insistence, since his house was so much bigger than her flat. And then after Christmas he was going to take the boys skiing, as his Christmas present to them. He had tried to persuade Sasha to go with them, but she'd refused.

True to his word, since the boys' return to school in September, Gabriel had mounted a determined assault on her refusal to accept that they could all have a future together. It had started with some clever by-play which had resulted in the boys insisting that Gabriel was included in whatever they were doing. Even their daily journey to and from school was conducted not via public transport, as Sasha had intended, but instead via the comfort of Gabriel's Bentley.

When she had objected Gabriel had looked innocent, and reminded her that as she had refused his offer to buy her a car she couldn't do the school run herself, and since he was now based in London, and living only a

few doors away, it made sense for him to take the boys
to school and then drop her off at her part-time job.

Sasha had managed not to retaliate. The power of
money was indeed something to be reckoned with.
While she had struggled to find rented accommodation, Gabriel had obviously had no difficulty at all in
buying the elegant London townhouse in which he was
currently living—all four floors of it. When she had
suggested that it might be rather large for him, he had
replied, 'Nonsense. It's the perfect size for us.'

He had courted her, flirted with her, teased her and
become the boys' hero. And not once had he over-
stepped the mark and tried to take her to bed…and
*that* disappointed her?

Well, it certainly left her feeling frustrated, Sasha
admitted ruefully. Her heart and her body seemed to
be filled with one long nagging ache for Gabriel. But
was satisfying that ache enough to risk the boys' happiness for?

Gabriel was being very determined and very thorough about taking apart all her arguments against them
being together. At half-term he had wanted to fly them
all to the Caribbean, where his yacht was berthed, but
Sasha had rejected this proposition. Instead of arguing
with her, Gabriel had simply and very good-naturedly
suggested that instead they spend the holiday in London, having a variety of days out.

'You take the boys on your own,' she had suggested,
especially when she had learned that one of the boys'
chosen destinations was Madame Tussauds.

'It won't be the same without you, Mum,' Nico had
complained.

'No, it won't,' Gabriel had agreed softly. And so of course she had gone, and somehow Gabriel had managed to be always at her side as they moved through the exhibits—tantalisingly close, and yet out of reach.

He hadn't caused a fuss when she had refused an allowance. Nor had he attempted to put any pressure on her to change her mind. Her job didn't pay very well, but at least it was a job—even if some evenings she felt almost too tired to move. Luckily they were close enough to Hyde Park for Gabriel to take the boys there at the weekend to give her a break.

In the months since they had left Sardinia, Gabriel had both amazed and sometimes humbled her with the effort he had put into proving how willing he was to accept that he had to make his peace with his own past. She loved him more now than she had believed possible. But she still couldn't give in and agree to marry him. Trust was the foundation stone of the kind of relationship she longed to have with him. But right now there was a growing barrier to their mutual trust. It would be easy to feel sorry for herself, to wish she could simply place herself and her future in Gabriel's arms and be held there for ever. But she couldn't. Not now.

She was just about to take the boys' stockings into the cramped bedroom they shared—so very different from the large interconnecting rooms they had in Gabriel's house—when her mobile rang.

'It's me,' Gabriel announced unnecessarily when she answered it. 'I'm outside. Come and let me in. I didn't want to ring the bell in case I woke the boys.'

Unsteadily, Sasha went to open the door. Gabriel filled the small hallway, bringing with him the smell of the cold wet streets. He was, she saw, holding a thin but quite large rectangular gift-wrapped package.

'I've brought your Christmas present,' he said, indicating the parcel he was carrying without handing it over to her.

'You could have left it until tomorrow.'

'I wanted to give it to you tonight.'

Sasha shot him a wary look, wondering if he was being deliberately provocative or if she was guilty of hoping he might be. It was probably better not to put the issue to the test by informing him that she had been on her way to bed, she decided.

'Would you like a hot drink?' she asked him instead. Gabriel shook his head, and then held out his gift to her.

'Thank you—' she began.

'Why don't you open it now?'

It looked as though it might be a calendar, and that alone was enough to make her heart thump guiltily.

'Perhaps I will have that drink after all,' he told her. 'But I'll make it.' They were talking in the low-voiced whispers familiar to all parents. 'You've no idea just how much I want to kiss you right now and then take you home with me,' he told her huskily 'All of you. Oh, God, Sasha, I want that so badly—all of you with me, under my roof and my protection.'

She could hear the emotion in his voice and see it in his eyes. She felt as though something inside her was breaking apart. Her own eyes stung with tears she couldn't allow him to see. It would be so easy to give in now to regret and self-recrimination, to rail against what was happening. But she couldn't. Gabriel turned towards the kitchen.

'Gabriel.' He stopped to look back at her. This wasn't the way she had planned to tell him, but he was waiting and looking at her, so she took a deep breath.

'I know this isn't what you want to hear, but I can't marry you.'

Gabriel shook his head. 'Open your present. We'll talk about it tomorrow.'

He disappeared into the kitchen, leaving her staring unseeingly down at her gift. It was no use. She would have to tell him.

He came back, carrying two mugs. 'I've made herbal tea for you instead of coffee—is that okay?'

'Yes. Gabriel, there's something I have to tell you.'

'No, you don't. I already know.'

'Gabriel—'

'You're pregnant. You conceived when we made love in Sardinia, and you've been worrying yourself sick about what to do ever since your visit to the doctor.'

Sasha sat down. 'You know? But how? I haven't…'

He came over to her. 'I love you. I know you. This time I recognised the signs. You've been eating avocados with every meal; I thought in the Caribbean it was just because you liked them, but this time I guessed the real reason. You've looked pale and washed out every morning, the boys have mentioned that you've been sick, you've been wearing concealing clothes and besides…' He looked down at her and then away.

'Besides, what?'

'Well, I didn't plan to score a bullseye twice over, and getting you pregnant certainly wasn't something I intended to happen when I omitted to take any precautions, but I admit the thought did occur to me that if you *had* conceived again it could make our passage down the aisle swifter and easier. But then, when you didn't tell me…'

Sasha took a deep breath. 'You sound very sure that it's yours.'

Gabriel looked at her. 'Of course it's mine,' he said quietly, and then reached for her hands, drawing her up onto her feet and into his arms before she could resist. With one hand behind her head and the other pressed gently against the carefully hidden swell of her belly, he said softly, 'How could it possibly not be mine? I love you, and you are the most loyal, faithful, trustworthy and honest person I know. Had there been someone else you would have told me, and you would not have gone to bed with me. It may have taken me far too long to realise that, but I can assure you that I know it now. I love you,' he repeated. 'We have two wonderful sons and now, between us, we've created another new life.'

Sasha looked up at him. A mistake which immediately led to him bending his head and slowly and thoroughly kissing her.

It was impossible not to kiss him back. Impossible too to deny the telltale lurch of her heart and the fierce, hungry tension gripping her body. Automatically she leaned into him, shivering in delicious anticipatory pleasure.

'Why didn't you want to tell me?' His question brought her back down to earth.

'It was afraid to,' she admitted. 'I knew that if you found out you'd insist on us getting married…'

'And you don't want that?'

'What I don't want—ever—is for you to feel that I

married you because of this baby,' she answered him fiercely. 'You don't know how often I've wished that I hadn't held back, that I'd told you when you asked me in Sardinia that I loved you, that I'd agreed then to marry you, before I knew about this. That way at least you would never have been able to throw it back in my face—'

'Stop right there. There is no way I will ever throw anything back in your face, Sasha. I've learned my lesson. And I've made my peace with my ghosts. Open your present—please.'

She was trembling so much it seemed to take her for ever to remove the ribbon and then the wrapping paper. Beneath it was a layer of bubblewrap, and beneath that was...

Sasha stared at what she was holding, glanced up at Gabriel, and then looked back down at his gift.

'How...?' she began, and then stopped as tears spilled down her face.

What she was holding in her hands wasn't just a painting, it was her future—their future—depicted by an artist: two boys, a man and a woman, and in the woman's arms a baby.

'I managed to work out part of what you might be thinking while I was waiting for you to tell me about the baby. I thought that maybe this would tell you how I felt about it—about you, about all of us. I was going to tell the artist to put the baby in pink, but I decided that might be tempting fate,' he added ruefully.

'Gabriel.'

There was no holding back when she went into his arms. Not the love in her heart nor the joy in her eyes.

When he kissed her she felt the fine tremor in his body and knew that it betrayed the intensity of his own emotion. He kissed her fiercely and passionately, claiming her as his. And then, very slowly and tenderly, she kissed him. When he started to ease her away, she tensed at first, and then relaxed, trading smiles with him when the door opened to admit the twins, whose imminent arrival he had obviously heard before her.

'You were kissing,' Sam accused them both sternly.

'Yes,' Nico agreed. The twins looked at one another. 'Does that mean that you're going to get married and we can go and live at Dad's house, Mum?'

'You needn't have come to collect us. You only live three streets away—we could have walked,' Sasha protested in the flurry of the boys putting on their jackets and showing Gabriel what they had found in their stockings.

'If you were really concerned about getting me out of bed early on Christmas morning you wouldn't have let me stay with you last night,' Gabriel teased her in a discreet whisper. 'Do you realise it was four o'clock when you woke me up and sent me home?'

'Do you realise that the boys were up at five?' She laughed as Gabriel ushered them out to his car.

'Did you put the turkey in the oven, like I said?' Sasha asked.

'Of course. And I turned the oven on,' Gabriel assured her, winking at the twins as he pulled away from the kerb.

Sasha nodded her head.

The house that Gabriel had bought was enough to

make anyone drool with envy, Sasha admitted as she stood in front of the fire in the well-proportioned drawing room.

At Gabriel's insistence she and the twins had decorated the tree, and although its somewhat homely decorations looked out of place in the elegant room, they still brought a sheen of emotional tears to Sasha's eyes.

Her anxious inspection of the turkey confirmed that Gabriel had followed her instructions to the letter.

It had been agreed that the boys would open their presents here at Gabriel's, and now, as she listened to their excited cries of delight as they demolished hours of careful wrapping on her part, she exchanged amused looks with Gabriel.

'With any luck they'll be so tired they'll want to go to bed early tonight.'

Sasha laughed. 'I shouldn't count on it. If the boys don't wear you out wanting to ride their new bikes in the park then their sister will certainly exhaust me.'

'Isn't it time you looked at the turkey,' Gabriel suggested meaningfully.

Sasha got up, checking on the boys before heading for the kitchen, with Gabriel following her.

'When I imagined formally proposing to you it certainly wasn't in a kitchen,' he told her, as he closed the door behind them and then leaned firmly on it, taking her in his arms. 'I love you so very much. I hope you know that now. These last few months have been purgatory. Marry me, Sasha, and make me the happiest man on earth.'

'Yes,' she said. 'Yes. Yes, yes...'

He bent his head to kiss her, and then suddenly stopped to say accusingly, 'You said our *daughter!*'

Sasha laughed. 'Well, when I had my scan they said they thought it was a girl. Just as well, really,' she added.

'Why?'

She gave him a small smile. 'You didn't look carefully enough at the painting.' When he frowned, her smile broadened. 'The baby is wearing white knitted boots threaded with pink ribbon.'

# *EPILOGUE*

*Nine months later*

THEY HAD DECIDED not to hold the christening at the London church where they had been married shortly after Christmas, but here in Sardinia instead. The words of the service, spoken both in English and Italian, had been simple but well-chosen, and now they were back at the newly converted house, where five-month-old Celestine was the centre of attention, the guests cooing over her while the twins looked on with brotherly watchfulness.

'She's chewing her sleeve again,' Nico warned Sasha. 'I think she might be hungry.'

'No, she's not hungry. She's teething,' Sam corrected him scornfully. 'She wants to come out. She doesn't like lying there doing nothing, and it's my turn to hold her.'

'No, it's not. It's mine.'

'Actually, it's my turn,' Gabriel told them both firmly, deftly removing his daughter from her basket and expertly cradling her against his shoulder in a way that still left him free to slip his other arm around the boys.

Watching them, Sasha couldn't resist reaching for her camera.

'She's going to wind all three of you around her little finger,' she warned, as she smiled lovingly at her daughter and discreetly slid her hand down Gabriel's shirt-clad back.

'If that's an invitation for later, then the answer is yes,' he murmured softly. 'Pity we've got such a houseful, though…'

'There's always the beach,' she reminded him teasingly as she leaned closer for his kiss.

Life could not give him another gift to rival that which he now held within his arms, Gabriel thought to himself: Sasha, the twins, and now their daughter.

'I think when he made me the boys' guardian Carlo wanted this to happen and for us to be together,' he told Sasha quietly.

'Yes,' she agreed. 'He knew how much I loved you, and perhaps he sensed that you loved me—even before you acknowledged it yourself.'

'I can acknowledge it now,' he said, looking from his daughter and the twins to Sasha. He bent to kiss her. 'Now and for ever, Sasha.'

\* \* \* \* \*

# REQUEST YOUR FREE BOOKS!

**Harlequin** *Presents*

PASSION
GUARANTEED
SEDUCTION

## 2 FREE NOVELS PLUS
## 2 FREE GIFTS!

**YES!** Please send me 2 FREE Harlequin Presents® novels and my 2 FREE gifts (gifts are worth about $10). After receiving them, if I don't wish to receive any more books, I can return the shipping statement marked "cancel." If I don't cancel, I will receive 6 brand-new novels every month and be billed just $4.30 per book in the U.S. or $4.99 per book in Canada. That's a saving of at least 14% off the cover price! It's quite a bargain! Shipping and handling is just 50¢ per book in the U.S. and 75¢ per book in Canada.* I understand that accepting the 2 free books and gifts places me under no obligation to buy anything. I can always return a shipment and cancel at any time. Even if I never buy another book, the two free books and gifts are mine to keep forever.

106/306 HDN FERQ

Name _____ (PLEASE PRINT)

Address _____ Apt. # _____

City _____ State/Prov. _____ Zip/Postal Code _____

Signature (if under 18, a parent or guardian must sign)

Mail to the **Reader Service:**
**IN U.S.A.:** P.O. Box 1867, Buffalo, NY 14240-1867
**IN CANADA:** P.O. Box 609, Fort Erie, Ontario L2A 5X3

Not valid for current subscribers to Harlequin Presents books.

**Are you a current subscriber to Harlequin Presents books
and want to receive the larger-print edition?
Call 1-800-873-8635 or visit www.ReaderService.com.**

* Terms and prices subject to change without notice. Prices do not include applicable taxes. Sales tax applicable in N.Y. Canadian residents will be charged applicable taxes. Offer not valid in Quebec. This offer is limited to one order per household. All orders subject to credit approval. Credit or debit balances in a customer's account(s) may be offset by any other outstanding balance owed by or to the customer. Please allow 4 to 6 weeks for delivery. Offer available while quantities last.

**Your Privacy**—The Reader Service is committed to protecting your privacy. Our Privacy Policy is available online at www.ReaderService.com or upon request from the Reader Service.

We make a portion of our mailing list available to reputable third parties that offer products we believe may interest you. If you prefer that we not exchange your name with third parties, or if you wish to clarify or modify your communication preferences, please visit us at www.ReaderService.com/consumerschoice or write to us at Reader Service Preference Service, P.O. Box 9062, Buffalo, NY 14269. Include your complete name and address.

*One unbreakable legacy divides two powerful kingdoms....*

*Read on for a sneak peek at*
BEHOLDEN TO THE THRONE *by* USA TODAY
*bestselling author Carol Marinelli.*

\* \* \*

"LET's go now to the tent and make love...." Emir's mind stilled when he tasted her lips; the pleasure he had forgone he now remembered. Except this was different, for he tasted not a woman, but Amy. He liked the still of her breath as his mouth shocked her, liked the fight for control beneath his hands, for her mouth was still but her body was succumbing. He felt her pause momentarily, and then she gave in to him. But there was something unexpected, an emotion he had never tasted in a woman before—all the anger she had held in check was delivered to him in her response. A savage kiss met him now, a different kiss than one he was used to. The gentle lovemaking he had intended, the tender seduction he had pictured, changed as she kissed him back.

"Please…" The word spilled from her lips. It sounded like begging. "Take me back…."

Except he wanted her now. His hands were at the buttons of her robe, pulling it down over her shoulders, their kisses frantic, their want building.

She grappled with his robe, felt the leather that held his sword and the power of the man who was about to make love to her. She was kissing a king and it terrified her, but still it was delicious, still it inflamed as his words attempted to soothe.

"The people will come to accept…" he said, kissing her neck, moving down to her exposed skin so that she ached for his mouth to soothe there, ached to give in to his mastery, but her mind struggled to fathom his words.

"The people…?"

"When I take you as my bride."

"Bride!" He might as well have pushed her into the water. She felt the plunge into confusion and struggled to come up for air, felt the horror as history repeated—for it was happening again.

"Emir, no…"

"Yes." He must know she was overwhelmed by his offer, but he didn't seem to recognize that she was dying in his arms as his mouth moved back to take her again, to calm her. But as she spoke he froze.

"I can't have children…."

* * *

*Can Amy stop at one night only with the enigmatic emir? Especially when this ruler drives a hard bargain— one that's nonnegotiable…?*

*Pick up*
*BEHOLDEN TO THE THRONE*
*by Carol Marinelli on December 18, 2012,*
*from Harlequin® Presents®.*

*They're Wilde by name,
unashamedly wild by nature!*

Discover a deliciously sexy new
Wilde Brothers family dynasty tale
from *USA TODAY* bestselling author

# Sandra Marton

Caleb Wilde, infamous attorney, has a merciless
streak and a razor-sharp mind…until one New York
night changes everything. Now, he's haunted by the
memory of tangled sheets, unrivalled passion and
one woman—Sage Dalton. But when he learns of
the consequences of their night together, Caleb will
stop at nothing to claim what's his!

## THE RUTHLESS CALEB WILDE

Available December 18, 2012.

Bound by blood, separated by secrets...

*USA TODAY* bestselling author

# Kate Hewitt

introduces *The Bryants: Powerful & Proud,*
a stunning new trilogy.

Architect Chase Bryant has spent years appreciating
beautiful structures, and Millie Lang has all the right
angles! A passionate affair on a desert island is just
what he needs. As long as they keep their hands on
each other and off messy emotions, all will be fine.
But are they prepared for the Pandora's Box
of emotions that their intense passion unleashes?

Find out in

# BENEATH THE VEIL OF PARADISE

**Available December 18, 2012.**

www.Harlequin.com

HPI3117